WEB OF SIN #2

LIES

Book #2 of the WEB OF SIN trilogy
Aleatha Romig

New York Times, Wall Street Journal, and USA Today
bestselling author of the Consequences and Infidelity series.

COPYRIGHT AND LICENSE INFORMATION

2018 Edition License

This eBook is licensed for your personal enjoyment. This eBook may not be resold or given away to other people. If you would like to share this book with another person, please purchase an additional copy for each recipient. If you're reading this book and did not purchase it, or it was not purchased for your use only, then please return to the appropriate retailer and purchase your own copy. Thank you for respecting the hard work of this author.

LIES – WEB OF SIN BOOK 2

Blurb

The twisted and intriguing storytelling that you loved in Consequences and Infidelity continues with an all-new alpha anti-hero in the dark romance series Web of Sin, by New York Times bestselling author Aleatha Romig.

I am...

That's no longer an easy statement.

Who am I?

Since Sterling Sparrow, a man so handsome he takes my breath away and so infuriating he pushes me in ways I've never known, came barreling into my life like a category five hurricane, I can't even finish that simple statement.

In twenty-six years I've lived three lives—been three different people.

Renee. Kennedy. And now, Araneae.

They say that I was named after the spider to make me resilient.

Sparrow would then be a bird.

Birds eat spiders.

I prefer to consider myself a cat. It ups my chance of surviving the world I'm now living.

Maybe that's only wishful thinking because according to Sterling, my number of lives is running out.

There are people who want to harm me, to learn the secrets they claim that I possess.

The only person to offer me protection is Sterling Sparrow.

Can I trust a man who willingly put me in the sight of danger?
What is real?
What are lies?
Have you been Aleatha'd?

Lies is book two of the Web of Sin trilogy.

WEB OF SIN BOOK TWO

LIES

O, what a tangled web we weave when first we practice to deceive-
Walter Scott

PROLOGUE

Araneae

The end of Secrets, book #1 of the Web of Sin trilogy

With an air of the status he said I deserved, I made my way through the people and back onto the tall stool. The liquid in my drink quivered as I lifted my glass. With the rim to my lips, I hoped the contents would ease a little of the strange feeling the lady in the bathroom had given me.

I replayed the scene. She was slender with blonde hair pulled back in an elegant twist, diamonds dangled from her ears as well as her fingers, and her gown was long and emerald green. If I really thought about it, the eerie feeling began before she asked about my bracelet. I felt it as our eyes met.

My neck straightened as the energy around me shifted, telling me he was near even before his hand landed upon my shoulder or voice came to my ear.

"I told you not to talk to anyone."

"I haven't," I whispered back.

"Then how the fuck did you get that drink?"

I turned to face him, my eyes shooting lasers—if only they could.

His large hand grasped my upper arm. "We're leaving."

My gaze went from him to his hand as the pressure on my arm built. "Sterling, you're hurting me."

Instead of releasing his grip, his fingers blanched. His mouth barely moved as he growled in my ear. "Get down now, or I'll put you over my shoulder. We're leaving."

Since there was nothing I'd put past him, my heels quickly moved from the bar beneath the stool to the floor. "Is everything all right?" I asked as I stood. "Did it work?"

Our words were low. "You're safe."

Was I?

As we began walking toward the elevator with my arm aching under his grasp, for not the first time, I questioned his statement. From whom did I need protection?

"Mr. Sparrow—"

"We're leaving," Sterling said, interrupting Evelyn.

A commotion behind us caused both of us to turn.

"Araneae?" the woman from the bathroom questioned, her pronunciation was like that of the real spider. "Oh my God, is it really you?"

My lips opened as Sterling's grip loosened, and he reached for my waist, pulling me against him.

"Why? How?" she asked, her cheeks red and blotchy and her soft brown eyes flooding with tears. "My God, why? How are you here? And why are you with him? Marrying him?"

The doors to the elevator opened, and the smile on the man inside faded as Sterling escorted me aboard.

"Talk to me," she pleaded.

"Get us downstairs," Sterling barked as the man pushed the appropriate button.

I reached out and stopped the doors from closing. "Who are you?"

"Araneae," Sterling said.

I moved my hand back, allowing the doors to close but not before I heard her answer.

"I'm your mother."

My knees went weak as I collapsed into Sterling's arms.

STERLING

"*A*raneae," I called repeatedly as the elevator doors closed, and her limp body collapsed against mine. My voice rose with each floor we descended until her head rolled back, and panic flooded my bloodstream. This was more than a reaction to what she'd just heard. "Araneae, you're all right," I reassured, uncertain if she could hear me.

Was she?

What the fuck happened?

She had to be. That was what I'd told her...you're safe.

Her feet slid on the shiny floor of the elevator as her body dangled in my grasp. Placing two fingers on her neck, I prayed to God, one I'd long ago stopped believing in, asking him, her, or it, for a miracle that I sure as hell didn't deserve.

I didn't.

Araneae did.

I prayed for a pulse.

Thump, thump—the swish of blood in her veins pulsated beneath my finger.

I sighed with a bit of relief as I called her name again, my voice coming out more as a growl. My free hand gently slapped her cheek. "Araneae, fucking wake up."

She didn't.

"Mr. Sparrow," Jamison said, his voice barely penetrating the rush of adrenaline swooshing through my ears.

I turned to see his widened eyes as his back flattened against the wall.

"Stop the elevator," I demanded, needing more time than we would otherwise have, while simultaneously, in one fell swoop, I lifted her, cradling her lifeless body with her legs bent over my arm and face fallen against my chest. The elevator jerked and an alarm sounded as Jamison did as I said. "Take my phone from my pocket," I yelled over the shrill siren, pushing my hip his direction.

With a bit of hesitation, his eyes moving between the pocket of my jacket and me, he reached forward.

I extended my hand, the one holding Araneae's legs, as he handed me the phone. With it in my grasp, I hit the button to call Patrick and turned back to Jamison. My tone left no room for discussion. "Get this damned thing moving again."

"Get the car behind the building, now," I barked into the phone.

With shaking hands, Jamison hit the button, quelling the alarm and returning the elevator to motion. Thankfully, this particular elevator only stopped at two floors—the club and the back of the restaurant—leaving no concern that anyone else would enter. I narrowed my gaze toward Jamison. "She walked out of this club tonight. If I hear anything different from anyone, it won't bode well for you or for them."

Jamison's Adam's apple bobbed as he nodded. "Of course, sir. She was faint, but she-she," he stuttered, staring at her in my arms, "was much better by the time we reached the bottom floor."

"For your sake and your family's, that better be the story I hear."

His head nodded. "It will. You have my word."

My attention went back to the call as Araneae's lips parted. The hand in which I held the phone uncharacteristically shook. "Get here now. Call Dr. Dixon and have her meet us at the apartment. I don't give a fuck where she is or what she's doing. Get her there!"

This wasn't happening. This wasn't happening.

No matter how many times I said it, I couldn't make it true.

A small bit of saliva pooled behind her lips.

I'd made my statement—declaring her off-limits.

Who was willing to challenge me, right the fuck in front of me?

The drink.

My body tensed, knowing in my gut that was the answer. Right under my goddamned nose someone had gotten to her.

She wasn't lying in my arms because of the news she'd heard or because she'd seen her birth mother. That had been jarring and fucking unexpected. I never would have guessed that Rubio McFadden—senator and potential presidential candidate, not to mention an underworld kingpin and the Sparrow outfit's biggest adversary—would show up with the crowd that was there with his mistress instead of his wife.

His mistress, Annabelle Landers, was a federal court judge

as well as the widow of Daniel McCrie. It was a small fucking world that ran the underground of Chicago. And it was about to get smaller.

Having Annabelle present at tonight's gathering was one possibility I hadn't explored.

As soon as I saw her at that table with McFadden, I knew our stay had to be short. I was anxious—too anxious—to stake my claim. Now, Araneae was suffering the consequences.

The elevator came to a stop as I looked at Jamison. "Is there somewhere we can stay out of sight until the car arrives?"

"Yes, sir—"

The vibration of my phone interrupted him as I pushed the button and read the text from Patrick.

"HERE. WHAT THE FUCK HAPPENED? WHY A DOCTOR?"

I wasn't sure how Patrick had done it—how he'd gotten here so quickly. I didn't care. I also didn't respond to him. I turned back to Jamison. "Make sure no one sees us."

Jamison's head bobbed. "Yes, yes...let me..." He hurried away. A few seconds later he was back. "It's clear to the doorway, sir. No one will know. As far as the story goes, you both walked out of here."

I hesitated as my eyes searched. "Cameras?"

"No. Strict club policy. Can't have cameras in a place that doesn't exist."

"For your sake, that better be the case and the story I hear."

As I flung open the door at the back of the building, Patrick's door flew open and he raced our way. "What happened?"

"I'll tell you in the car. We need to get the fuck out of here."

Settling in the backseat with Araneae still cradled in my arms as the back door closed, for a moment something happened, something that I couldn't recall ever occurring, not since I was too young to remember. The lump growing in my throat since Annabelle came rushing our way grew bigger. Araneae's paling complexion blurred as moisture filled my eyes. Releasing her body and legs to the seat, I held her face close.

She was positioned as she had been on the beach of the lake in Ontario. That vision came back: her beautiful soft brown eyes staring up at me, asking me for answers, and trusting that I'd give them, that I'd help her.

My voice cracked, the lump now a dam holding back what I refused to release. "Come back to me, sunshine. I can't lose you now. I won't."

The door slammed and my neck straightened as Patrick put the car in motion.

Sniffing back the emotion I didn't recognize and wouldn't acknowledge, I moved on to what I knew, something familiar and comfortable—anger, rage, and determination. Clearing my throat, my voice grew louder as I released her face, still secured in my lap and gripped the door handle. "Dr. Dixon?" I asked, my fingers blanching as the wrath within me built.

I could tear the fucking handle off the door, but that

wouldn't save Araneae, nor would it exact the revenge that I planned to inflict.

"She's on her way, Sparrow. She was on call but said she'll get someone else to cover. She understands there's an emergency." His eyes met mine in the rearview mirror. "You know she wouldn't let you down." He pounded the steering wheel as our speed increased, and he weaved in and out of traffic. "Tell me," he demanded, "What happened and who? Who's going to die for this?"

"Not Araneae. Not on my watch." I shook my head, recalling the club. "Fuck. I started with Hillman. I wasn't..." The realization hit me. The person who was responsible was me. I was the one who didn't do my job. Pushing that away, I tried to think about what happened. "...I wasn't watching like I should have. She should have been safe."

"Hillman?"

I recalled the impromptu meeting I'd conducted. "It would have caused World War III if I had gone straight to Rubio. Wendell Hillman's his bookkeeper, his consigliere." Patrick knew that. I was simply talking to talk, to recall anything—everything. "I told him that she was here. She was found and most importantly, she was mine."

Patrick nodded.

"Neither Rubio nor Hillman did anything personally. I was with Hillman the whole time. McFadden was in my sight too..." I replayed it all in my mind.

By the blanching of his fingers, Patrick's grip upon the steering wheel was as intense as mine upon the door handle. Araneae was important to us all. We'd planned her acquisition together. They knew how imperative having her with us was for many reasons.

Up until recently, the plan and execution had all been in theory. However, now that she was with us, we all saw her light. How could we not? She brightened every fucking room with simply her presence.

I had a fleeting memory of Patrick telling me that Araneae had demanded that I call her. As he relayed her message, he tried to hold back, but the idea of her commanding me had him laughing his ass off. We all knew she was like no other woman I'd ever had, how she pushed my buttons, and how she made everything...different.

"Fucker," I went on, concentrating on the story I'd been telling, "wanted to talk to her. Like I'd allow that."

"Hillman wanted to?"

"Wanted to. I wouldn't allow it."

"Did she talk to anyone?"

I shook my head. "Not any of them. The conversation was intense. I didn't want her to hear what could have been said. I told her to sit at the bar and not speak to anyone." I looked down and smoothed her blonde hair away from her beautiful face. Her skin was too cool. For the second time, I pushed two fingers against the side of her neck.

The faint thumping was still present.

Whoever the fuck did this will die.

"She didn't do what you said, did she?" Patrick asked, pulling me away from my murderous thoughts.

"Of course the fuck not. She got up. I think she went to the bathroom."

Patrick's head shook. "How long was she out of sight?"

"Not long. As soon as I noticed the empty stool, she was back." I recalled seeing her across the room as she returned. "She was so fucking stunning standing in that doorway." My lips momentarily curled upward. "Damn, she walked back into that room with all the poise and regality of the queen she was born to be. Chin held high in that one-of-a-kind dress. Every eye was on her. I was so fucking proud to say she was mine."

Patrick's reflection met mine again. "How is she, boss?"

"Still a pulse. I can barely feel her breath." I laid my hand over her chest, not as I'd done before but to try to sense movement. "Her chest is moving. She's breathing." My eyes popped up to look outside, assessing our surroundings. "Damn, we need to hurry."

"Do you think we should go to a hospital?"

"No. Whoever did this...that's what they expect. I'm not letting someone else get a second chance at her." I met his eyes again. "She ordered a drink."

"Fuck." This time the sentiment was from Patrick.

I nodded, my hand mindlessly resting on her chest, monitoring its up-and-down motion as the one from the door moved to her hair, as silky as her dress. "That's when they did this," I went on. "It had to be." I tried to remember the contents of the glass in her hand. "I'm not sure how much she drank. She had it to her lips when I got to her." My fists clenched and unclenched. "I want the name of the bartender, some young brunette whom I haven't seen before."

"Reid will find out."

"Jamison in the elevator said there aren't cameras anywhere. Club policy."

"Has that ever stopped Reid?"

"Get him on speaker now. I want him working on this."

"Sparrow?" Patrick said, bringing my eyes to the rearview mirror. "She's going to be okay. There's too much life in that woman to snuff out."

"Fucking A."

"And," he went on, "that World War III you mentioned, it's on. Whoever did this is going to pay."

"Reid here..." His voice came from the car's speakers. "It's about fucking time I got your call. What the hell is happening? Why's the good doctor on her way...?"

ARANEAE

The fade into consciousness happened slowly, like the melting of ice. The water was still present. It just changed form.

I'd read that once in a book.

The quote came back to me. No longer were the words a part of fiction or an unfathomable tale. I was now her, the heroine in my own unimaginable story.

Wasn't that what they said, that truth was stranger than fiction?

The ice wasn't melting fast enough, my clouded mind couldn't process. Every limb—make that every muscle, nerve, cell—in my body had quadrupled in size. The weight was excessive. Even opening my eyes took too much effort.

Something had happened but I couldn't remember.

Maybe I didn't want the ice to melt or to remember. Maybe I needed more sleep.

Time passed as dreams played like spliced pieces of film

behind my closed eyes, fragments of incomplete scenes that didn't make sense. Quentin Tarantino would be proud. Nothing was in sequence.

I was surrounded by tall trees, such as in the wilderness of Colorado but with a different view, more trees than mountains. A chill settled over me as I walked along a lake's shore, the sun on my cheeks and pebbles beneath my feet. And then I was back in Boulder as Louisa showed me a new Sinful Threads garment. The dress was stunning as I ran the spun silk through my fingers. "I'm a spider, you know?"

Why did I say that? Why would I say that to her?

"Kenni—"

The way she looked at me alerted me that I'd spoken out of turn. I wasn't supposed to tell her, to tell anyone.

"I-I..." My stomach twisted with the shame that came with revealing a secret that wasn't mine to reveal.

Or was it?

After all, if I was the spider, shouldn't I be the one to tell?

Her expression morphed as my pulse kicked up its pace. The swooshing of blood was background music growing faster and louder as the repetitive beat reverberated through me. Instead of my pulse, it morphed into tribal drums broadcasting a signal, a warning of impending danger.

I had to get out of there. I couldn't explain my statement, and Louisa would want it. She was my best friend. I trusted her with my life, and yet I hadn't. There was someone else, someone I wasn't supposed to defy, someone who would be upset.

I ran down the hallway, beyond Winnie's desk. She called out to me, calling out the name Kennedy. I didn't answer as I hurried out onto the street.

The door swung open, but the scene was wrong. I turned back to the entrance of our office building. Sinful Threads was etched into the glass. Our office was there, but I was no longer in Boulder.

My head bowed, bringing into view a sidewalk where my feet were planted, wearing ridiculously tall shoes. I didn't own expensive shoes like those. Why was I wearing them? My gaze inched upward. My legs were covered in silk stockings, and farther up, I was wearing the black dress—the one I'd just been holding.

The plunging neckline wasn't what I usually wore, but I had...I had...

A memory of a red dress was there, but before I could reach for it, it flew away with the wings of a sparrow.

A sparrow?

Why not simply a bird?

I couldn't make sense of my own thoughts.

I lifted my chin, taking in my new surroundings. The breeze between the tall buildings, its scent a combination of Lake Michigan and exhaust fumes, blew my long hair. Like a sticky web, the tresses encircled me, binding me as I turned a complete circle. Not once, not twice, the world blurred as my speed increased.

The buildings beyond me came closer, closing in on me as I spun.

Perspiration prickled my skin, drawing the expensive silk closer to my body as I turned faster and faster.

No longer was I Kennedy but now a small dancer trapped in a little girl's musical jewelry box.

Suddenly, the music stopped. A strong hand grasped my arm as my feet fought to maintain their balance. "Ah!" I gasped as the man came into view. With my free hand I reached up, covering my mouth with the tips of my fingers to stop the scream I wanted to release.

My hand dropped. I couldn't shout or even talk. Words were unable to form as his eyes bore into me. With the growing pressure on my arm, I was held captive, unable to back away or go forward.

Hell, I couldn't move at all.

I gasped for breath as the dark stare accelerated my already-too-fast heartbeat. Second by second, I stood still, the expensive shoes cemented to the sidewalk, paralyzed in his sight.

"Kenni, this isn't real." My own voice rang in my ears. Though I'd made the proclamation myself, the name I'd spoken was no longer mine.

"Araneae..."

The deep tenor rumbled like thunder.

And then everything was gone.

I was gone.

My feet were no longer on the ground.

I was flying...no, floating in a cloud of nothingness.

The fog had returned, surrounding and supporting me as I became aware of the bed below me covered with the softest sheets I'd ever known, as if Sinful Threads had broadened our merchandise line, now creating sheets. The cover over me was warm. It was my arm that was once again bound.

I blinked to see what I could only feel as annoying beeps came into range.

My left arm was secured to something, restricting its ability to move, not allowing it to bend.

The light within the room assaulted my eyes as I strained

to focus.

My heart rate accelerated as I made sense of what I'd been feeling. In my arm, held in place by some kind of tape, was a needle.

Fuck!

A wave of panic washed over me.

There was a needle in my arm.

I jumped away, yet my arm followed. "What the hell?" I squeaked more than said as I clawed at the sticky tape, my fingernails digging at my own skin.

An unfamiliar woman wearing unbecoming green scrubs came rushing toward me. "Ms. McCrie, please don't do that. You'll remove the IV or worse, break the needle."

"IV?" My gaze moved from my reddened arm to her face. Her clothes indicated she was a nurse or doctor. Not much older than I, she had beautiful skin a warm shade of brown, and her dark eyes were filled with both fatigue and concern as she lifted my arm and inspected for any damage I'd inflicted. Her black hair was pulled back too starkly. I imagined that with a different hairstyle and other clothes, she could be quite pretty. Even now she was attractive. "Why?" I asked.

"It's a saline solution to help you, flushing the drugs from your system."

That didn't make sense. I didn't do drugs. I never had. Well, in Colorado there were legal options, and of course, I had an occasional drink, but never drugs, not the kind that would need to be flushed from my system.

My raw and dry throat scratched as my eyes filled with tears. I started to speak again, "Who are you? Where am I?"

Ms. McCrie. The words she'd said came back.

McCrie. Araneae McCrie.

Memories were returning as more tears flowed.

"Araneae." She said the name the same way Sterling said it. *Sterling.*

My memories were building blocks, rebuilding what I'd momentarily lost.

My chest filled with emotion. "Sterling? Where is he?"

She held a cup before me, bringing a straw to my lips. "He's here. He had to step away. Drink some water. It'll help your throat."

I nodded before my lips pursed and I sucked. The cool, clear liquid made its way over my tongue and down my throat, like rain to a desert, rehydrating what had been on the verge of demise.

More memories returned. I remembered the plane ride, two of them, and two on a helicopter. The cabin high in the trees with Paul Bunyan's lake was coming back...and the return trip to Chicago. I was mad at him. He'd ruined what had been good, and then...I thought we made up, but the rest was gone, like a switch had been flipped.

What happened on the plane?

How did I end up with an IV flushing out drugs?

When I stopped drinking, I asked again, "Who are you?" My eyes roamed the room. I was in a bedroom, not in a hospital or clinic. No medical facility was this luxurious.

Was I in Sterling's penthouse?

The palm of the hand I could move—the one not connected to an IV—ran over the blanket that had been keeping me warm, taking in the exquisite softness and quality. The windows were covered with drapes, their color a light beige contrasting the chocolate-colored walls, as sunlight seeped from the edges. It was daytime. I just didn't know what time or what day. The bed I was in wasn't hospital issue either. Its sleigh style was constructed of dark, heavy wood. The light ceiling and darker walls were bordered with white carved molding, the color matching the wood of the baseboards, bookshelves, and doors.

Somehow, I knew that this was his home. Sterling had once told me that his mother lived in the castle. From what I could see, he had constructed one within his penthouse, significantly statelier than the cabin where we'd been.

"My name is Renita," she answered. "Renita Dixon. I'm a doctor, a cardiologist, and I've been with you since last night."

My eyes opened wide at her introduction. "Cardiologist? Oh God." My free hand came to my chest. "What happened? Why do I need a cardiologist?"

Her grin broadened, showing a gleaming white smile. "No, you didn't need a cardiologist. Your heart is fine."

"Then why?"

"You did need medical care, and let's just say that Mr. Sparrow called and I answered."

That was my confirmation. This was Sterling's home.

I tilted my head toward the IV. The clear tube ran from my arm to a bag secured on a silver post. "Do I still need that? I'm awake and it's...uncomfortable."

Dr. Dixon scooted off the bed and bent down. "I'd like a little more liquid output before removing the IV."

Oh God. The muscles of my core clenched.

Do I have a catheter?

I did.

I let out a long breath and leaned back to the pillows, closing my eyes. "I know I'm at Ster—Mr. Sparrow's apartment. Did you say that he's here?"

Did I want him to see me like this?

"He is," the doctor answered. "Mr. Sparrow has been in here with you for most of the night."

My eyes opened. "He has?"

"Yes, he's been talking to you, saying your name. I honestly don't think he slept at all. You've had us all worried."

"All?" I asked.

Dr. Dixon nodded. "In the years I've known them, I don't recall seeing Mr. Kelly or Mr. and Mrs. Murray nervous." She nodded. "Like I said, you had us all concerned."

"Kelly? Murray?"

"Patrick Kelly and Reid Murray, his wife too. Mr. Kelly and Mr. Murray have been with Mr. Sparrow for as long as I can remember."

Well, well, wasn't this informative?

I decided not to mention anything she was saying to Sterling. As memories continued to flood my mind like a dam had been broken, I recalled something about him not wanting me to talk to people. It was part of the reason I had been upset with him.

Did that rule include the doctor he'd left alone with me?

Common sense would say no, but I also remembered enough to recall that Sterling Sparrow couldn't be equated with common sense.

"What happened to me?" I asked, sitting forward as my body ached. "Oh, I'm sore, like everywhere. Dr. Dixon, I don't use drugs. I don't understand."

"The soreness is normal. Your body has been through a trauma." She smiled in a way that told me she was accustomed to difficult patient discussions. "I believe that Mr. Sparrow wants to be the one to tell you."

Sighing, I wanted to ask about patient and doctor privilege or maybe HIPAA rules, but I didn't. Her response was the one answer that would stop me from asking more.

In the short time I'd been with Sterling Sparrow, it was abundantly clear that if he chose to be my only source of information, there was little I could do to change that. My tongue darted to my still-dry lips. "Then could you tell him I'm awake? And may I have more water?" My stomach rumbled. "And maybe something to eat?"

"Yes to all. The food and water will also help with the removal and dilution of the chemicals." She took a step toward the door. As she pulled it inward, raised voices came into range.

Her wide eyes darted to me as she pushed the door back into place. "Maybe we should wait a bit?"

I tried to hear until the door was fully shut. "Was that Sterling and a woman?"

What woman would be here with him? And why was she yelling at him?

Surely Patrick and this mystery guy Reid were somewhere close. Wasn't she breaking his *not around others* rule?

"Ms. McCrie..."

"Araneae, please." My eyes narrowed. "What do you know?"

Dr. Dixon shook her head. "Nothing really. The reason Mr. Sparrow was called away was because someone was here to see him."

"Dr. Dixon, please tell me who," I prompted.

"His mother."

Genevieve Sparrow.

STERLING

*S*eated on the ottoman of a plush leather chair in the sitting room that I rarely used, my feet planted, knees spread, the fist of one hand held tightly by the other, and my jaw clenched, I reminded myself again this raving lunatic in front of me was my mother and deserved a semblance of respect. That was all she deserved—the appearance of it—and she was losing that license by the second.

With her skinny arms alternating from waving to slapping her sides, she'd barely shut up since she'd stormed in uninvited to my home. There were few who had that privilege. Hers was about to be revoked.

It was barely after ten in the morning, and she looked as if she'd spent three hours in a salon chair. She probably had— after her personal trainer, blue-light shower, and a hearty breakfast of fruit and oatmeal.

Giving her my attention when what I really wanted was to be back upstairs was quickly losing its appeal.

"Mom, go home."

"I-I just don't understand how you could do this to me."

My head shook. "I guarantee that nothing that I have done involving Araneae has in the least way been about you. Other than a sentence or two, you haven't even crossed my mind."

"Sterling, my phone started ringing last night. Last night! The calls continued into the night, each person asking me if the rumors were true—if my son would..." She shook her head. "Well, needless to say, my sleep schedule was completely thrown off."

Unfisting my fingers, I ran both hands through my hair as I inhaled deeply. As the sweetness of her overpowering perfume filled my senses, I regretted my choice to breathe. It was the same perfume she always wore, her trademark calling card. The scent preceded her upon her arrival and remained after she was gone.

The heels of her pumps clipped the floor each time she stepped from the rug to the marble. I was ready to tell her to sit her skinny ass down or at least stay on the fucking rug. Between the *tap, tap, tap,* her sickeningly sweet aroma, her running mouth, and my lack of sleep, my head was pounding.

"Look at you," she said, gesturing my way. "You're not dressed."

I was dressed, in sweatpants and a t-shirt. If Dr. Dixon weren't with Araneae, I'd be wearing less. All through the night I'd wanted to climb into the bed beside her and hold her until she woke. She appeared so small and frail lying in the middle of that big bed with the damn tubes.

"You're not even at the office," my mother went on. "Don't you realize the signal you're sending? Do you want people to think you are hiding out after you'd gone missing last week? Do you want them to think you're embarrassed to be seen with that...that—"

Standing, I decided that I couldn't take it any longer. "Stop right there, Mother."

"Why, Sterling? Why would you track her down? Why would you want to fulfill your father's prophecy? You know that no matter what he did or said, there was always a reason behind it, usually to inflict harm or agony. The man was evil and you're playing into his hands, fulfilling his wishes. You should have left her dead. It was better for everyone."

"Allister is gone," I said. "This has nothing to do with him or you. And I didn't disappear. Sterling Enterprises was handled from the cabin. I do have an office here too, you know? I don't need to be sitting on fucking Michigan Avenue to get work done."

"Language." Her head shook as her painted blue eyes opened wide—well, as wide as they could considering the number of surgeries she'd had to erase wrinkles. Those *procedures*, as she called them, also erased the elasticity that skin was supposed to have. "The cabin," she continued. "Don't tell me you took *her* to that beautiful place. As her name indicates, she will infest everything if you don't get rid of her now. She's the devil's spawn." Her hands slapped the sides of her thighs.

I doubted the fabric of her designer dress was covering Kevlar underneath. She'd probably be bruised by the time she left. It wouldn't be from me, but at this point, I didn't give a damn.

I took a step closer, my height towering over her. "I. Said.

Stop. And you have that wrong, Mother. The devil's spawn would be me."

Her neck straightened. "Sterling Sparrow, I warned you about her since the day Allister put that ridiculous notion into your young head. What Daniel did, what he learned, what he knew...bringing her back is only opening old wounds. The girl was dead and buried as far as the right people were concerned. Why bring her back? Why risk your standing?"

"The only thing that I've risked is her. It wasn't intentional, but I'll regret that forever and spend the rest of my life making up for it. So you better start to understand that she's here. She's staying here, and she's not a risk to anything that I've done or will do concerning any part of Sparrow." I forced a smile. "Oh, and Mother, she's also not a girl. She's a woman."

My mother's eyes blinked and lips puckered as if she'd tasted something sour. "I am your mother." Her tone was that of disgust. "Do you think I want to hear about the latest whore you've bedded?"

The night at Araneae's side had been long; patience was not currently a virtue I possessed. My voice rose. "Araneae McCrie is not a whore."

"Like mother, like daughter," she huffed as her fist came to her hip and she spun my way. "Tell me you didn't bring her here."

"I just said she was *here*." I pointed at the floor. "Here means this location. Besides, after last night, where the hell else would I take her?" My mother didn't know about the poisoning. No one besides those who'd been in this apartment during the night—Dr. Dixon, Patrick, Reid, Lorna, and me— did. That was how I planned on keeping it.

And until Araneae woke, I wasn't leaving this apartment,

not even to go another two floors down to where Reid and Patrick were making lists and following up with our teams on leads. When we made lists, you better hope your name wasn't on them. Let me say that if my two associates worked for Santa, they weren't collecting the names of those who were *nice*.

Dr. Dixon said that based on the blood poison concentration level, Araneae would wake. The doctor had run tests throughout the night. Thankfully, it appeared that Araneae hadn't consumed an excessive amount. Stopping her when I did from finishing her drink was one of the few things I did right last night.

According to our sources—our ears out and around as well as those on the ground and what I was getting from my mother's rant—the story Jamison had repeated in the elevator was what was being circulated: Araneae McCrie appeared from the shadows, materializing in a place that doesn't exist. She wasn't alone but with Sterling Sparrow, a statement to everyone that she had not only the Sparrow realm protecting her but the king himself.

McFadden's expression was priceless the moment he realized that Araneae and Kennedy were the same person. That alone would have made the entire night had it not been for the poisoning.

I'd told Araneae that she'd been in her biggest enemy's fucking grasp. She had been, at the dinner for Sinful Threads, sitting at the same table. Patrick had been watching. Still, last night, it was amusing to watch the wheels turn. Rubio McFadden had been close enough to stop the potential decimation of himself and his campaign, and he'd missed the opportunity.

One might have thought he'd consider familial ties as those that would protect her. Rubio has already proven he had no such lines.

I knew without a doubt that last night while we were in the club, McFadden never left his chair. That didn't mean he was off our list of suspects. When you're the top of your outfit, you kept your hands clean. I did too, but I would gladly make a fucking exception for him.

If the goal of the poison was to have Araneae collapse and die with a room full of witnesses, Annabelle's poorly timed scene played more into our hands than it did for whoever spiked Araneae's drink.

Araneae McCrie, a woman who never knew her birth parents—or even if they were alive—was simply stunned. That was the way it appeared as she collapsed behind the closing elevator doors.

Thank you, Annabelle. As soon as your daughter wakes, I'll clean up the fucking mess you made.

While I'd been lost in my thoughts, my mother had continued her rant as she perfected her trek—on the rug and then off the rug.

"This is done for now," I declared. "Go home. I have more important things to do."

"More important than your mother?" Her tone softened. "No matter what you think you were promised, you can't keep her like she's a pet." She scoffed. "A pet spider you can keep in a jar." Her beady eyes turned directly to me. "She's a ticking time bomb. When that bomb goes off, it will annihilate not only your target, but the world as we know it. We're talking mass casualties."

"I think I'm a little better versed in explosives and how to use them. The truth is..."

I took a deep breath and again ran my hand through my hair. My mother wasn't getting the truth that was on the tip of my tongue—the gut feeling I had that Araneae was not the prophesied oracle that she'd been forecast to be.

I began again, "The truth is that *this world* is in need of rearrangement. She won't blow it up—I will. First, I need to decide who will be named on the list of casualties."

"I lost my husband. I don't want to lose you, too."

"I hate to break it to you, Mom, but you don't have me. You gave up that right a long time ago. I simply tolerate you."

"And you think bringing back Daniel's daughter, parading her in front of Annabelle, is going to help your cause? Sterling, I remember when Araneae died—when we all believed that. Annabelle and I have had our differences, but she's still a mother—or she wanted to be. What you've done..." She shook her head. "Did you stop to consider how this will affect others or don't they matter?"

"I didn't parade her in front of Annabelle. I never imagined that she'd be there. Why the fuck wasn't Pauline with Rubio?"

"Sterling," she admonished. "Pauline can't stand the man. I don't blame her." She shrugged, like discussing mistresses was a conversation to be had over tea. "If your father were still alive, I'd be envious. Had your father taken his slut out and about to boring dinners and events, it would have been a relief." My mother shook her head. "The difference was that she was just that. Annabelle is at least a refined woman."

Again my hand went to my hair. "Fuck, Mom, how can you—?"

"Sterling?"

Mother and I turned the direction of the foyer as Araneae came to a stop on the bottom step of the staircase.

I couldn't look away as my heart beat faster. Her long yellow hair was pulled back in a ponytail, and her sexy, slender body was covered in a long robe. She was pale and moving slowly, but I didn't care; she was awake, and to me she was stunning.

"Hmm," my mother huffed under her breath. "Now I see what you've been busy doing."

"Mother, I mean it..." My voice was a low growl. "Adjust your bitchy attitude or leave and don't come back."

Araneae took one more step down as she tightly held onto the banister. "Mrs. Sparrow, it's an honor to meet you."

After a quick nudge with my elbow, my mother found her voice. Too damn bad she couldn't have lost it about twenty minutes sooner. "Miss McCrie, the rumors are true."

"Rumors?"

Shit, I needed to stop this.

"A phoenix rising from the ashes."

"Hardly, just a rough night—"

"Traveling can be difficult," I said, interrupting as I stepped forward, my eyes on Araneae, silently pleading that she stop talking before something that we'd both regret was spoken in front of my mother.

"In Sterling's plane, I presume. It must have been awful. More like finding the golden ticket, if you ask me."

Before I could tell her again to shut the fuck up, Araneae responded.

"I suppose Sterling did that—found the golden ticket. I'm certain he'd agree that since finding me, it's been an all-expense-paid trip to Charlie's Chocolate Factory. Mrs. Sparrow, I came downstairs to apologize for the way your son was speaking to you." Araneae's head tilted as she grinned. Even with the pallor, her soft brown eyes shone. "You see, it's my fault that he hasn't gotten much sleep. But now, after meeting you, I see that an apology on my or his part is undeserved."

Genevieve huffed her response.

Fuck, Araneae was amazing.

I turned to my mother as my eyebrows rose and eyes widened with the surprise of Araneae's comeback. Regal and deadly. Hell yes, this woman was made for me. I cleared my throat. "Well, there it is. I think that's your cue to leave."

My mother's lips pressed together as she reached for the handbag she'd tossed onto the chair when she'd stormed in. Turning to me, with her chin jutted up and fire burning in her gaze, she said, "We're not done."

"No, but we're damn close."

With a quick, bitchy nod to Araneae, she turned on her toes, her heels clipping the floor, and stalked to the front door.

As it slammed closed, I let out a breath and moved forward, making my way to Araneae. Reaching for her waist, I pulled her close. "Damn, it's good to see those eyes open." I looked around, my gaze going to the upper-level landing. "Did Dr. Dixon approve of your walking all the way down here by yourself?"

Araneae's lips turned upward. "No. After she disconnected me, I waited until she stepped out of the room, and then I snuck out."

"I should spank your ass."

Pink filled her cheeks as the tips of her lips rose. My

earlier assessment was confirmed. Araneae McCrie was made for me.

"Can that wait?" she said. "I have huge holes in my memory..." She twisted her left arm showing where the IV had been. "...and in my arm. I'm also starving. Can we find food while you fill in the holes?"

My lips quirked. "One of my favorite things to do, but eating at the same time could get messy. Do you like chocolate?"

Araneae's head shook as she leaned into me. "You're incorrigible."

"Insatiable." In one fell swoop, I picked her up, lifting her from the floor into my arms.

"Sterling," her voice squealed as a smile filled her face and light glistened from her eyes.

She was the most beautiful sight I'd ever seen. After last night, I wasn't sure I'd ever see her or her light again. "Sunshine, those feet aren't touching the ground until Dr. Dixon clears you to walk. And we'll talk about what happened. When we do, we'll discuss following my orders."

She shook her head. "You're not my boss."

My forehead wrinkled. "I am. Tell me, do you think it's a good idea to argue that fact?"

"I could." She let out a breath. "However, I'm pretty sure it won't do me any good."

My grin broadened. "As a matter of fact, it may get you in more trouble than you're already in." I began to walk, carrying her in my arms toward the kitchen. "Now, let's get you some nourishment so you can regain your strength. After having your stomach pumped, I can only imagine how you feel."

"My stomach pumped? I don't remember any of that."

"That's probably for the best."

Her cheek fell against my chest. "Okay, I want to eat." She turned her face up to mine. "Are you upset with me at how I spoke to your mom? I kind of insinuated that your lack of sleep was from—"

A laugh rumbled through me. "Fuck no. Next to seeing you standing and awake, it was the best part of my day."

She sighed as her cheek again fell against my t-shirt. "I recall something about being mad at you."

I bowed my head to kiss her hair as I continued walking. "Probably. Someone lately has mentioned that I can be an asshole."

"That someone was right. You can be." She looked up. "Just not right now."

"See, you can't stay mad at me. Now, let's concentrate first on food. Lorna can make you whatever you want to eat."

ARANEAE

L orna?

Sterling was right. I couldn't stay mad at him. I could be mad and he could be an asshole. I remembered that. However, staying that way, I doubted it.

In a very short time, the man whose arms I was in had turned my life upside down. He was infuriating, overprotective, and domineering. And yet even with the holes in my memory, as he carried me—hell, the way he looked at me even in front of his mother—he was able to do things to me that I'd never before known, making me feel safe and adored. This sense of well-being was foreign to me, almost unbelievable. It wasn't something I realized I'd been missing until now. I hadn't felt this secure and content probably since the afternoon I first boarded a plane to Colorado.

Looking at Sterling's handsome face, I almost forgot to look around at the apartment that I hadn't before seen and didn't recall entering. I'd looked beyond the drapes in the bedroom where I'd awakened. Surrounded by blue sky, we were somewhere high within the Chicago skyline. From my limited knowledge, the first floor—which obviously was much higher than that in the building—was more modern chic than the grandeur of the bedroom. Large windows filled exterior walls, blanketing the rooms with natural light. Marble floors, area rugs, and sleek furnishings were a testament to Sterling's style as well as wealth.

Unlike the story that he'd told me where he described his father's office as dark and musty, Sterling's living space was light and open. We turned a corner and came to a stop, entering the kitchen. I had the sensation of walking into a photo within an architectural magazine. Black granite countertops, stainless steel appliances, and shimmering tile backsplashes were only the beginning. However, it was more than picturesque. It was welcoming.

"Why does a single man need this nice of a kitchen, especially one who said he doesn't cook?"

"He doesn't cook. I do," said a woman carrying vegetables from what was probably a pantry. Maybe a little older than me, she was petite yet fit, with a runner's body. Her long red hair was piled on the top of her head in a messy bun, and her bright green eyes shone without the aid of much makeup. Dressed in blue jeans and a Cubs t-shirt, she didn't look like the staff at the cabin; she appeared at home.

Her smile bloomed as she dropped the produce on one of the counters. "Ms. McCrie, I'm Lorna. It's so good to see you up and about." She turned her attention to Sterling. "Maybe one day he might even let you walk?"

Sterling pulled out a chair at the long slate-topped table and gently sat me down.

"Lorna, how about some food for Ms. McCrie?"

"Food? Oh, that's right." She laughed. "I forgot."

I liked her.

As Lorna continued whatever task she'd begun with the produce, Sterling turned to me. "You're right. I don't cook, but this kitchen isn't just for me. Lorna makes sure we all eat."

All?

"I try, but these men like to disappear, sometimes in the middle of the night for days at a time with no notice, I may add. When that happens, I end up eating the same thing for every meal. But hey, it frees up some time for other things."

He shook his head. "Lorna is Reid's wife."

"Or Reid is my husband," she corrected with a wink my direction.

"When she married him," Sterling went on, "she got more than she bargained for. Patrick, Reid, and I are a package. You get one and you get us all."

My brows rose. "Oh?"

Sterling smiled. "Not like that, sunshine. We have limits on what we share."

"Good to know."

"Housing is one. It's easier that way. Reid and Lorna as well as Patrick all live here." He shrugged. "Not on these floors. We'll have some privacy. Their apartments are one floor below. All of the floors are connected and protected."

Protected?

I had this vision of bulletproof walls and windows or maybe an infrared force field that sizzled with high-end technology making the building appear as if the floors he discussed weren't present. Maybe Sterling was like the comic book superheroes and he'd brought me to his secret lair.

As I let that thought settle, I realized what he'd said about Reid being married, the same as Dr. Dixon had mentioned. "So this mystery man really exists?"

"Mystery man?" Lorna asked.

"Reid. I've heard his name, but so far, that's it. Oh..." I grinned at Sterling. "...I take that back. I think I heard his voice once."

The way Sterling's dark stare gleamed, making my insides twist, I was certain that we were both thinking about what happened in the office of his cabin after I overheard Reid's voice. Just the memory recirculated my blood.

How could I be sore from whatever happened and yet want the man who was now seated beside me?

"Oh, that man is real," Lorna said, "even when he works twenty-four seven."

"Things have been busy," Sterling replied.

"I know." She looked at me. "And don't expect to learn more than *busy*—like what it entails. I guarantee you won't find out."

My cheeks rose.

"Now," she said, "what can I make for you to eat?"

"I can cook," I volunteered.

"That's great. Another day, we can cook together, but today, how about you let me do it? Having caveman over here carry you from counter to counter could get a little crowded."

"I like her," I whispered to Sterling with a giggle.

"That makes one of us."

Lorna's laugh filled the kitchen.

"Sparrow," Patrick said, his footsteps preceding his entrance by milliseconds. As we both turned to another doorway, the opposite direction as we'd entered, Patrick's eyes widened and feet came to a stop at the sight of me. "I mean, *Mr.* Sparrow." He nodded my way, his blue eyes smiling. "Ms. McCrie, it's good to see that you're up. I didn't realize..."

"Thank you, Patrick. I'm glad to be up. I just need someone to fill me in on what I missed."

"What's the last thing you remember?"

Lorna set a cup of coffee in front of me. "Did I hear you like cream?"

"Yes, thank you. I can do this myself."

She shrugged. "Then what would I do?"

I turned back to Patrick. "The plane and getting ready to land, nothing after that." My eyes opened wide. "It wasn't another airplane issue, was it?"

I knew the answer before I finished the question. If it had been, I wouldn't have been the only one attached to an IV with a doctor present.

"No, that wasn't it," Sterling said as he and Patrick stared back and forth, leaving me waiting for one or both to share information.

"Oh, I just remembered," I went on, "we were going somewhere...an engagement. I was nervous." I shook my head. "I really don't recall more. Did we make it? What happened?"

There were more looks passed between the two men.

"Are you going to tell me?"

Instead of answering, Sterling stood, pushing the chair under the table and turning to Patrick. "Do you have something for me?"

"If we could bother you for a minute?"

"We?" I repeated. "Maybe one day soon I'll meet the infamous Reid"

Lorna smiled. "Once you do, you won't forget him."

I grinned up at Sterling. "Yeah, I know someone else like that. So, Sterling....details?"

"I told you not to ask for details," Lorna reminded me.

"This is different. It isn't random. It's about—"

Sterling's lips came over mine, stealing my words and refocusing my attention. Once the kiss ended, his dark eyes shone inches away from mine, causing my pulse to kick up as I swallowed.

"No more questions. After you eat, we'll talk about what happened." He looked up at Patrick. "I won't be gone long." His expression lightened. "And don't let Lorna fill your head with stories that aren't true."

Nodding, I realized that this was his way of saying that Lorna was safe, someone with whom I could talk. I wasn't used to seeking permission and wasn't sure I ever would, but it was nice to receive it.

"And you," he said pointing to Lorna, "food. Remember, that's what you do. No lies about things she doesn't need to know. And above all, she's not to walk anywhere until Dr. Dixon gives her clearance."

"Did I hear my name?" Dr. Dixon asked, entering the kitchen and looking my way. "Imagine my surprise when I came back to the room after a call with the hospital and my patient had disappeared."

Spank your ass, Sterling mouthed.

Though he hadn't said the statement aloud, from the way the temperature rose and my cheeks filled with heat, it felt as though he'd announced it to the entire room. My increased pulse from moments earlier jumped another few notches. Smiling, I lifted my coffee cup to my lips and waited for a wink or any sign that he was joking.

It didn't come.

I couldn't decide if that made me nervous or anxious. Whatever it was, Sterling Sparrow could elicit a variety of emotions with simply a look.

Dr. Dixon and Lorna chatted about what food would be best for me to eat as Patrick and Sterling disappeared, leaving the direction Patrick had come. While Dr. Dixon helped herself to a cup of coffee, I decided I needed a tour. It wasn't like we were in the wilderness. We were in downtown Chicago.

How big could this place be?

As I thought about that, I also tried to find words to explain to myself what was happening—here, in this apartment.

Normalcy.

Camaraderie.

Friendship.

In this place, with the absence of Genevieve Sparrow, there was a shift in dynamic, a sense that things were completely different than they had been with the staff at the cabin or on the plane.

The barriers that were present in those locations didn't seem to exist here, even with Sterling. While each person had their role, they all worked together, looking after and caring for one another. It was as if while here, behind closed doors— or infrared technology—these people were more than colleagues, more than employer and employee.

They were a family.

It wasn't the kind of family brought together by birth but by life.

Sterling had told me that he'd been to actual war with

Patrick and Reid, that he trusted them implicitly. It seemed as though marrying Reid brought Lorna into that equation. If I were Sterling's, as he'd proclaimed, it would also include me.

That realization enlightened and warmed me. A man like Sterling Sparrow wasn't one-dimensional. He wasn't all intensity and work. He had other sides, some that he'd shared with me and others that he shared with these people. This was his inner circle and he'd brought me here.

Of course, I loved the Nelsons and the way they'd included me. Yet I was still the one outsider, the one whose name was different. This gathering was different.

Could Sterling Sparrow be more than my lover and protector? Could he be my family?

Whoa, Kennedy, you're making some big leaps.

Wait, no...Araneae.

I shook my head.

I didn't even know my own name. How could I even guess at the future?

As the chatting around me continued, I shook the thoughts away. It was probably the drugs or whatever had happened last night. I wasn't a little girl in need of a fantasy family. I was a woman with a full life even before Sterling swept in like a cyclone, disrupting everything in his path. Besides, by the way Genevieve Sparrow responded to me, I couldn't foresee a *welcome to the Sparrow family* party in the future.

"Ms. McCrie, would you like breakfast or lunch?" Lorna asked as Dr. Dixon sat in the seat Sterling had vacated.

"Oh my God, it's Monday," I said, my thoughts of the Nelsons opening doors to my memories.

"Yes, it usually comes after Sunday," Lorna said.

"I need to be at work." I quickly stood, holding onto the edge of the table as the room slowly spun.

"Araneae," Dr. Dixon said, her voice coming from a tunnel as she reached for my hand. "Please sit back down."

Nodding, I did as she said. The little bit of coffee in my otherwise-empty stomach percolated. A flush of heat followed by a chill coated my skin in goose bumps. As I reached for my own upper arms I flinched. My right one, not the one that had the IV, was tender to the touch.

What had happened?

STERLING

*P*atrick and I walked in silence to the elevator within my apartment. There was shit going down and yet somehow, I had to put aside the image I had in my mind, the one of me doing what I'd just threatened, my hand-print reddening Araneae's ass—make that plural, handprints. After what she's been through, she wasn't ready, but when she was, I was the man for the job. After disobeying my simple demands and drinking that drink, she should be happy if that's the only thing I do.

She didn't realize how important she was. Sneaking out on Dr. Dixon, the thought made my blood boil. What if she'd fallen on those stairs? The next picture in my imagination was of her at the bottom of the staircase, not standing but sprawled out—injured.

That was the problem with what I did, the life I lived. It wasn't difficult for my mind's eye to conjure up gruesome images.

Where Patrick and I were headed wasn't the elevator that connected my five floors to the outside world, not the same one that my mother rode up and thankfully, down. The one she and others rode connected us to the world. Not just anyone gained access to that elevator. If anyone unexpected made it past the well-paid and faithful security guards, Reid's technology stopped their ascent before the elevator ever got close to the top of the building.

I should reconsider my mother's clearance.

This elevator that we were about to enter was different—it transported us within the world we'd created within my five floors.

The doors were hidden behind a pocket door. Laying my palm on the sensor beside the doors, the screen came to life and the elevator opened. This elevator only had four options: P, A, 2, and G. The penthouse consisted of the two floors where Araneae and I now lived. Only the first floor of the penthouse was accessible from the elevator. 'A' stood for apartments, where Patrick, Reid, and Lorna resided. That particular level had been subdivided into three complete living spaces, each with multiple bedrooms, bathrooms, a kitchen, living area, and offices. Level A was only accessible from P, not allowing for guests or entertaining within their apartments.

It was all right. None of us were the entertaining type.

Though Patrick, Reid, and I did most of our business from the next two floors—both accessible from 2 on the elevator's control panel—we each also had private offices in our own living quarters. 'G' was our direct route to our private garage.

Even the fleeting thought of the empty apartment on the same floor as Reid and Patrick's made my chest ache. The loss wasn't something I dwelt upon. Nevertheless, I'd come to acknowledge that the pain would never fully go away.

"Reid will add Ms. McCrie's palm print to the security," Patrick said as the elevator doors closed.

I shook my head. "No." Although he didn't question, I answered, "There's no need. She isn't leaving the penthouse without you or me, so she doesn't need access to the garage. There's no reason for her to go to your floor." I rarely did. "And she sure as hell isn't going into the work space."

"Have fun with that conversation."

My lips quirked. "Yeah, I probably will."

"Are you going to tell her everything about last night now that she doesn't remember?"

I ran my hand through my hair. "I don't know. I was expecting a full-out battle, and now I have the option to let it slide. I hadn't even asked her what she remembered. I was too happy that she was awake, walking, talking—oh fuck, you should have heard her with my mother."

"Now that is a conversation I might enjoy."

I took in his growing smirk. "What?" I asked.

"Happy looks good on you, Sparrow. It's been—"

"Yeah, don't get used to it," I said, interrupting him, somewhat surprised I'd been the one to use that word. When was the last time? I shook the thought away. "Someone crossed us last night. I won't be happy until that person or persons are no longer an issue."

The elevator stopped, the doors opening to a stark concrete hallway with one steel door and another sensor.

"She's blissfully unaware," I said, considering what I was going to do. "Part of me wants to keep her that way. When we walked out of the club last night, before she collapsed I wasn't happy with her for getting that drink or leaving my sight. She wasn't thrilled with my response. I saw it in her eyes. And then when Annabelle made her announcement...damn, I don't know if I want to fill in all those gaps."

"She's either going to find out from you or someone else."

"Not if I don't let her leave the apartment."

"Do you want me to be honest?" Patrick asked.

"You're going to tell me that she'd have something to say about that."

"Has she asked about Sinful Threads?"

"She hasn't. Shit," I said, "with everything else, I haven't even thought about it."

"She will. That company is her life."

He was right. I wouldn't be keeping her in the apartment even though that was the safest option.

"Don't worry about Sinful Threads right now," Patrick went on. "I thought about it, and since I still have her phone, *she*..." He emphasized the pronoun. "...messaged Louisa and Winifred, telling them that she isn't feeling well—it was probably the traveling. She hopes to be back in full swing by tomorrow but is available for emergencies."

"Damn, you're a lifesaver. Was there anything else?"

"Yeah, it's about that Francesca guy at the warehouse here in Chicago. There's something about him that I don't like."

During the few interactions I'd had with the man, he was more than willing to take my money at the expense of Araneae's business. "I agree that he's slimy. Let's keep an eye on him and be sure he's not the tip of some iceberg. Then...we'll make some decisions on his future."

"Future employment?"

"Future, period," I clarified.

Patrick nodded with a grin. "Good plan."

I placed my palm on the sensor near the door. The added security was necessary. We were entering the heart of our operation—the Sparrow outfit.

The steel door slid into the wall as our large work space came into view.

Immediately, my blood pressure lowered. No matter the chaos of the world, this room was my Zen. Everything here soothed me—the concrete floors, the large screens on the walls going up nearly fifteen feet, the multiple systems that constantly monitored anything and everything. I even liked the smell—concrete and technology. We were set up for everything. There were treadmills and free weights. Sometimes ideas and decisions came better with physical exertion. Because of that, there were also showers as well as a kitchen area. This giant space was our control central, the heart and soul of the outfit—reinforced and impenetrable. If necessary, we could exist on this floor for a long time.

Floor *two*, where we'd entered, was the securer level of the two working floors, accessible exclusively by our elevator and another one equally as protected that only connected it to floor one. Each of those elevators opened to a locked steel door like the one we'd just passed.

No one entered this floor but us.

This was where the three of us did whatever was needed to be done, no matter how filthy, unfathomable, or inhumane. This was where judgments were passed and sentences were decided.

Sparrow Enterprises, the company that excelled in real estate, had prime property on Michigan Avenue for everyone to see with thousands of worldwide employees and even more private contractors. That was where the upfront side of Sparrow resided. My assistants there were trustworthy—to a point.

The two Sparrow worlds didn't mix—except in here where no one else could observe.

The underground world of Sparrow operated fully from these two floors of the building. The floor marked numeral one on the panel had a private second entrance to the outside. Others worked there also—crews and their leaders ultimately overseen by Reid and Patrick came and went. Meetings occurred. Floor one was where the administration met with capos and associates. These people came from all walks of life. Some stayed in the shadows while others walked in the daylight in front of the cameras. They were the people who pretended to run the city as well as those who wanted to.

Decisions that appeared to the world as coming from others were first run through us.

Though my decision was final, rarely did I disagree with Patrick or Reid. Their word was as good as mine.

It was an unspoken fact that Sparrow was the name that ran Chicago.

On occasion, people had forgotten. Reminders were a bitch. Those people didn't forget again, if they were around to have a second chance.

It wasn't uncommon to have many associates on the floor that we called number one. That was why it was only connected to our residences via this floor. While the underground world of Sparrow didn't hand out W-2s at the end of the year, it had its share of well-paid employees. Everything that occurred there could be viewed from here. In this line of work, complete trust was earned not given.

STERLING

*a*s our footsteps neared, Reid's chair spun toward us. He'd been studying twenty screens with numerous readouts on each. His abilities when it came to technology and multitasking were truly unmatched. There was nothing he didn't or couldn't understand. If he found something unfamiliar, he learned it.

When I asked him questions or for clarification, he could rattle off verbatim definitions or complete manuals. What took others days or weeks literally took him hours. He wasn't the world's best conversationalist, but when you were hunkered down in a bombed-out school waiting to kill or be killed, having a quiet partner with a mind assessing every possibility was better than someone with the gift of gab.

Patrick and I'd learned that while Reid's words were often few, the ones he spoke were important. The emotion he'd shown on the phone last night—through the car's speakers—was a rarity, another example of how Araneae had gotten to all of us. The only other person who witnessed Reid's emotion was Lorna. Though I was hesitant to recognize it at first, the two of them had something special. When she was near, he became someone different than the man who was one of my most trusted friends and colleagues.

Currently, there was something in his expression that said he had information.

"What do you have?" I asked. "Is it the bartender?"

Instead of answering, Reid said, "Stephanie has called for you three times. That woman's nothing if she isn't annoying."

I pulled my phone from my pocket. Stephanie was my number-one assistant in that office on Michigan Avenue. The screen came to life. "Well, she's called me four times directly. I guess I need to turn my ringer back on."

Reid nodded. "Lorna said Ms. McCrie is awake. I'm glad."

"Me too. Any idea why Stephanie is calling?"

"From the look of her computer screens..." Reid could screen share with anyone at any time without their knowledge. "...she's spent the day rearranging your schedule. There were a few meetings you didn't make."

"Fuck. Araneae has me all—"

"Sparrow," Patrick interjected, "it's all right. Shit, after last night, we're all spent. The three of us combined probably haven't slept three hours."

"I doubt you two called me down here to remind me that I missed sleep and a few meetings." As I waited for their information, I typed out a quick text to Stephanie, explaining that I'd be in the office after one o'clock. I didn't offer any explanation or even an apology that her morning was fucked up. It was my name on the top of that building. Shit happens.

"The bartender is..." He pulled up a picture on one of the large screens. "Amanda Smith."

"Sounds like a fucking alias." I nodded toward the screen. "That's her."

"It's not an alias," Reid replied. "She's working at the club to pay for veterinary college in Urbana."

"That's a long drive from the club."

"She only works weekends," Reid answered.

"And according to a very reliable source, she does more than bartend," Patrick offered.

"Tell me how she's there." No one got into the club as a patron or an employee without connections and a vow of silence.

"Her aunt is Antonio Hillman's maid. Officially she works for his wife, Clarice."

Antonio was Wendell Hillman's son. Antonio's dirty work for the McFaddens wasn't as hands-on as his father's. He excelled in money laundering. Offshore and dark-web accounting with enough shell corporations connected to him to cover a fucking beach. He was also—from many of his various entities in order to keep campaign-finance reports clean—one of the biggest donors to the McFadden campaigns. Antonio had his eye on some posh White House position.

Cleaning money wasn't limited to the McFaddens. The Sparrows did it too. Knowing the players on both teams kept the Sparrows in power.

You weren't in charge if you didn't know what was happening across the entire city.

The muscles in my neck tightened. "That's too fucking close of a relationship."

"She drove back to Urbana last night," Reid said, "but we have an interview crew on their way. They know not to be specific. We don't want word getting out that Araneae was drugged. They'll know if Amanda was involved."

I gritted my teeth.

Women.

That was my line—the one I hated to cross.

Just because I hated it didn't mean I wouldn't do it. We now lived in the world of equal opportunity—women killed as easily as men. Women may be my line in the sand, but Araneae was my line in the fucking concrete. No one touched her. No one. "If it was her, tell the crew to take care of her. And don't hide it. Clean their tracks, but make a statement."

"Got it, boss," Patrick replied.

I turned around to leave. "I'm getting back to Araneae."

"There's something else," Reid said, stopping me in my tracks and turning me back to him. "It's Judge Landers."

Annabelle Landers, Araneae's biological mother.

"What about her?"

"Her docket has been cleared for the next two weeks."

"And this is relevant...why?"

"Because," Patrick said, "she was admitted under another name to St. Michael's Hospital in East Chicago, Indiana."

"Indiana? For what?" My mind swirled with the possibilities. "Why not Loyola, Rush, or Northwestern? There are highly acclaimed hospitals right here." I reached for a chair, spun it around, and sat down, straddling the back. "Wait. Why was she admitted?" I recalled her reaction from last night at seeing Araneae.

"Psych," Patrick replied. "According to the patient records, she admitted herself."

"You're sure it's her."

"Yeah, it's her. When patients admit themselves for psychological evaluation, they can leave whenever they want. I would assume the false name is to avoid the consequences to her appointment." Reid took a breath. "There's more. She has injuries that were documented on the admittance paperwork."

"Can we assume it was Rubio who helped contribute to her *injuries?*" I asked, knowing that there was no depth too low for that asshole to go.

"No actual proof like a video recording," Reid answered. "Using traffic cams, I can track him from the club to her place. Her home is deficient of technology. She doesn't even have a dot or echo. The only way for the interior of her house to be seen or heard is via her computer, phone, or security system. By the time she and Rubio entered, all of that technology was surprisingly offline. According to our eyes on the street, the senator has a bandage on his cheek this morning. Shaving incident. He joked about it at a press conference."

"Right because I'm sure he shaves with a cheap-ass Bic. Fuck him. At least she fought back." I stood. "Fucker needs to pick a fight with someone who knows how to fight back."

"I think he has," Patrick said. "I'd be happy to kick his ass."

"We all would," I agreed. The sad truth was that even killing him wouldn't stop it all; however, it would make me feel better. No, our plan involved a lot more.

"She's not talking," Reid began, "yet the staff is concerned that the injuries are self-inflicted. You know that I've been digging from the beginning into Ms. McCrie—for almost a decade. The reason she was presumed to no longer exist was because of one very strong firsthand witness." He pulled up a photograph of an obituary from the Chicago Tribune dated five days after Araneae's birthday.

The McCries, Daniel McCrie and wife, the Honorable Judge Annabelle Landers, regret to announce the unfortunate loss of their daughter, Araneae McCrie. The infant passed away less than an hour after birth. The family has decided that there will be no public services. Condolences may be made in the form of donations in their daughter's name to the University of Chicago School of Law.

"I've seen this," I said. "Obviously, it's a lie." I recalled my mother's visit. "My mother said something today about this. According to her, she remembers when this happened and Annabelle was devastated."

"From eyewitnesses at the club last night," Patrick said, "McFadden was livid after you two left, red-faced and about to blow. Landers was in shock—white as a ghost. Hillman— Wendell—got them out of there. McFadden's driver was waiting. Hillman and his wife went to their own home. From Reid's hacking into city cameras, McFadden's driver took Rubio and Landers to her home."

"The driver waited for over an hour, drove McFadden home, and then returned to Landers'. He personally drove her to Indiana. From that point, she admitted herself. I'm not trying to make assumptions," Reid added. "Maybe she's known and stuck to the story for twenty-six years—that her daughter died after birth. If that's the case, she has probably kept the truth from her lover too. He might have taken that deception out on her. Then again, if she didn't know, it could have been more than she could handle."

"Why, if she knew, wouldn't she have told Rubio?" I asked.

"Because she can't trust that son of a bitch," Patrick offered.

"Pauline McFadden was Daniel McCrie's sister," I said, putting the pieces of the puzzle together.

Patrick shook his head. "We didn't say it wasn't fucked, but that information isn't new. We all know the judge has been his companion since McCrie died ten years ago."

"I bet they have some great Thanksgiving dinners." I shook my head. "For not the first time, I wonder what Daniel McCrie knew," I said, thinking aloud. "I always figured he knew Araneae was alive. I guess I figured Landers did too. There are too many holes in this history."

"We'll probably never know," Patrick replied. "It's hard to say. The birth happened at a small rural hospital. It was right after all the shit hit the fan."

Reid lifted his hand. "Boss, before you go back upstairs, let me mention again about the Marshes. This has been a thorn in my side forever. No matter what I try, I can't find them. They existed for roughly sixteen years. Before Araneae and after, they evaporated into thin air." Reid let out an exasperated breath as his palm slapped the desk. "Sparrow, I've spent over ten years on that quest. I don't fucking fail. They are the ghosts in this story."

"What about the hit?" I asked. "There's the rumor that Byron was killed, prompting Josey to hide Araneae. She confirmed that her adoptive father had died before her adoptive mother drove her to the airport."

"It didn't happen," Reid said, his head shaking side to side. "I'm not saying Ms. McCrie is lying. It was probably what she was told. Yet there's no accident report. No coroner's report.

Not even a report of the car that he drove going to a junk-yard. Nothing."

Reid pulled up the picture that Araneae carried with her of her and her two adoptive parents. On the giant screen it was grainy and the crease appeared to be a huge fissure.

"Even facial recognition," Reid went on, "doesn't work. I have everything that should lead to them: their IDs from when she was with them, the résumé Byron submitted to Boeing, even passports. Nothing checks out. Everything on the résumé, from the references to the degrees, is unverifi-able. Yet he was hired by Boeing. It's not like a grocery store. You don't get in there without verification."

"Not with all their government contracts," I said. "It means one thing. I'm not saying to give up, but damn, they had help disappearing." I leaned forward on the back of the chair.

"And appearing," Patrick said.

"Ms. McCrie became Kennedy Hawkins days after Daniel McCrie died. I've got the timeline, just not the players," Reid said.

I ran my hand through my hair. "How do I tell Araneae that the parents she knew don't exist and the one she doesn't remember is in the hospital with a possible psychotic break?"

"McFadden," Patrick interjected, "is a powder keg ready to blow. He'd lined all his ducks in a nice row, and now the appearance of Araneae has set them all out of kilter."

"How is Araneae's Chicago office?" I asked, changing the subject. We'd beaten this horse into the ground more times than I could count.

"Almost ready," Patrick answered. "Our guys are working on security. She'll need an on-site assistant. I was thinking that instead of taking out a help-wanted ad or using a head-hunting service, we put someone there we know is trustworthy."

I nodded. "Make it happen." I returned the subject back to Landers. "You know, maybe we've misjudged the good judge. I'm wondering if she's in bed with McFadden because of what she knows or because she didn't have a choice?" I thought about that. "I don't know. I'm thinking about what my mother said a little while ago. I'm not saying Genevieve Sparrow doesn't lie, but she was pretty worked up too. Annabelle was extremely upset to see Araneae with me. If she was acting, she's one hell of an actress."

"My fucking assessment," Reid said, "is that everyone is lying in one way or another. Over the years, rumors became fact and facts were lost. Most of this shit happened when the three of us were kids. This mess was created by the generation before us, and like every other fucking mess they made, we're the ones picking up the pieces."

ANNABELLE

Twenty-six years ago

The vaguely familiar man sitting across from me shook his head as he stared my direction. I was covered with only a hospital dressing gown. I wasn't in the hospital but at my doctor's appointment—my obstetrician—in an examination room smaller than my closet. The person who entered and was waiting for my reply wasn't my doctor. Though I believed I'd seen him before, I didn't know him.

"Judge Landers?"

I wrung my hands resting on my lap as my feet dangled from the examination table. This man wasn't my husband.

Daniel and I'd met in law school, the University of Chicago. A gregarious man, I found myself immediately in lust with not only his handsome face but also his personality. Daniel McCrie could, as the saying went, sell a glass of water to a drowning man. His finesse and manipulation of the English language was mesmerizing. In law school I used to chuckle to myself as he would orate his closing statement for a mock criminal defense. With a memory that surpassed the multitude of crib notes I'd taken, he would rattle off statutes and cases, defendants and dates, like he was singing a song. Not only accurate, his argument radiated passion that could be sensed throughout the large classrooms.

He was going to be a great—no, the greatest—criminal attorney in the history of criminal defense. That was what I told my parents when I first introduced him.

We were compatible in the way magnets attract.

Opposites.

While I was more patient and open-minded, when Daniel made up his mind, he saw no other options. I was an excellent student and felt no need to broadcast the news. He on the other hand thrived on recognition. Like the iron-rich material that made up real magnets, when we were too heated our attraction lessened, but our determination grew.

The wedding happened in a quaint historic chapel in Cambridge, Wisconsin. It was a small fairy-tale wedding, timed directly after graduation and before our bar examinations. After a monthlong European honeymoon, the fairy tale ended as real life took over.

The next years were filled with pressures and stresses as we each found our way in the real world. Daniel joined a well-known firm and worked to make his name in the world of criminal defense. With a keen interest in finance as well as his knowledge of precedent-setting case law, he thrived on the big cases—the ones that caught the interest of the public. At first, he was only a co-counsel until the day that one of the partners asked him to be lead.

The case gained national prominence—and so did Daniel McCrie.

There's a saying that one case can make or break an attorney's career. I'd seen it break others, reducing a competent attorney to nothing more than an ambulance chaser. That wasn't the case with Daniel. That one case opened up a world of possibilities. He was asked to become a partner.

To my utter shock, he declined, instead deciding to open his own practice.

His bold move was stupid in my opinion. We had money. We both came from wealthy families, yet the costs associated with his decision were astronomical. He didn't listen to me. His success was legendary.

My passion had been prosecution.

Where do attorneys go when that is their forte? To work for the state prosecutor.

The office was nothing like Daniel's nor was the pay. My compensation came in the form of administering justice. With the encouragement of Daniel's family as well as the backing of a few of his clients, seven years after graduating law school, I ran for judge for the Illinois Circuit Court. To my disbelief, I won the election. At thirty-three years of age I was sworn in as a circuit court judge.

Four years later, with Mother Nature knocking on my chamber door, I told Daniel the one thing I wanted that our marriage hadn't provided.

I wanted a baby.

We had material possessions: money, houses, cars, and vacations. His legal/financial advising practice was booming. With my time for re-election nearing, I was ready to take some time away from the bench and do what we hadn't discussed since law school—begin a family.

Though cautious, Daniel agreed. "A baby?"

"Yes, I'm not getting any younger."

"Annabelle, you know who some of my clients are?"

"Some. You don't tell me much and that's the way it should be. I can't talk to you about a case I'm trying. You shouldn't talk about your clients. The two worlds might cross."

Daniel nodded. "That's what concerns me about a child."

"No." I went to where he was sitting. "I'll take time away from the court." I shrugged. "It's been an honor. If people are willing to re-elect me after some time off, I'll go back. If not, we will do fine on your income."

He exhaled. "We can try."

And try we did. I took my temperature. We had charts. We scheduled afternoon "meetings." His sperm count was checked and so was my ovulation. The hands of time continued to turn.

Now, here I was, in my thirty-fifth week of a complicated pregnancy, my first to go this far—the miscarriages were heartbreaking—and I was being faced with a choice that threatened my dream.

"How did you get in here," I asked. "In my doctor's office? Why are you here?" Tears leaked from my eyes though my voice held no emotion. Years on the bench had taught me to hide that shit.

The older gentleman shook his head. "You wouldn't answer our requests. We were running out of options. Judge Landers, your time to make this choice is about up. As we speak, raids are occurring at your home and your husband's office. You're an intelligent woman who knows the law. You understand the gravity of this situation."

I did.

Was I willing to do this? Could I?

I didn't have an answer.

ARANEAE

*H*aving a cardiologist help me with a shower seemed a bit like overkill. The woman specialized in the health of people's hearts, and here she was walking me into the bathroom of the room where I'd awoken. The room itself as well as the attached bathroom was lovely and impersonal. I hadn't asked if this was also Sterling's bedroom, but I had the feeling it wasn't. Then again, the bedroom he called his own within the cabin didn't have any pictures or personal mementos, nothing that said it was his own—well, other than it was.

"Your color is better since the oatmeal and fruit," Dr. Dixon said. "And you made it back upstairs, but that doesn't mean I'm going to let you fall in the shower on my watch." The part she didn't say, the part hanging in the air like a neon sign, was that she wouldn't want to be the one to explain a fall to Sterling.

He may be more open in this apartment; however, he was still Sterling Sparrow.

Dr. Dixon was right: the food had helped and I had made it upstairs. The trip to the second floor was slow, reminding me of what Sterling had said about hiking to the lake in Ontario. The hike back up to the cabin took three times as long as the hike down. I'd say the same could be said for those stairs.

It's an apartment.

Who needs so many stairs?

As for food, Dr. Dixon decided that I shouldn't eat anything too heavy or spicy. Oatmeal and blueberries fit the bill. After giving it time to digest, it was more satisfying than I would have believed.

While I wanted to find my phone—which was probably with Patrick—and call Louisa and Winnie, I doubted I'd find it while Patrick and Sterling were MIA. According to Lorna, they'd gone to what she called their lair. It sounded a lot like a bat cave, but Batman fought criminals, working on behalf of the Justice League. I wasn't convinced that title of superhero would apply to Sterling.

Strangely, that didn't bother me as much as I thought it should.

According to him, I had somehow been born into this world. Maybe I was a villain too. If Spiderman was a hero, couldn't Spiderwoman be an anti-hero?

Each exposed secret revealed another lie about my life— the life I thought I had—and yet I believed that despite the little that had been shared with me, the truth was still veiled in lies.

And then there was the hole that was last night. Neither truth nor lie, it was gone.

Dr. Dixon explained that amnesia or memory loss associated with trauma wasn't uncommon. It also wasn't usually permanent. She recommended not dwelling on it. The information would return in its own time. That sounded a lot like the information from Sterling Sparrow. The difference was that his information wasn't locked away in the recesses of my mind. It was his to share as he saw fit.

Instead of worrying about my phone or retrieving my memories, after finishing breakfast I asked Dr. Dixon about taking a shower. Apparently having unwanted drugs in my system and my stomach pumped—the only information I'd officially received—gave me a sense of yuck.

Yes, that was my official description of how I felt, as if my skin was covered in a coating, not lotions and creams but something I wanted gone.

On our long walk back upstairs, she explained that my body needed to expel the chemicals I'd consumed—another clue, they'd been consumed—therefore, it did and would continue to remove them in any way possible. The IV and catheter—another yuck—from earlier, and once I woke, my eating and drinking, all worked together to help remove in a normal way, whatever had been left after my stomach was pumped. The body's other method for removal was perspiration. As happened when I stood too quickly in the kitchen, apparently throughout the night, I'd been wracked with bouts of perspiration and chills. The best way to describe the result would be to equate it to a very bad hangover, when even your pores emitted the odor of the offending liquor.

I'd had that terrible experience once with vodka after an off-campus party my senior year at St. Mary of the Forest. It was my first experience with alcohol, and after that night and the next morning, it was my last experience for about three years.

Vodka and I still weren't friends. Wine and whiskey, that's a different story. Though in general, other than occasionally, drinking wasn't my thing.

Even though I'd washed my face and tried to clean myself prior to going downstairs, I now can only imagine the first impression I gave to Genevieve Sparrow.

Right, Kennedy, next time you meet her, be freshly showered and dressed up. You two will become best friends.

I didn't think so.

Dr. Dixon directed me to the long vanity. "Araneae, there's a seat in the shower. I recommend you sit as much as possible. Your strength will return. Your blood saturation levels are normal. Just give yourself time."

I nodded as she turned on the shower. Immediately, warm steam escaped the glass enclosure. As the humidity built I had a flashback, a memory of Sterling on the plane. He was standing by a shower, every inch of his body on display. Yet it wasn't erotic or even comforting.

No, this memory was frightening.

My body quaked with a chill.

"Are you going to be all right?" Dr. Dixon asked, reaching for my hand.

I looked up into her big brown eyes. "I don't know."

Was I?

The image that had skirted over my memory was so different than the man at the bottom of the stairs. Maybe I was confusing things in reality with the hodgepodge of dreams.

"The water's warm. Let me help you."

Letting go of the counter, I untied the sash of the robe. Beneath the covering I only wore panties, ones I recalled putting on while on the airplane. The dress hadn't allowed a bra and this room was basically devoid of clothes. I'd taken a look into the closet and opened a few drawers. As I opened the plush long robe, I recalled Sterling's decree that no one but him would see me naked.

It was a risk making assumptions when it came to him, but in my mind, the doctor who had just taken care of me qualified as an exception.

As the sleeves pulled over my shoulders, I winced. The soreness wasn't from the arm that had been attached to the IV. No, this was my upper right arm. My gaze darted to the discolored skin. The marked area wasn't prominent—shades of blues and greens—yet it was distinctive in the undeniable shape of four strong fingers.

I rolled my arm to see the darker oval of what could be assumed to be the print of a thumb.

My eyes fluttered closed as I tried to recall what had happened.

Dr. Dixon stepped forward, her eyes narrowing as she inspected the bruise. "I saw this last night." Her gaze met mine. "Would you like to tell me what happened?"

"I-I don't remember." I gently rubbed my other hand over the evidence.

"I want you to know that I would do anything for Mr. Sparrow. But first and foremost, I'm a doctor. I have him to thank for that, but right now you're my patient. I'm here if you need someone. I won't—"

I shook my head. "Dr. Dixon, I'm not lying or covering up. You saw him downstairs. It doesn't fit in character." Though I recalled another scene with a different character. "I don't remember what happened to my arm."

"She was falling and I caught her."

ARANEAE

$\mathcal{W}$e both sucked in a breath and turned toward the deep voice rumbling from the doorway, dominating the bathroom. It wasn't simply the sound of Sterling Sparrow that stole my breath; it was the authority of his presence. Swallowing, I scanned the man who'd suddenly appeared.

More haggard than usual, Sterling was still the handsomest man I'd ever encountered. Though his gaze and set jaw said business, his posture seemed more relaxed. With one arm lifted to the doorjamb, the muscles of his bicep bulged. In the time it took to blink, my gaze moved lower to where his lightweight sweatpants hung low from his hips, revealing the V of his torso. In that small toned area between his t-shirt and pants, made visible by his uplifted arm, was the area with the trail of dark hair.

"Mr. Sparrow," Dr. Dixon said, focusing my gaze back to

his. No doubt she was wondering the same thing that I was
—*what did he overhear?*

The dark expression I recalled not liking was back as the
tendons in his neck pulled tighter with each word. He
lowered his arm. "Thank you, Dr. Dixon, for your assistance,
professionalism, candor, and discretion. I can guarantee that
Araneae is safe with me."

"Sir, I-I wasn't..."

My pulse kicked up as they spoke.

"You were," he said, "and given what you see, you should."
He stepped forward and gently reached for my arm. As his
dark stare scanned the bruise, his fingers intertwined with
mine. "I caught her before she hit the floor. Not all bruises
are as justifiable." With one finger from his other hand, he
turned my face from side to side.

What was he doing?

Returning his attention to Dr. Dixon, he went on, "I mean
it. Thank you, Renita. One day, if you haven't already, you'll
save a life, and I don't mean regarding cardiac care." He tilted
his head toward the running shower. "Is she strong enough
for that?"

"The drug is mostly gone."

It was as if I wasn't standing there, my robe partially open,
as they continued to talk, to discuss me.

"Yes," Dr. Dixon went on, "she asked to shower, and I
believe she's up to it. I wouldn't recommend leaving her in
there unattended. That's what we were about to do. I was
going to help, be sure she had the strength. After that, I
recommend rest for the remainder of the day. Each day will be
better."

"Hello, I'm the patient. Talk to me." I didn't say it aloud though the words were on my tongue and fighting to jump off.

Sterling nodded. "I think I have it covered from here. She's released from your care. I'm sure there are other patients in need of your expertise."

Released from her care...

That was Sterling's way of countering what the doctor had said before we knew he was here. If I were released, I was no longer her patient.

Dr. Dixon nodded. Our eyes met in the large mirror, the one slowly being covered in the warm moisture. "You are going to be fine, Araneae. However, if you start feeling ill or something doesn't feel right, tell Mr. Sparrow or Mr. Kelly to contact me. We'll reinstate your care, and I'll be here as quickly as possible."

Before I could respond, Sterling did.

"Patrick has already taken most of your things to your car in the garage. It seems as though we're done."

Dr. Dixon stood taller. "Thank you. Goodbye, Mr. Sparrow. Ms. McCrie..." She smiled my direction. "...it has been a pleasure meeting you."

I forced a scoff. "Maybe next time it could be less traumatic."

"I'd like that."

Reaching for my shoulders, Sterling gently turned me toward him as Dr. Dixon's footsteps disappeared into the bedroom and the sound of the door to the hallway alerted us that she had departed. Though I was confused and unsure about...well, everything, under his gaze I melted toward him, wanting—and in my weakened state, shamelessly needing—

the man from downstairs, the one concerned about my well-being, the one who protected me.

The pounding of his heart thumped loudly below the soft t-shirt as I laid my cheek and upper body against his strong solid torso. In seconds, Sterling's t-shirt dampened as tears of exhaustion and uncertainty escaped my closed lids. As I struggled for breath, his strong arms encircled me with warmth, moving downward until they rested upon my lower back. When he didn't speak, after taking a deep breath, I did.

"I need to know what happened."

His chin above my head nodded. "I'll tell you everything. There've been too many lies."

I looked up at his stony expression.

"From you?"

"No, everything I've told you is the truth."

There was a certainty in his words and expression that I believed.

Letting go of my waist, Sterling took a step back and after untying and kicking off his shoes, he reached for the waistband of his sweatpants.

"What are you doing?"

When he looked back up, the gleam in his eyes gave me a glimpse of the other man, the one who was more than intensity, the one with an overpowering need to protect and an equally consuming desire. It was only a peek, but he was there.

"Sunshine, you wanted to shower. I'm helping you."

My lower lip disappeared behind my teeth as his pants lowered, revealing that again there was nothing underneath. *Nothing* was a terribly inaccurate description. There was definitely *something* underneath—just not boxers.

"Wait," I said. "Dr. Dixon wasn't going to join me."

"I'm not Dr. Dixon."

He wasn't.

"But..." My words trailed away. Arguing this wouldn't get me anywhere.

Stepping in the shower, Sterling adjusted the temperature as his wide chest and broad shoulders deflected the shower's spray. Turning my way, he reached out, offering me his hand. If the surroundings and our attire were different, with his expression and gesture, he could be asking me to dance.

With a tug to the still-partially-tied sash, I allowed the robe to drop before lowering the panties to the floor that was now littered with our clothes. As if accepting the invitation to dance, I placed my hand in his much larger one and stepped into the glass enclosure.

Sterling's attention went to my arm and then to my cheeks. "Last night, someone slipped something into your drink at the party we attended."

I'd been poisoned. I suppose I'd known that from the clues. That wasn't the same as having it confirmed.

My knees weakened as I lowered myself onto the shower's bench, my eyes on him, not the part of his body that was now at eye level and more than partially erect.

His words had my full attention.

"I didn't know," he went on. "I hadn't been away from you for long."

His jaw clenched between each sentence.

"I'd made my declaration." He ran his fingers through his now-wet mane. "You are safe. The person who's responsible will be dealt with as well as anyone associated with him or her. You're now safe."

You're safe.

It was as if he needed to keep repeating it.

I wasn't sure if it was for me or for him.

"We stepped into the elevator to leave," he went on, "and you collapsed."

"My arm?" I asked.

"I reached for you."

He reached out again with an open palm for me to stand. I didn't. Instead, I took a deep breath of the heavy, humid air. "Sterling, I remembered something that happened on the plane. It's bits and pieces, but I recall being upset. I was more than that. I was..."

Did I want to say it? Did I want to admit it?

His eyes closed and opened slowly. "Araneae, come here." Again his hand was extended.

This time I did as he said, moving to my feet.

He lifted my chin, bringing my lips to his. "I will fucking kill anyone who harms you, with my bare hands if necessary. Anyone. That doesn't mean that I won't also do whatever I feel is necessary to keep you safe, even if it seems like too much at the time."

I forced a smile. "Like having a cardiologist help me shower and watch me eat breakfast."

"Like that..." His hands at my waist moved to cup my behind. "...or taking it out on this mighty fine ass to help you understand the importance." His lips brushed my forehead. "This world I've brought you into is dangerous. Above all, remember, you're ultimately safe with me. Trust me."

I wanted to believe him, to trust him.

Reaching for his chest, I looked past his wide shoulder. "We better hurry or the hot water will run out."

Sterling shook his head. "No, it's instant hot. We could spend all day in here and it wouldn't cool a degree."

Wow. That's cool—or hot.

"Still, all day is a long time, and I'm not quite back to full energy."

The gleam from his dark stare was back, the one that did twisty-turny things to my insides. Reaching again for my shoulders, Sterling said, "Leave the energy to me."

Nodding, I allowed Sterling to slowly turn me until I was facing the tile wall.

"Hold on, sunshine."

I still wasn't sure what happened last night, but as I faced the damp tile, I knew one thing.

I wanted to trust Sterling Sparrow.

A minute earlier, I would have thought that I wasn't up for what this man could give me. That was sixty seconds ago. Sixty seconds can change many things. Widening my stance, I leaned forward, my hands on the tile as I closed my eyes.

Mentally preparing for something else, Sterling startled me as a gentle warm rain covered my hair. With the shower's wand he methodically sprayed my hair and skin in cleansing water. The next was the cool sensation of shampoo combined with the sweet aroma of grapefruit and oranges. As his long fingers massaged, I was transported to a country grove filled with citrus trees.

Conditioner came next, followed by the fresh clean scent of bodywash and a soft cloth. With a tenderness I didn't expect, Sterling tended to all of me, caressing my aching muscles and washing away the aftereffects of the poison. Through it all his lips kissed and filled my ears with reassurance.

"You are amazing. So strong. I knew you'd come back to me. When you walked into the club last night, every eye was upon you. They all saw you as I do. They saw the queen you are." Sterling ran his hands over my skin, over my breasts, teasing my hardening nipples, to my waist where he pulled me against him. I leaned my head back as his lips came to the sensitive area behind my ear. His whisper was more of a growl, his words a declaration. "You're mine, Araneae. One day you'll believe it as much as this sexy body of yours already does."

As his words rumbled through me, looking down, I watched the last bit of bubbles slide down my legs, onto my feet, and down the drain. Turning in his hold, I reached up to and palmed his prickly cheeks. "Thank you."

His head tilted. "I'm sure the good doctor would have done as well. With the exception of emergencies, only I get access to that pussy."

A smile tugged at my lips. "Sterling, I'm not sure of much, but I am sure I want to trust you."

His forehead dropped to mine. "There's still more that happened."

"Will you tell me?"

"Yes."

He'd repeated his mantra about a man's word multiple times. If Sterling told me yes, he would do it.

"Can we get out of here first? I believe you that the water will stay warm, but in the meantime, we'll shrivel into prunes."

ARANEAE

Sterling turned off the water and helped me from the shower. After drying ourselves with thick, plush towels, we'd wrapped them around our bodies when he again swept me off my feet.

I slapped at his shoulder. "Stop doing that, I can walk to the bed."

"You're not going to *that* bed." He tilted his head toward the bed where I'd awakened. "You're coming to ours."

Ours?

Out the door and down a hallway, we turned at what I recognized as the landing above the stairway to the foyer. "Aren't you worried about someone seeing us...um, not quite dressed?"

"No, sunshine. Strict orders: the upstairs is only ours, off-limits to others unless given the clear."

My lips curled upward. There was something reassuring about knowing we had that layer of privacy. Sterling continued walking until we entered another hallway, one with a set of double doors at the end. With a twist of the knob and a kick of his foot, one door opened. The room within was significantly larger than the one we'd just left. On what appeared to be a corner of the building, windows filled two of the walls, saturating the room in sunlight. I looked out beyond the uncovered panes. In the not-too-far distance was the glistening expanse of Lake Michigan. Closer, the majority of the buildings were lower than we were. It was stunning to see the city of Chicago sprawled out at our feet.

"The city is gorgeous," I said, taking in the scene.

"It's deceiving..." His gaze darkened. "There are multitudes of things happening all the time, things that go unnoticed, that occur right under people's noses and yet remain invisible. That's part of what I do—make certain that it stays that way. Underground is named that for a reason.

"Average people need a sense of security to go on with their everyday average lives. They crave it and will give up anything for it, even believing what they see and hear." He stiffened his neck, looking out to the city beyond me—beyond us. "That sense of well-being they desire isn't real. It's a combination of their imagination and belief systems. They can't comprehend that the darkness where I brought you exists. So even when it's laid out in front of them, their minds see something else. It's the only way a city such as Chicago can exist. It's the only way it can thrive. It's the only reason tourists still come and millennials snatch up overpriced apartment space in the city when on any given weekend during the summer, there can be forty to fifty reported shootings." He turned back to me, still holding me in his arms. "That doesn't include what goes unreported. And yet people continue to visit and to live here. They support the arts, sports, and higher education because those are what they want to see. The universities, museums, and aquarium, the NFL, NBA, MLB, or NHL franchises are what people want to associate with Chicago.

"It's my job to make sure that when people look out at a view like this, they only see the shiny buildings and blue lake."

In his hold I could feel the tension his words evoked. Sterling Sparrow took whatever he did seriously.

I was certain it was more than real estate.

Turning my head, I looked suspiciously from the view of the city toward the large four-poster king-sized bed. The bed on the plane had been similar.

My change of focus lightened his mood as he took in my expression and his lips quirked.

"What's going on inside that beautiful head of yours? I think it's more than the city. I see the wheels turning."

Warmth filled my cheeks. "The bed."

"The posts or the height?"

"Sterling..." I tried for my most admonishing tone, but it came out somewhere between anxious and enthusiastic.

Gently sitting me near the foot of the bed, he pulled back the covers. Coming back to me, his smile grew as he tugged at the place where I'd tucked the towel, loosening its hold around me. "I believe I've mentioned that you're mine."

My eyes narrowed. "I seem to recall hearing that a time or two." I shrugged. "For the record, your saying it doesn't make it true."

The towel was now open and lying upon the bed.

"Oh," he said, his eyes following the trail his finger left behind as it skirted from my collarbone to my breasts. "I have done and will do more than say it. I'll prove it. And besides that, I also told you that I'm going to have you in every way possible." He shrugged, bringing his gaze back to mine. "I'm tall."

"I've noticed that, too." My grin grew as my heart rate accelerated.

"I knew you could be observant. While I'm sure you can figure out good uses for the posts, as for the height, it's perfect for taking your ass."

My eyes widened as I swallowed. "You mean spanking?"

Offering me his hand, Sterling helped me stand and move to where he'd pulled back the covers. With a gesture, he encouraged me to step onto the platform, sit, and turn.

"If that explanation helps you sleep, sunshine, by all means, go ahead and tell yourself that's what I meant."

I lay back, my damp hair falling to the pillow. "I-I...don't think...I've never—"

Bending closer, his finger came to my lips. "You need rest. Dr. Dixon's orders."

I reached for his hand. "I need to call Louisa and Winnie."

"Don't be mad."

That was never a good opening line. Letting go of the connection, I propped myself forward on my elbows. "What did you do?"

"I didn't do anything. I've been mostly preoccupied with you. Patrick, on the other hand, contacted both of them—on your phone, by text. He pretended to be you and told them that you weren't feeling well. You hope to be better tomorrow."

Sighing, I lay back again. "I should be mad, but I'm not. I'm tired."

Sterling leaned down, giving me a chaste kiss, a mere brush over my lips. Such as his touch earlier, the kiss was light, yet the effect was exactly the opposite, making me want more. As he began to stand, I reached for his neck. With my free hand, I did as he had done and untucked his towel, now falling from his waist.

"Araneae, you said you're tired. Dr. Dixon said—"

Pulling myself upward, it was my turn to quiet him with my kiss. When our lips parted, I scooted over and sat up; lifting the sheet I stared into his gaze. "I know there's more to last night than you've told me."

He nodded.

"I know I was mad at you before we left the plane. I think you were upset with me, and I have the feeling that even though I recall making up, there's more to that, too."

Sterling didn't answer, yet if this were a poker game, his body was betraying him. His breathing had deepened and his Adam's apple bobbed.

"There's a lot I don't know," I went on. "What I do know for sure is that since I've met you, my world has gone crazy." I tilted my head. The sunlight behind him shadowed his features, making them darker and more intense. His body was responding to my invitation, though his expression was unsure. I sweetened my tone. "When we were at the cabin, you introduced me to a great nap-inducer. Think of this as a therapeutic request, to get my mind off what else happened and aid in my sleep." I sat taller and dropped the sweetness. "However, no utilization of bedposts or..." I shook my head. "...*anything* else...that...just no. Think of this as you and me— us together behind the infrared force field, helping me sleep and follow Dr. Dixon's orders."

"Who told you about the force field?" Sterling asked as the bed dipped and he joined me on the incredible mattress covered by the most luxurious sheets.

I shook my head. "I made it up."

He nodded.

Seriously?

Turning his way, my palm went back to his scratchy cheek. "I believe what you said the other day, that what we're about to do is a workout."

Sterling smiled. "Oh, don't worry, sunshine. It is and I'm up for it."

Lying back, I returned his grin, knowing that he was—*up*.

Though we were both ready, we didn't start there. Unlike our first time, I was about to learn that this was to be a marathon, not a sprint. The fact that I'd initiated what was about to happen didn't sideline Sterling's control when it came to orchestration.

Kiss by kiss, he inched down my exposed skin, toward my toes, parting my legs as he progressed. My pleas for more invasive techniques went verbally unanswered as each lick to the inside of my ankles and nip of my calves worked in tandem to revive the senses that had been quelled by the poison.

By the time he made it to my inner thighs, my entire being quaked with anticipation.

Though earlier I'd been lethargic, similar to the story of Frankenstein's monster, the shock of Sterling's power brought me back to life. His touch was the conductor, allowing his own electrical current to flow between us, infusing and radiating, as my hands gripped the soft sheets and my spine arched. Like a bolt of lightning to the monster, his tongue struck my core. Whimpers and moans multiplied, growing in intensity, filling the large bedroom and possibly echoing to the streets below.

Sterling wasn't satisfied with merely bringing me back to life. He wanted more. Holding my hips in place, he teased and taunted. His unimaginable technique was beyond my scope of understanding. I couldn't try to conceive of what he was doing as the ministrations of his fingers joined the torment.

My thoughts were too focused on his next move and the way I'd react—neither seeming to be under my control. The pressure he elicited as my body wound tighter moved beyond pleasure, teetering on the verge of pain, when with my orgasm within grasp, everything stopped.

And all at once, as his warmth covered me, we became one.

"Sterling." His name flew from my lips as my core held tight.

"You're mine."

The words reverberated through me.

I couldn't be sure he'd said them aloud through the fog of my current mental state. However, I was certain that despite my repeated protests, I was—his.

The muscles of his back flexed under my touch as more slowly than ever before, he eased in and out, each meticulous thrust moving deeper yet not quite to where I needed him. My hands roamed downward, gripping his tight ass as, unimaginably, the desire within me amplified.

"More, please," I whispered, shocked at the depth of my own wanton need.

"We're not rushing." Kisses to my lips, neck, and collarbone abraded my skin with his overgrown beard. His teeth and tongue besieged my breasts and inundated my pebble-like nipples. With agonizing slowness, he continued the torture.

When the time came that he finally filled me completely, there was nothing else on my mind but him. What happened last night or even the last couple of weeks was outside my grasp. Every nerve in my body, every synapse in my brain, was focused on the one man who did things to me I'd only read about.

My legs wrapped around Sterling, needing to be closer, as he figuratively lifted me upward.

Though the soft sheets were literally beneath me, I had the sensation of my body on the edge of a cliff. While the view was spectacular, my toes were curled over the ledge and I was primed to jump, to plunge into the relief of my pending orgasm. That wasn't Sterling's plan. Instead of experiencing the release of climax, his proficiency took me still higher. Controlled and rhythmic, he elevated me beyond the cliff to the sky and beyond.

The electricity he'd shared grew and multiplied until it was too much for me to bear. The stars behind my closed eyes grew bigger and brighter until the supernovas exploded, sending shock waves throughout my universe.

Somewhere I'd heard that noise didn't travel in space. Yet the room around us filled with sounds as words I failed to articulate came streaming out and the contractions within me continued. With my nails gripping his shoulders, Sterling's sounds joined mine to become a symphony of pleasure.

The muscles under my grasp tightened, and his baritone roar overtook our melody as my undoing became his too.

Slowly, reality seeped back into my consciousness as our breathing evened and hearts slowed to resume their cadence.

Even though there were probably fires that Sterling needed to tend, he didn't. Instead, he gently rolled beside me, wrapped me in his arms, and held me against his chest.

"You are safe."

It was the last thing I heard as my eyes closed against his skin. Within a cloud of our union and the rhythm of his heart, the sunlit room beyond disappeared.

STERLING

While I handled things on Michigan Avenue, Reid and Patrick and their teams worked on leads from the party at the club. There was no stone they'd leave unturned. Reid and some of his team worked cyberspace while others hit the pavement. At the same time, Patrick and his team visited people who had been in attendance.

After what happened to Araneae, Sparrow had a statement to be made. It wouldn't go without bloodshed and we all knew it. No one fucked with the Sparrow outfit—no one. In reality, everyone in that damn club, guest or staff, was a suspect. In my mind, it wasn't adding up with McFadden. The fire in her apartment and the plane going down were associated with her name—he had the power to make those things happen. Nevertheless, I took responsibility. I was the one who brought her to light—or the dark more aptly.

It was after she came to Chicago two weeks ago that the rumors again flew.

The stopped plane in Wichita could fit into the equation. While McFadden didn't recognize Kennedy as Araneae at the party at Riverwalk, it was his guy on the plane—Walsh. Facial recognition didn't lie. The fact that Walsh hadn't been seen since the incident could mean one of two things: McFadden eliminated him or Walsh went into hiding for screwing up.

We weren't exactly certain of what happened last night; however, we now had the results of Dr. Dixon's tests. The toxin Araneae ingested was GHB, a rather well-known and easily accessible club drug. Usually, it renders a person weak and confused. In some cases—such as with Araneae—the victim loses consciousness. Amnesia was common; however, what usually didn't happen was death.

The natural assumption associated with this knowledge was that death wasn't the perpetrator's goal.

Though I hated to admit it, that realization took McFadden off the list of conspiring suspects. He'd risked a fucking plane with hundreds of passengers and had her apartment torched to stop her from revealing what I didn't think she knew. He wouldn't have been satisfied with simply rendering her unconscious. Besides, he was fucking shocked to see her there with me.

The guilty party was someone who wanted her compromised.

The questions were who and why?

Midafternoon, Reid called with some answers.

"Our crew went to Urbana and paid Amanda Smith a visit. They arrived three hours ago."

Amanda Smith—the bartender.

"Why are you just telling me now?"

"Listen. I wanted answers to bring you, not more questions."

"Fine. What did she know?" I asked.

"Our men were too late. She was dead on her kitchen floor, throat slashed from ear to ear, probably bled out in seconds. Her fucking dog was dead beside her. It was a hit and a statement."

"Fuck, just not one made by Sparrow," I growled.

"That's the thing. It was."

Standing from my desk, I walked to the door of my office and closed it to the hallway and Stephanie's outer office. Pacing toward the windows, I said, "Explain."

"It's fucked up, Sparrow."

The view of Millennium Park and of Lake Michigan beyond was gone, covered in the crimson of the blood I planned to spill.

Who went rogue?

What was happening?

My neck straightened as I fought to maintain a semblance of rational thinking. "Give it to me straight."

"The contact from the club—remember, the guy who gave us Amanda's name—he became more forthcoming upon further persuasion. He's the one who told Patrick that Amanda did more than bartend. Her side job of screwing or sucking off important men included other shit—she didn't mind combining work with pleasure. That included drugs supplied by some of her customers. There was another couple at the bar."

Was there?

I tried to think back. I was concentrating on Araneae as

well as Hillman, McFadden, and the rest of the men in my discussion. "I can't recall."

Fuck! I can't allow her to take me off my game like that.

"Praxton McBride." Reid left the name hanging in the air.

My free hand twitched. I knew that fucking name. "He's one of ours, on Hanson's crew, been around for a couple of years. Hanson told me once that the kid's coming along. I've only seen him maybe once."

"Twice, then," Reid corrected. "He was one half of the couple at the end of the bar, sitting there with his girlfriend. Hanson got McBride into the club about six months ago as a reward for a big score. McBride likes the atmosphere, likes showing off like he's rich. He and his girlfriend have a thing with Amanda. Apparently, McBride and his whore of a girl-friend like three-ways."

My stomach knotted. "What the fuck would that have to do with Araneae?"

"He swears he didn't see you bring her in...too caught up in his own bitch—his words not mine. They thought she was alone. When they noticed her down the bar, he and his woman talked about the possibility of inviting her to their private party in one of the rooms upstairs from the club. Looking for something more exciting, they decided it would be more fun if she didn't remember.

"He sang like a fucking bird, spilling his guts, apologizing. Explained that they've done it before, and it's more fun to ask the second time when the bitches don't remember you already fucked them."

My throat tightened.

"When Ms. McCrie left her drink," Reid went on, "McBride gave Amanda the vial, told her he'd pay her for the three-way, and she'd get the night off, could make double if she fucked someone else. All she had to do was slip the GHB to the glass. They were going to take it from there."

With each of Reid's sentences, words, sounds, my blood pressure built. I was a fucking gasket about to blow. "He swears?" My words were separate and distinct. "Tell me that he's still alive."

"Yeah, you could call it that. Hanson has him. Hanson wants no part of this. When McBride went rogue, killing Amanda, Hanson called Patrick, informing him what happened, totally unsure why McBride would kill the little bartender. He didn't know about Ms. McCrie. We've tried to keep those details quiet. Hanson told Patrick he assumed it was a drug-related; she stole his stash or pissed him off by not swallowing. He fucking didn't know it involved Ms. McCrie.

"McBride," Reid said, going on, "didn't realize the mistake he and his girlfriend made until you came to get her. And then he just about shit himself. Well," Reid said with a scoff, "by now he has. Anyway, last night he threatened Amanda. During the night, he must have gotten scared that she'd talk, so he took care of her."

I remembered now. There was this kid looking at me with wide eyes who quickly turned away. I didn't recognize him, hadn't given it much thought, not with Annabelle and Araneae. "Fucker made a deadly mistake."

"We have him and Leslie."

"Who the fuck is that?"

"His bitch, the one that picked Ms. McCrie for their three-way."

"Fuck."

"Sparrow, we can take care of this. Keep your hands clean."

The fist of my free hand balled and unballed. "No fucking way. I made a goddamned statement to the McFadden outfit, I never thought I'd need to make one to the Sparrow too. Once I'm done, every fucking person from the top to the bottom will hear it loud and clear. Call the crew leaders together, Hanson included. We're going down to the lake in East Garfield Park."

My nostrils flared as I imagined the scene. "These two like to fuck unwilling women? We'll give them a fitting end, one that will spread through the ranks faster than shit from the damn geese moves through that shithole lake. No one fucks with Araneae, and no one under my name has a reputation for rape. After tonight, the capos will clean up their fucking crews or next time, it will be one of them."

ARANEAE

As I moved, the aches throughout my body brought me back to consciousness. There was the now strangely familiar reminder that Sterling and I'd been together. Memories of me pleading for more of what only he could give brought warmth to my cheeks as well as tightening in my nipples. Those were the aches I wanted. The way that even behind my closed eyes, my temples throbbed and muscles throughout my body felt sore, similar to the aftereffects of recovering from an illness, reminded me of my new reality: someone had tried to poison me. Scratch that. Someone *had* poisoned me. My hand rubbed over my upper right arm.

I contemplated what was real and what was covered in lies.

Sterling had caught me before I hit the floor. It made sense. It fit the scenario I'd been given. Why then did I believe it wasn't the entire story?

Somehow, unimaginably, I had become a woman who'd been sucked into a world she didn't understand. Then again, in Sterling's soft bed within this apartment, I felt safe.

Was I? Or was I acting like the people he'd mentioned, those who craved security so much that they didn't see the lies and deception staring them in the face?

The thoughts twisted my stomach, taking me down a rabbit hole; like Alice, I was in a strange land, unsure of whom I could trust.

The incredible softness of the sheets against my skin gave me the sensation of floating. I liked that better than falling. Maybe it wasn't a rabbit hole but a cloud. I just couldn't see beyond the fog. Forcing the uneasiness from my mind, I concentrated on the softness around me.

I should talk to Louisa about the idea of expanding Sinful Threads into bedding. After all, people spent more time in their bed than in a dress.

Louisa.

I needed my phone.

My eyes sprang open and closed again just as quickly to the bright sunshine still filling Sterling's bedroom. No, wait. He said it was *ours.* I shook my head.

"Saying it doesn't make it true." I'd said that to him just this afternoon, yet somehow, I was beginning to doubt that statement. It seemed as though Sterling Sparrow had that ability—to speak and make it so. As if he could declare the sky green and the grass blue and that would be what the world saw.

As my eyes adjusted, I assessed my surroundings more closely than I had when Sterling brought me here. First and foremost, I was alone. I'd known that before my eyes opened.

Sterling Sparrow had a palpable energy that was verifiable even without visual confirmation. Though the pillow beside me held the indentation—I leaned down and inhaled—and the fresh, spicy scent proving that he'd been here, the coolness told me that his departure wasn't recent.

Throwing back the covers, I made up my mind that I was going to get more answers.

The room wavered, not the spinning that occurred in the kitchen yet enough to twist my stomach and still my progress. I hesitated on the edge of the tall bed, my feet resting upon a wooden beam that was like a step. I'd noticed it when Sterling helped me into the bed, but now I was giving it more thought.

Who had a bed that required a step? And what the hell did he mean about my ass?

No. Oh hell no.

A breath in. A breath out.

The queasiness lessened.

Looking to the bedside stand, I searched for a clock. There was one on the other side of the bed—Sterling's side. I'd only once before been involved in a long-term relationship. It probably shouldn't have happened, and while for me it was long-term, in reality it was only a little under a year.

He'd convinced me to move in with him. Doing so was our first mistake, and even then, we didn't make the move until nearly four months into the dating. This was insanity that I was living with Sterling after less than two weeks.

The clock read 5:03 PM.

Turning back to my bedside stand, I saw a piece of paper beside a cell phone. It wasn't mine, but it was there.

Curiosity won. I picked up the phone and swiped the screen. A code screen came up.

Really, Sterling? You're going to leave me a phone that I can't use? Asshole.

I smirked to myself.

He really did have that talent, and no, it wasn't a virtue.

Placing the phone back down, I picked up the paper—it was a note.

Sunshine,

I hated to leave you, but there are things that can't be avoided. First, so you aren't surprised, the outside door to our room is locked.

What? My eyes darted to the set of double doors as my pulse surged, forcing blood through my veins.

Before you panic, keep reading.

Too late...was this a good time to call him an asshole?

It's locked from the inside. You control the key.

My smile tugged at my lips. Okay, Mr. Sparrow, I may jump to conclusions when it comes to you. I continued reading.

I meant what I said about others seeing your pussy, and lying there all curled up, you were too peaceful and beautiful to disturb and do anything but pull the blankets up to cover your sexy body.

You may have noticed the phone by this note. (Not sure yet of your observation skills.) It has six numbers programmed into it and your outgoing number is blocked on two.

Great. What's the damn code?

Once you're awake and clothed, call Lorna. She's expecting your call. Dr. Dixon and I agreed that another staircase journey should wait for tomorrow but food cannot.

Why wasn't I consulted on this treatment plan?

There is a pitcher of water on the armoire and more in a refrigerator hidden behind one of the doors. Look around. Lorna will bring you food. The other phone numbers are for me, Patrick, Reid (yes, he is real), Louisa (her private cell), and Winifred (her private cell.) Don't forget you already texted them once today.

I promised you contact with Sinful Threads and your friends. I keep my word.

. . .

This phone is sufficient for communication. For today and tonight, don't fight me—we can save that for when you have more strength.

I trust you'll remember the rules we discussed. Don't mention anything private or about me to Louisa or Winifred. To them and Sinful Threads, you remain Kennedy Hawkins.

I will be back as soon as possible. Make yourself at home—because it is —in our room. Did your own deception help you sleep?

Until I return,

Sterling

My own deception?

"*By all means, sunshine, if that description will help you sleep...*"

Shaking my head, I turned the paper over.

Nothing.

I stood and spoke to no one, "Asshole, just because you give me the greatest sex of my life, doesn't mean you can control everything. How the fuck am I supposed to call without a damn code?"

Slowly, I spun, taking in the room. Could he hear me? Were there cameras?

I couldn't see any, but that didn't matter.

Clothed?

How the hell am I supposed to do that, I wondered, as I walked naked around the room, approaching the tall windows. The view was simply spectacular in an urban fashion. I missed the mountains and wilderness of Colorado, yet there was beauty in a city like Chicago.

Getting even closer, I peered downward. I wasn't certain of how high we were, but by the sight of tiny cars on narrow strips of street, we were about as high as you can get. The more my vision narrowed on the workings of the city below me, the more I pondered about the illusion Sterling mentioned.

I wanted to see the beauty.

Walking around without clothing was something that I was never comfortable doing, yet in this new life, everything seemed different. Maybe it was Sterling and the way that even though he could be infuriating, he was also adoring.

Never before had anyone made me feel as at ease in my own body.

Opening a door that I knew was *not* to the hallway, I first found an attached workout room. The discovery made me giggle. Sterling Sparrow did work out. There was a treadmill and free weights, an elliptical machine, and another contraption with weights and cords. High on one wall were three TV screens.

Going back to the bedroom, I found the pitcher of water. Opening the cabinet doors beneath, I also discovered the refrigerator as well as a liquor reserve and a stash of books. I picked up one. These books weren't for show. Their spines were creased and pages furrowed. Lifting one to my nose, I inhaled. There was something about the scent of a real book that made me smile. These had that aroma, but also a faint spicy aroma. These were Sterling's books. He'd held them and read them. The man who took responsibility for the city below liked fictional classics.

I would have taken him for a mystery/crime suspense reader or perhaps nonfiction. Then again, maybe that was what he lived—mystery and crime. Perhaps the fabricated tales from the likes of Charles Dickens, Herman Melville, and George Orwell provided him with an escape from the darkness that surrounded him.

Closing the cabinet, I realized I'd just discovered another tile in the mosaic that was Sterling Sparrow.

Near the window was a sitting area with a long chaise and other furniture including overstuffed chairs. There was also a small table with two chairs, perfect for eating dinner alone when he wasn't up for the conversation of his housemates.

It was an assumption on my part, but it seemed to fit.

"Okay, Mr. Sparrow, how am I supposed to be dressed when your room contains no dressers or clothes?" The question was out of my mouth when I opened another door to a giant bathroom. The tile was dark and masculine, yet with the large window above the sunken garden tub, it gave it a light and airy feel. I stepped closer to the tub. Sunken into the floor with only a small lip to catch water, it was more like a small pool than a tub. I'd never seen one like it before.

Standing still, I inhaled. The entire room was saturated with the aroma of Sterling: his choice of bodywash and cologne, not overpowering but reassuring. The shower was bigger than the one at the cabin, with a panel of controls that would give the helicopter a run for its money. The vanity was long with raised colored-glass bowls for sinks and an array of lighting options for the mirror.

After taking care of business and washing my hands, I opened the drawers and cabinets.

Within the cabinet containing both the cosmetics that I'd packed and what could basically be considered a department store makeup counter's worth of new cosmetics—everything from creams and lotions to eye shadows and mascara—I found another note.

The code to open your phone is the same as the one to open the safe in your Chicago hotel room.

I know everything about you because...

I'm ready to hear you finish that sentence.

Sterling

Because you're creepy as shit with your spying and knowledge? That was my retort though I knew it wasn't the answer he wanted.

Though there was a robe on a hook in the bathroom, I walked past it as I made my way back out to the bedroom to the one last door I hadn't opened.

When I opened it, I found the clothes.

The closet was bigger than my bedroom in Boulder. The walls were lined with open racks of clothes as well as drawers and compartments for shoes. Divided down the middle, one side contained a variety of men's suits mostly in shades of gray and black. Starched button-down shirts all present in color groupings ranging from dark to light. It was a perfect rainbow, not one color out of place.

OCD much?

Farther down the closet were the clothes I thought I preferred he wore: blue jeans and casual shirts. Even the drawers on his side of the closet were organized with precision. Gym shorts, t-shirts, socks, and ties.

What I could only assume was now my side of the closet was also full. Though all my clothes that I'd packed from Boulder were present, so were many more I'd never seen before. I ran my hand over the luxurious materials.

My clothes too were hung in groupings: skirts subdivided by color, dresses divided by color and length, blouses by color and sleeve length, sweaters color, suit jackets color, casual clothes were there too. Jeans, capris, and tops.

It was like walking into a boutique where everything was my size. Drawers contained various items of lingerie from bras and panties, to stockings and socks, and of course, sexy as well as comfortable sleeping attire. There was even an array of workout clothes.

The shoes on my side were another matter altogether. The racks slid out like drawers, each one containing a half-dozen pairs of shoes. Heel length varied, as did the designers. There were boots of all styles, sandals, pumps, even athletic shoes.

I shook my head as I took it all in.

Standing naked in a sea of clothes, the reality overwhelmed me. My mind went to Louisa, her baby, and Boulder. Uncontrollably, tears spilled from my eyes. I sank to the posh bench in the middle of the room, pulled my knees to my chest, and with my arms wrapped tightly around my legs, gave into the grief.

My forehead fell to my knees as my lungs fought for air, and I choked on the boiling emotion.

I wasn't going home—ever.

This was now my life.

Such as it had been with the decision of my name—Hawkins or McCrie—and discussing my medical treatment, somehow within the last two weeks I'd lost control of...everything. As my tears finally slowed, I thought of something.

No, I hadn't lost control of everything. I wiped away the tears.

I still had Sinful Threads.

I just needed to get back to it, to the part of my life that was mine.

Opening drawers, I found what I needed to dress and laid them on the bench where I'd been. Within minutes, I was back in the bathroom brushing out my sex-mussed hair, washing my face, and brushing my teeth. The reflection in the mirror continued to morph as did the woman I was, including my name.

I stared beyond the surface into my own eyes. "*Think of Josey. Think of the risk she took for you...think of how strong she was. She was your example. She didn't send you away to be locked in a tower. She'd never settle for that. You may be back in Chicago, but that doesn't mean your life is over. You and Louisa built a life, one you love. Don't let Sterling Sparrow or anyone else change that.*"

I heard the words in my head. They began in my voice and ended in hers, my adoptive mother's. Just as she'd said the last time I saw her—listen to my heart, she was there. With a heavy heart for the decisions that landed me here, I lifted my chin and made my way back to the closet.

Wearing clothes I'd brought from Boulder—a small protest, but mine nonetheless—with my hair secured in a messy bun, which was about my only option without showering again, I was ready to take back the part of my life that I could.

My first stop was the telephone.

When the screen came to life, I entered the last four digits of my mom's telephone number.

My mom.

Josey Marsh.

A regained memory sent my mind reeling as I sank to the floor.

My mother. My birth mother.

I remembered.

ARANEAE

Splices of disjointed memories filled my thoughts: foremost among them, an older blonde woman sitting with Senator McFadden. I recalled wondering why it wasn't his wife, the woman I'd met at the Sinful Threads dinner. The senator was looking at us—at me—with a darkened expression as we stood in the entryway to the club. His appearance was much different than the jovial senator and possible presidential candidate whom I had previously met. He wasn't alone in staring me down. The entire room was turned our direction.

And then she, the blonde, was in the bathroom. She reached for my wrist. My body shivered as I relived the coldness of her touch. I ran away...back to...Sterling? No, to the bar where he'd told me to sit.

I remembered.

My hand went to the bruise on my arm now covered with a sleeve. I didn't get the chance to tell Sterling about the

woman or her comment about my bracelet. Sterling was angry
—no, maybe not angry but intense.

I wasn't falling when he grabbed my arm. I was sitting
and he wanted to leave. I told him he was hurting me. He
didn't loosen his grasp as his determination to leave
intensified.

She—the blonde by McFadden's side, the same woman in
the bathroom—called out to me. She knew my name as
Araneae. When I asked her who she was, she answered, *I'm
your mother*.

I sucked in a breath, pushing myself off the floor and
running to the closet. I started pulling open drawers. I
recalled one with velvet padding especially constructed for
jewelry.

I couldn't remember which one it was as I pulled drawer
after drawer until I found it. Once inside, I lifted the velvet
covering that protected all the jewelry from dust and the
silver from tarnish. Flinging it back, I surveyed the contents
as my heart beat erratically.

Where is it?

Relief flooded my system as I found it.

My bracelet.

Placing the gold chain and charms in the palm of my hand,
I secured my fingers around the entire bracelet.

I wasn't sure who that woman was, but she wasn't the
mother I remembered, the one who watched my track meets,
sat and studied with me, taught me to sew and nurtured my
love for silk, or dried my tears.

I took a deep breath.

Fuck them all.

I was done with crying. Placing the bracelet back in the

compartment within the drawer, I gently closed the lid and slid the drawer in place.

Reminiscing was over. I needed answers.

Walking back into the bedroom, I knew who possessed my answers: Sterling. He could help.

I scrolled the numbers on the phone. It didn't take long. There were only six.

STERLING.

My finger hovered.

No. Fuck him, too.

I'd given him the opportunity to tell me about last night and he hadn't.

I wasn't letting him off the hook—I would confront him, we would talk. It just wouldn't be on the phone.

I'd waited twenty-six years for answers. I could wait another few hours or however long it took for him to return. In the meantime, I wanted *my* life back.

The one I was living was too confusing.

It was time to be Kennedy again.

Instead of Sterling, my first call was to Patrick. As soon as he answered, I spoke, "I want my laptop."

"Ma'am?"

"My laptop. It's a computer that's portable. It was in the plane. I need it now."

"Mr. Sparrow—"

"If I thought Mr. Sparrow would bring it to me, I would have called him," I interrupted. "The business day is officially over. I need to catch up on Sinful Threads, and I can't do that on this cheap-ass burner phone."

"It's not actually a—"

"Sterling told you to listen to me." There was something

powerful about making my demands known and not waiting for his excuses. "I'll be waiting. Hurry. I've already missed too much of today."

I hung up.

The next call was to Lorna.

"Ms. McCrie," she answered.

"Please, Lorna, call me Ken-Araneae." Maybe if I wore a nametag, I could remember who I was. It could be two-sided —flip it when I'm Kennedy, flip it again when I'm Araneae.

"Araneae," she said.

"Yes, I wanted you to know that I'm awake, but honestly, I'm not hungry, and I don't feel right having you or anyone else waiting on me. I'll come down and look for something when I am hungry, *if you're all right with me rifling through your kitchen.*" I added the last part as an afterthought.

"The kitchen is Sparrow's but coming down is the concern. He said—"

"Between you and me, I don't care about the end of that sentence."

"It's your decision," Lorna said. "I'd be more than happy to bring you something. That is what he wants."

"I appreciate it. It's not what I want. If you see Patrick, please tell him to hurry. I need my laptop."

"I believe I saw him take it to Sparrow's office."

"His office?"

"Yes, on the same level as the kitchen."

Like a bud growing stronger, hope bloomed in my previously heavy chest. "Is his office...accessible?"

"It isn't locked if that's what you mean. However, it's an unwritten rule of sorts that unless it's being cleaned, it's his personal space."

I looked around the bedroom where I was. This was his personal space. He'd said this entire level was *our* personal space. He'd invited me into his personal space, or perhaps a better explanation would be that he pulled me in kicking and screaming...I wasn't sure. Either way, Sterling had been the one to blur the line of his space and mine.

"If I came down, would you show me where it is?"

"Araneae, I don't..."

"Bread crumbs, Lorna, something, please. I'll say I found it on my own."

"Officially, I'm saying don't come down until tomorrow. Unofficially, I'm coming up to the penthouse. You aren't falling on my watch." It was the same thing Dr. Dixon said.

"Unofficially, regarding the office?" I asked.

"Sometimes Sparrow listens to music. Jazz is his thing when he's relaxing, which he sometimes does in his office. If you hear it..."

"Thank you, Lorna."

After hanging up the call and putting the phone that was apparently not a cheap burner in the back pocket of my jeans, I went to the double doors. It wasn't so much a key that I possessed, but access to a large lock button that twisted below one of the handles.

Turning it, the mechanism clicked. Tentatively, I pulled the door inward, wondering if it was really that simple.

I would have thought that there would have been a higher form of defense, something other than an old-fashioned lock. Then again, if no one could access this apartment or even see it—I wasn't sure about that last part—except the people Sterling trusted, then I supposed an old-fashioned lock did what it was designed to do, which was keep out people who respected the symbolism.

With each step along the hallway toward the stairs, my strength returned. Dr. Dixon explained how my body needed to eliminate the poison. Perhaps, my crying fit was an answer I hadn't realized I'd sought.

By the time I reached the stairs, Lorna was standing at the bottom, her head shaking as I reached for the banister and began my descent. Meeting me halfway, she smiled. "He's going to be mad."

I nodded. "No doubt."

She didn't help me as Dr. Dixon had done; instead, we took the steps together.

"And you're not worried?" she asked.

"If I say no, I'm a fool. If I say yes, I'll overthink this. I'll keep my mind and computer usage on work. I did it yesterday on the plane. He can't expect me to stay locked away in a gilded cage." My feet stilled as the sound of music came into range. My cheeks rose as my smile grew. "Thank you."

She lifted her hands in surrender. "I know nothing. You called and said you weren't hungry, and I stayed in my apartment."

"Oh, when you said up, you meant from the other floor—your apartment. I'm sorry you rushed up here." We were now at the bottom of the stairs. Standing beside her, I could see that Lorna was a good three inches shorter than me, yet there was a spirit within her that was impossible to miss.

She grinned. "I don't mind. I probably shouldn't tell you this."

My eyes widened. "Oh, please don't let that stop you."

"In the six years Reid and I have been together, Sparrow

has never brought a woman into this place." She shook her head. "I don't know all of why you're here or even what happened to you last night.

"I know you drank something you shouldn't have, but I don't know more.

"Anyway," she went on, "I hope you'll stay. This place gets lonely when they're out doing whatever they do." Her smile grew. "And more than that, you give him shit. He needs that in his life."

"I don't think he's used to it," I answered honestly.

"That's the thing. We're kind of a family around here—or a pack. My man is fucking tough, smart, and capable of just about anything. So is Patrick. They could easily make their own way in the world without Sparrow, but they won't. I do my best to keep this place..." She gestured about. "...all of it, a place where they can relax and unwind. We joke and laugh. We even grieve, but at the end of the day, in a pack there's only one alpha. That's your man."

My man?

"I'm not sure," she went on, "if he asked for that position or it was thrust upon him, but no matter how it happened, it's his."

"So," I asked, "I shouldn't give him shit?"

"No, you should because no one else will get away with it. One more thing..." Her green eyes widened. "I hope you don't mind a bit of unsolicited advice. I tend to say what's on my mind."

"Lorna, when it comes to all of this..." It was my turn to gesture. "...and Sterling, I'll take whatever you have. I'm not certain of anything."

She reached for my hand. "I remind myself every time

Reid leaves my sight: tomorrow isn't a guarantee. I don't know the specifics of all they do, but they deal with some heavy shit. He may piss me off." She nodded. "He does, and I may piss him off, but before he walks out the door, even in the middle of the night, we kiss one another and reaffirm our love. He's not dying without that being the last thing I said."

I blinked away the moisture filling my eyes. "I think Sterling and I are a little too new for love."

She shrugged. "It's not something you can control." Squeezing my hand, she dropped it. "Hey, I'm getting out of here before he finds you. Do you have that phone?"

"Yes." I nodded.

"Then if he's here, you don't have long."

"It has a tracker?"

"Oh, rule number one. Those three men will know where you are at any moment."

I looked past her toward the source of music. "Well, fuck. Then I better hurry."

"Araneae?"

My gaze went back to her green eyes.

"For what it's worth, seeing him with you makes us all happy. I hope you decide that one day it makes you happy, too."

"Thanks, Lorna."

"If they don't find you, call me before you go back upstairs. I don't want you falling."

I nodded as I went farther down the hall, the music growing louder with each step.

ARANEAE

The melody of Dizzy Gillespie's signature trumpet came from beyond the partially closed double doors as I came to a stop, and memories of his office in Ontario filled my mind. There was something about entering that accelerated my heartbeat, its pounding threatening to drown out the tune. No. I wasn't overthinking this. I was simply getting my laptop.

Pushing one of the tall doors inward, I stepped inside Sterling's personal space. Similar to the rest of his apartment, the first thing to catch my attention were the floor-to-ceiling windows filling one wall. Despite the fact that it was after seven at night, the cobalt blue summer sky still shone. I stepped closer. It was the same view as from one side of his bedroom. Turning, I took in the room.

Sterling definitely had a thing for light and open; most of the office fit the bill. Perhaps he also leaned toward modern with some glass, chrome, and accent lighting. The word eclectic came to mind. That was not to insinuate that the decor was a hodgepodge, but more of an interesting combination that seemed to work. The focus of the room was a large wooden desk with ornate carvings. Next to the rest of the furnishings, it was a bit stuffier and more pretentious. If I didn't know Sterling as I do, I may even think it was overcompensation for other inadequacies.

Sterling Sparrow had no need to overcompensate.

In one corner by the windows were two large chairs near a round table, complete with a chessboard. I brushed my fingers over the elaborate marble pieces. They weren't set up to begin play, but instead as if a game were in progress.

Keeping in style with the furniture, the paintings hanging upon the walls, spotlighted by the accent lighting, were an interesting collection. In other parts of the apartment accessible to more people, I'd seen some stunning photography, mostly of cities. This was art. It was altogether different. Walking closer to each one, I read the names of the artists and shook my head: Jean-Michel Basquiat, Jasper Johns, and Andy Warhol. These famous artists had works hanging in places like the Met in New York, and Sterling had his own private collection.

I searched the room until I came to my carry-on, near Sterling's chair on the other side of his desk. Sitting, I pulled the bag into my lap and unzipped it. I could say it was just as I'd left it, but it wasn't. I'd left it sitting on the table in the plane. It was as Patrick had left it.

Not thinking about where I was, my mind was focused on access to the Wi-Fi as I booted up the laptop. In my preoccupied state, I didn't hear the door open farther or footsteps or anything until the deep clearing of a throat startled me. With my eyes still on the screen in my lap, I froze. Perhaps it was because I couldn't feel *his* presence or maybe it was that the pitch of the throat-clearing was slightly off, but whatever the reason, I sat perfectly still, knowing that whoever had entered the office wasn't Sterling. I was also pretty sure it wasn't Patrick. As my gaze moved from the laptop to the man at the door, I drew a breath as I flinched back in Sterling's chair.

"Ma'am," the incredibly large man in the doorway said.

My eyes widened, looking at this person I didn't know. My first impression was that he resembled Michael B. Jordan, not the basketball player, but the actor. He had the same stunningly ebony skin and dark eyes. His hair was short, more like the character in *Creed* than the one in *Black Panther*.

Who was he and how did he get here?

I forced myself not to retreat as he took a step closer. Wearing jeans and a t-shirt that stretched across his wide chest, he had heavy boots on his feet that made me wonder how I hadn't heard him approach.

I contemplated my next move. The phone I'd been given was in my back pocket. Maybe I could call Sterling or Patrick or even the mystery man, Reid.

With his hands gripped behind his back, the man came to a stop in front of the wooden desk. "It's good to see you're feeling better."

I swallowed. "I-I am, thank you. And you are...?"

"Reid, ma'am, Reid Murray." He leaned forward and extended his hand. "I'm sorry. I assumed you'd be able to figure that out."

My face blossomed into a true smile as I reached forward and took his hand. "Oh, goodness, I've heard all about you, but they seemed to have left out a few details."

His handshake was quick and solid. A small smile came to his lips as he stepped back to parade rest and nodded. "It was my height, wasn't it? It's because I'm an inch taller than Sparrow. He doesn't like to mention it."

I shook my head, leaned back, and let out a small laugh. "Yeah, that was it. It's good to meet you, Reid. Are you here to kick me out and send me back upstairs?" *To my room.* Damn, that sounded juvenile.

That small smile on his face grew bigger. "I'm here to enter the Wi-Fi code into your laptop and make sure you're all right."

"Really?" I sat the laptop on Sterling's desk and pushed it Reid's direction. "And Sterling...I mean, Sparrow..." It seemed as though that somewhere along the line with this inner group, the Mr. had been dropped. "...knows I'm here?"

Reid was bent over, looking down at my screen as his fingers flew incredibly fast on the keys, and yet still he was able to scoff—he actually scoffed—at my question.

A few seconds later, he pushed the laptop toward me and turned it until the screen was my way. "Yes. He knows. He said something about discussing it with you later."

Oh shit. That didn't exactly sound good.

"Do you know when later will be?" I asked, thinking of the memories I'd recalled from last night. I had things to discuss with him too, things one hell of a lot more important than my disobeying his stupid note.

"No," Reid responded. "He and Patrick left earlier today and have been dealing with a few things. They'll be back when they can."

"If I asked you what that means—dealing with a few things—would you tell me?"

Reid shook his head. "No, ma'am, I wouldn't."

"If I asked you to stop calling me ma'am because it's making me feel old and I get the impression that you're older than me—probably not by a lot, but still—would you call me Araneae?"

His lips quirked. "I could try."

"Thank you, Reid. I'd like that."

"I hope you won't mind if I make a recommendation," Reid said.

"Not at all. What?"

"You should confirm that the ringer on your phone is turned on. I believe Sparrow plans to call you when he's able. And he likes his calls answered."

Jeez. I'm sure he does.

"Okay. By the way, the phone in my pocket isn't my phone."

Reid nodded. "I know."

It was like all three of them shared a brain. What one knew, the other two did also.

Reid went on, "Good night, Araneae. Please don't forget to call Lorna before going up the stairs. None of us want you hurt again."

Hurt?

Was that what poison did or was he talking about something else —like my arm?

Pushing that thought away, I replaced it with a mental image of Lorna and Reid together, recalling what she said about reaffirming their love. Now that I've met them both, the thought brought a smile to my face.

And then my lips pursed as one of my hands went to my hip. "Is she the one who told on me?"

"Your phone—the one you're carrying," he clarified, "told on you." His gaze narrowed. "Wait, are you saying that my wife knows that you're down here?"

"No, of course not."

His smile returned. "I see why she likes you. Don't forget, she's one floor away, and I'm only two away if you need anything."

"Thank you, Reid."

The vibration tingled my butt before the sound of the ring filled the office. Standing slightly, I pulled the phone from my back pocket.

STERLING was on the screen.

My gaze darted back to the man across the desk.

Reid nodded. "Good luck with that one, ma'am."

I wanted to remind him that it was Araneae, but before I could, he exited as quickly as he entered.

I pushed the green button. "Hello."

For a long enough time to cause my heart to race, my greeting was met with silence. I was about to speak again when Sterling did.

"Unlike the lock on the bedroom door, which I am seriously considering having replaced so that I can keep your ass in there when I say, the apartment is secure. You may not leave."

"May not?"

"Cannot. As in…are incapable of, not only forbidden but physically unable. Is that spelled out enough for you?" Before I could reply, he continued, "Obviously, following rules voluntarily is not your strong suit. The choice for you to go against my will regarding leaving the apartment has been taken away from you."

I lowered my voice. "Tell me if I'm on speaker or if anyone else can hear me."

"Tell you?"

My teeth ground together before I enunciated the words. "Tell me."

"No, Araneae, no one can hear you but me."

"Then, fuck you. I simply wanted my laptop."

"You had a phone."

"A phone," I repeated. "Not *my* phone. I still don't have that."

"Your office space is ready for you tomorrow. Patrick will be with you throughout the day, every day. He's hired a temporary assistant. Winifred will be here next week to train her."

"Wait," I said, my mind scrabbling with all he just said. "What?"

"Did I stutter?"

"No, asshole, you didn't stutter. I'm simply getting sick and tired of you making all these decisions. It's one thing to have all your stupid rules here in your apartment, but Sinful Threads is mine."

"My rules are not stupid. They are for your—"

"Yeah, I know," I interrupted, "my safety."

Sterling changed the subject. "Reid has been working on Sinful Threads' security nationwide."

My free hand went to the top of my head as I stood. My voice was saturated with the exasperation coursing through my bloodstream, growing louder with each sentence. "See, like that. Louisa and I make decisions together. By the way, that's what partners do. One does not unilaterally do things like rent office space in fucking Chicago or beef up nationwide security. Jesus, Sterling, Sinful Threads has a budget. We have expenses. Sinful Threads is not about you. Don't you have real estate to buy or sell and a city to run?"

Sterling's tone deepened. "If it's about you, then it's about me. What I do is also about me. I will be home around nine. If things change, I'll call this number. Keep your calls limited to the six numbers you've been provided. Keep your computer usages to only business regarding Sinful Threads. For fuck's sake, eat. I know you haven't, and, sunshine, if you even as much as think about touching an exit to the apartment, not only will you not be at your new office tomorrow, sitting will be off the table too."

"Sterling, wait, I remembered—"

The phone went dead.

"Damn you, Sterling Sparrow." Pulling the phone away from my ear, I stared at the dark screen and shook my head. I couldn't even be sure he'd heard what I said. In my mind I imagined him moving the damn phone away from his own ear the moment he was done speaking his royal proclamations.

And then on the desk before me, the screen of my laptop went dark. "No, no, no." I reached out and violently shook the mouse. Immediately, it came back to life. "Gah! Asshole, I even give you credit for my screen falling asleep." I looked around the room and continued to speak aloud. "I don't know if you can see or hear me, but you, Sterling Sparrow, are infuriating. And I will repeat, an asshole, which as I've mentioned multiple times isn't a virtue."

Taking a breath, I laid the phone on the desk by the laptop. Going to the highboy in the corner of the room, I opened one of the tall doors. Just as in the bedroom, there was a small refrigerator hidden inside. I pulled out a bottle of water, thinking that despite the craziness of the world I'd entered, maybe I was getting accustomed to a few things.

Originally, I'd planned to retrieve the laptop and go back upstairs, but now that everyone knew where I was, the point was moot. Looking around at the crazy paintings with the jazz music playing, I decided I'd stay. I liked the change of scenery.

My gilded cage had grown.

As I walked back to Sterling's desk, I lamented on what I'd remembered about last night—about the blonde woman and Sterling's power play. Those thoughts were there, but it wouldn't do me any good to overthink them or worry about the impending conversation. Besides, I was feeling better and had a life to regain.

Sitting back down in his big chair, I scooted closer to the desk. As I opened my emails, I also lifted the phone, swiped the screen, and after entering the four-digit code, I pushed the name *LOUISA*.

"Why are you calling me from a blocked number, and are you feeling better?" my best friend asked before saying hello.

I let out a long sigh. "How did you know it was me?"

"Well, the text message saying you'd be calling from a blocked number and to answer it was my first clue."

I shook my head. Fuck you, Sparrow. "Yeah, sorry, I forgot I'd sent that. It's been a long day."

"Are you feeling better?" she asked again.

"I am. I think it was something I ate—*or drank*." I left the last part unsaid.

"Oh, food poisoning sucks."

"It does."

"Hey," Louisa said, "Winnie is excited to come visit you

next week. She has a friend in Chicago she hasn't seen in a while. That and training someone, she's practically giddy." Before I could ask more, Louisa went on, "I can't believe the deal you got on that office space. I was kind of pissed you didn't discuss it with me first, but damn, girl, I agree you couldn't pass up that deal for downtown Chicago."

Now, if only I knew what kind of a deal I got.

"How are *you* feeling?" I asked. "Will you survive without her?" Winnie was really the main assistant for both of us. There were others who worked in the office, Cindy and Paul, but Winnie was our go-to person.

"For a few days, no problem. And I'm feeling the same. Ready to see Little Kennedy."

Kennedy.

"Okay," I began after a drink of water. "Can you catch me up? I plan to hit the ground running tomorrow."

"Sure. Let me get comfortable. Where do you want to start?"

ARANEAE

*I*t was after eight o'clock when my stomach reminded me of one of King Sparrow's directives.

"For fuck's sake, eat."

Turning off my laptop, I packed it in my carry-on to take upstairs. I wanted to be ready for work in the morning—I'd been away for too long. After talking with Louisa, I felt better, more caught up. We'd spoken for over an hour, ending our call a little after seven o'clock. After that, I called Winnie. Her excitement at commuting back and forth between Chicago and Boulder was contagious—and at first surprising. I hadn't realized it was a commuting thing. I thought she was only helping to train someone else. And since I hadn't been the one to propose the original promotion—because apparently an increase in salary was involved too—I spent more time listening than speaking.

She told me a little about her friend. They'd grown up

together near Boulder and Leslie had come to Chicago for college and never went back. Winnie said she should arrive to the office Monday morning and planned to stay through Wednesday. In the meantime, she'd help the new person via calls and teleconferencing. She'd booked herself a room in the same hotel where she'd booked mine nearly two weeks ago.

That timeline seemed unbelievable to me. It was difficult to comprehend all of what had occurred in such a short time. Supposedly, God created the world in seven days—one week. In double that amount of time, Sterling Sparrow had blown my world to kingdom come.

After turning off the music and lights in Sterling's office, I left the carry-on by the stairs and went on a search for the kitchen, remembering the way Sterling had carried me. However, Patrick had come from another way. I wandered, wanting to see more of the apartment. Walking from room to room, I made a few wrong turns on my self-guided tour. Of course, I could call Lorna; however, I thought it was silly. This was an apartment—a big-ass apartment, but an apartment nevertheless. Eventually I'd find the kitchen, and once there, I was perfectly capable of making myself a sandwich.

My feet stopped as I entered a big open living room with stylish furnishings, complete with a fireplace. Like Sterling's bedroom upstairs, this room had two full walls of windows. Like a moth to a flame, the glass drew me closer. Standing where the windowed walls met, I stood mesmerized as the sky and the city below me were blanketed in the hues of pinks, reds, and purples cast by the rays of a spectacular sunset.

It was amazing to see the beauty of nature even in the middle of one of the largest cities in the United States.

Before my eyes, lights throughout the city came to life. As

the sky darkened, their glow shone bright spheres of illumination from windows and along the streets below. Higher in the skyline, colorful words advertising proprietorship glistened from the tops of tall buildings.

As I stared into the growing darkness, it was easier to believe that the world Sterling mentioned lurked within the shadowed areas of the city, those not contained within the bubbles of light.

Warding off the chill those thoughts of an unseen darkness gave me, I continued on my tour. The door that Mrs. Sparrow had passed through was obviously one of the exits to Sterling's apartment. In his warning, he'd said exits—plural. I didn't know where another or others were located. His threat about me *even thinking* about touching one had me a bit concerned. I didn't want to come into contact with one unwittingly, not knowing what it was. From his tone on the phone, I doubted he'd believe my claim of ignorance, and even if he did, he wouldn't accept it.

For that reason, as I searched the first floor, closed doors were avoided.

He and I had enough to discuss tonight. I wasn't looking for another reason to provoke his punishment, well, any more than I'd already done. When I finally entered the kitchen, I realized I'd accomplished what I'd set out to do. I'd seen more of the first floor and found the way that Patrick had entered this morning.

A flip of a few switches and the entire kitchen was bathed in warm yellow light. The window that this morning had been filled with blue sky was now black, transforming the glass from a window into a mirror. The room's reflection made the kitchen seem twice as large.

My conscience had a twinge that I was trespassing as I rummaged through the refrigerator and opened cabinets. The saving grace was that doing so wouldn't lead me to an exit.

In reality, I didn't need to *rummage*. Inside the refrigerator, in perfect view, were two covered dishes, identical in contents, significantly different in portions. Removing the cover of the smaller portion released the delicious aroma of what appeared to be my prepared dinner.

Leaving the larger one where I found it because Sterling had said he wouldn't be home for another hour...

Was it weird to think of this place as home?
I couldn't even find the kitchen.

...I placed my plate with grilled chicken, sautéed onions and peppers, and small red potatoes in the microwave and retrieved one of the two salads I'd spotted with the meals. With the salad and my reheated dinner, I sat at the breakfast bar, and did as I'd been told—I ate.

It was as I was rinsing out the dishes that it happened.

The energy shifted.

I didn't need to turn or see. I knew he was there.

Sucking in a breath, I closed my eyes as the warmth of Sterling's body covered my back and the fresh aroma of body-wash filled my senses. I wasn't sure how he and Reid were able to move so quietly, but they did.

Sterling's deep tenor rumbled from my ears to my toes, sparking every nerve, setting the little hairs on my neck to attention. "It's good to see that you can at least follow some instructions. It's about time you fucking ate."

There were so many things I wanted to say and questions I wanted to ask. It was easier to come up with those things while he was away. Now, with his large hands on the edge of the sink, caging me between his outstretched arms, and his body coming to life behind me, I couldn't remember one of them.

Turning, I placed my hands on Sterling's chest. With the rapid beat of his heart beneath my palms, I took him in, every inch—from his tousled wet hair, dark eyes, and high cheekbones to his rigid freshly shaven chiseled jaw. My gaze lowered to the taut cords in his thick neck and the slow bob of his Adam's apple. His dark-blue t-shirt was darker where it was damp and his jeans hung low, partially covering his bare feet. "Where were you?"

"Making damn certain you're safe."

"You showered. Why did you shower?" The question came out unsteadily, as if my mind knew I didn't want to hear the answer even though my mouth couldn't stop from asking.

"Because, sunshine, sometimes what we do gets messy. You're never going to see any of that."

My eyes widened. "Sterling, what did you do? What happened? Were you safe?"

Where did that last question come from? Had I come to care if he were safe?

I had.

In one fell swoop he reached for my ass and lifted me. Spinning around, he placed me on the breakfast bar, the same one where I'd just eaten, and wedged himself between my outstretched knees. With the height of the counter, our noses were close enough to touch. We were eye-to-eye as he stared unblinkingly into mine.

I'd heard that the eyes were the windows to our soul.

If that were true, Sterling Sparrow's soul was as black as

coal, growing hotter by the minute, and nearly ready to combust.

I reached for his shoulders. He wouldn't answer my other questions. I had one more. "Did it work? Am I...safe?"

The silence of his non-answer disappeared in the swooshing sound of blood coursing through my own ears. As if in sync, our breathing quickened. Oxygen depleted as our lips grew closer. With each exhale, my breasts flattened against his chest as we breathed in one another.

His kiss was ravaging and unforgiving as he palmed the back of my head and pulled me toward him. Without hesitation, his tongue bore entrance, parting my lips, and seizing my tongue. Moans filled the air as my lips bruised and lungs fought for air. When he pulled back, there was more to his dark stare: the fire that had been smoldering was now ablaze.

"You are safe," Sterling said. "Never doubt it."

I didn't get the chance to respond before his hands moved to the front of my jeans, reaching for the button.

Covering his hand with mine, I stopped him. "Sterling, we're in the kitchen."

"Araneae, I need to fuck you."

I gasped as his lips came to my neck. Like his kiss, his movements were forceful and savage. He was a famished man and I was the dinner he'd yet to eat. The front of my cotton top shredded as he ripped it down the center, exposing my bra. One more tug and my bra was ruined. Easing them both from my shoulders, his lips followed the material as my nipples hardened. The air-conditioned air clashed with the fire from his eyes, two contrasting fronts coming together, leaving me the target of an impending storm.

Sterling's gaze came back to mine, asking—or maybe

daring—me to stop him. The primal need bearing into me, searching me, was more powerful than words could describe. I may never know what Sterling had done, where he'd been, or what he'd do in the future. Yet from the depths of my soul, I knew this powerful man needed what only I could give.

"We could go upstairs?"

With one motion Sterling opened his jeans, freeing his thick cock. The head of the hard, angry rod glistened in all its glory as the full length sprang forward.

"No one will bother us." He again reached for my jeans. This time, I didn't stop him as he skillfully released the button and lowered the zipper, easing them down my legs taking my panties with them. The fire smoldering in his gaze left my core in ashes as he spread my knees farther. "I told you. No one sees this but me."

Fisting his cock, his hand moved up and down. "Araneae, I meant what I said. I'll fucking kill for you. I'd do it again. That pussy—all of you—belongs to me."

Kill?

"Oh!" I didn't have time to think about what Sterling said because before I could even consider the ramifications, in one savage thrust he pulled me forward, stretched me, and filled me completely. With his hands on my ass, he continued to pull me close until my backside was on the edge of the counter and my legs surrounded him. Reaching for his shoulders, my nails clawed for leverage, for stability, for anything.

Sterling Sparrow was a force of nature, a category five hurricane, and all I could do was hold on. As a casualty of those hurricane-force winds—simply someone in the path of destruction—I fought to maintain a facade of balance where there was none.

His rhythm was erratic, his pace excessive. His focus wasn't on me but on his own satisfaction. And yet the pressure within me began to build, finally growing. Closing my eyes and holding tightly to his shoulders, I sensed the pending orgasm as I lifted myself, trying to get the friction I needed.

"Oh," I called, "it's almost..."

All at once Sterling slammed his hips at the same time he pulled me down. The friction was gone as his roar filled the kitchen. Unrelenting, he held me in place as his cock throbbed within me.

"Fuuck," he growled as his hands released me and he pulled out, leaving me teetering on the edge of the breakfast bar.

"What the...?" I asked as I scooted back to safety.

Taking a step back, Sterling's dark gaze scanned from my now-tangled hair to the tips of my toes.

My skin prickled as I realized that I was completely nude while minus his open fly, Sterling was still fully clothed.

Shaking his head, he reached for the hem of his t-shirt and pulled it over his head, further messing his hair and revealing his broad chest. With a grunt, he threw the soft shirt my direction. "Put this on."

The indignation within me bubbled over. "What the hell? You came. You couldn't let me go a little longer?"

His grin wasn't welcoming but sinister. "You know the rule: good girls get to come."

"You're a fucking asshole. You know that?" I fumbled with the inside-out shirt. "Why do I need this? You said no one would bother us."

"Just put on the damn shirt. We're going upstairs and discussing your ability to follow rules."

My bare feet landed on the floor with a thud. Despite Sterling's shirt hanging to my thighs and surrounding me in the amazing aroma of him, I put my fist on my hip and stared at the man who after tucking himself back in his jeans had leaned down to pick up my clothes.

"Really? You're going from that..." I pointed to the counter behind me. "...to a discussion of rules."

He stood straight. "Yes. And since you walked down the damn stairs, disobeying my request, I'm going to assume you can make it back up. If not, I'll pick up your fine ass and put you over my shoulder. While I might like that, once we're upstairs, I guarantee you won't."

Both of my hands slapped my t-shirt-covered thighs. "What you said in that note wasn't a request. I don't know if you realize it, but you, Sterling Sparrow, don't make requests. You make demands and issue fucking summonses and punishments for no fucking reason. A request begins with the word will or would. You should try it sometime."

Sterling's jaw clenched as a vein came to life in his forehead. "You have five seconds before I take matters into my own hands. *Will* you be walking or *would* you prefer that I carry you?"

Biting my tongue, I shook my head. "You're insane. Fine, asshole, I'll go upstairs with you—and walk on my own, thank you very much—not because you suddenly learned how to make a request but because I have things I too want to discuss."

"Then get your ass up there and we'll decide whose matter is more pressing. I'm going to put my money on mine."

Turning my back on him, I lifted my chin, straightened my neck, and walked barefoot in his damn t-shirt with all the dignity I could muster. Reaching for the carry-on at the foot of the stairs I lifted it in one hand while I took the steps one by one, walking like a fucking queen to where I'd been summoned like a child to my room to learn whatever it was that Sterling Sparrow had in store.

Well, Sparrow, you're going to explain my memories too.

ARANEAE

With each step toward the bedroom, my ire grew.

"Good girls get to come."

Asshole.

Son of a bitch.

Jerk.

I was running out of names to call Sterling Sparrow. Maybe there was an online thesaurus for insulting personal pronouns. I would add checking on that to my list of things to do.

Inhale.

Exhale.

Never in my entire life had I met anyone as exasperating, infuriating, or as maddening as Sterling Sparrow. He set off my last nerve, pushing me like I'd never been pushed. The way he'd stared at me when he'd first entered the kitchen made me feel as though he needed me. He'd done something

—something I would probably never know—and I was his relief or maybe reward. I wasn't sure exactly what I was, other than in that moment I believed that he saw me in the way a person saw the one he cared about.

He needed what I could give.

I was wrong. That was *not* what had just happened. I didn't give myself to him—he took.

No matter how upsetting he was, the man could practically induce an orgasm with his eyes and words, without a physical touch. As my mind went over what just happened, I realized that throughout the entire copulation, he had no intention of letting me come. It was all about him and his fucking punishments.

Dropping my carry-on onto the bedroom floor, I went into the closet and found a new pair of underwear and a pajama short set. Yes, it had lace around the boy shorts and camisole top, but no, it didn't scream sexy. Because at this moment, the last thing I wanted was for him to think I still wanted what he didn't provide.

Thankfully, as I reentered the bedroom, I was still alone.

My next move was to take the new clothes to the bathroom. As I shut the door, I realized the damn door didn't lock. Of course, it didn't. Sterling lived alone, according to Lorna. Why would a man who lived alone need a lock to a bathroom only accessible from his bedroom?

As the thought hit me, a smile came to my lips.

The bathroom didn't have a lock, but the bedroom did.

Sterling wanted to treat me like a child. I'd act like one.

It may be petty, but I wasn't the one who denied him an orgasm—not this time but maybe the next.

Pulling the door inward, I peeked back inside the bedroom and quickly scanned the room.

Still no Sterling.

I rushed to the double doors. Flipping the same lock I had in order to leave the room earlier in the day, I secured the outer entrance and turned my back to the door. My return walk to the bathroom was slower as the indignation within me morphed to a new level of satisfaction.

There you go, Sparrow.

Fuck yourself. Just don't use me to do it.

I had planned to rush my shower and ready myself for sleep, but with my newfound safety bubble, I changed my mind.

Hot water spilled from dual faucets, filling the large sunken tub as humidity and steam floated in the air. A handful of bath beads added the sweet aroma of lavender. Lifting Sterling's t-shirt over my head, I dropped it to the floor and stared at my own reflection. The bruise of my arm wasn't my only marking. While it was more distinct, both of my hips and—I could see as I turned—my buttocks were spotted with different degrees of discolorations.

I wanted to be mad, to have those additional bruises amplify my anger. The arm, yes, I could be upset about, but the hips I couldn't. I recalled times when Sterling's hold had been so firm that I'd imagined my skin was bruising, and during those moments, I didn't care. I wasn't troubled. No, in those situations, I was hot, bothered, and needy.

My breasts heaved with the memories. I'd never had a man take me, want me, possess me the way Sterling could. Unlike my arm, those markings weren't given in anger. They were given and received in passion. I'd noticed a few scratches on his shoulders, too. When it came to the zeal of our connection, I wasn't an innocent bystander, nor did I want to be.

Resecuring my blonde hair on top of my head, I repaired the bun he'd dislodged and waited for the tub to fill. Five minutes later, I eased into the tepid water, my skin turning pink as I settled to the depth, and water overflowed into the channel surrounding the mini-pool.

My solitude was short-lived. The bathroom door opened inward.

Sterling didn't speak.

My heartbeat quickened with each second of silence, yet I couldn't look away from his dark stare.

His gaze devoured me, penetrating the silky water as he stepped closer, towering over the sunken tub. Without a word, he shed his jeans—the only clothing he wore—and gracefully stepped down into the tub. Like Poseidon, the Greek god of water, his defined body was enveloped by the lavender liquid. Wave after wave rose, filling the channel as he lowered to the depth at the other end of the tub, and his feet came to the sides of my legs.

Never once did his dark eyes leave mine.

My neck straightened and lips thinned. Our stares were a battle of wills, both declaring our righteous anger. Neither one of us was issuing a plea for forgiveness—not him for his selfishness nor me for my pettiness.

In hindsight, I should have realized that a lock wouldn't stop Sterling Sparrow. He'd been the one to lock the door from the outside while I was sleeping. It made sense that he could also open it.

As he was about to speak, I found my voice.

"Sterling, I remember last night. I remember everything."

The darkness of his gaze eased a bit as he sat forward, causing the water to slosh. "I was going to tell you."

"Were you?"

Nodding, he asked, "What does *everything* mean?"

I gazed down at my arm and back to him. "I know this didn't happen when I was falling. I remember sitting at the bar in the club. You were upset. I told you that what you were doing hurt and you didn't stop."

His eyes closed and opened as he swallowed. "Araneae, I could say that I was trying to avoid what happened next. I could tell you that I was livid when I saw that you'd disobeyed my simple directions by ordering a drink, leaving the barstool, and especially leaving the fucking room." His tone grew deeper as his words came faster. "I had specifically forbade you from moving or speaking to anyone." His head shook. "You aren't stupid and they weren't fucking complicated commands." His fingers flexed beneath the water. "I could say other things." His broad chest rose and fell as he took a deep breath. "I'm not a man who apologizes for—anything. I don't always do what's best—sometimes it's downright wrong. But I do what I believe is right for the sake of those involved. That includes you."

Even in the warm, scented water, my skin became coated with goose bumps as a lump formed in my throat. I wouldn't —couldn't—be with a man who despite the way he made me feel sexually, would see me as inferior, as unworthy of an apology, who believed he had the unilateral right to make every decision without discussion.

Blinking, I broke our connected gaze. Looking down at

the water, I fought the release of the tears now prickling the back of my eyes.

Water sloshed again as Sterling moved closer and reached for my hand. "Araneae, I'm sorry."

The tears won their battle, overspilling my lids as I looked up toward his softening gaze. "You just said—"

"That I'm sorry. And for the record, I did catch you when you fell, but no, it wasn't by your arm. I'll tell Renita the truth or you can."

I shook my head. "What good will that do?"

He pulled my hand toward his lips until I was no longer sitting, but kneeling in the tub in front of him. After kissing my knuckles, he said, "Legally, none. Personally, it may once and for all show her the true asshole I am."

He tugged me closer, until I settled with my back against his chest, surrounded by his long legs and the lavender-scented warm water.

"You can be one," I said, "but not always."

Sterling kissed the top of my head and lifted my arm. His strong fingers gently skirted over the bruised skin. "It's not an excuse. I was wrong; that's not debatable. It's that you amaze me. You're so fucking strong, a spitfire full of sunshine. In the world I live in—where I brought you—I sometimes forget that you're also fragile."

My day, despite the naps, was exhausting. Tears silently descended my cheeks as I ran one hand over his leg, up and down, and he did the same over my arms. It wasn't sexual; it was more...personal, familiar, even soothing.

"Thank you for the apology," I finally said, swallowing the rest of the tears.

"Can you forgive me?"

Letting go of his leg, I spun until we were eye-to-eye. "Are you asking me to?"

Sterling nodded.

"Why do I get the feeling that you ask for forgiveness as often as you apologize?" Yes, I knew technically they were the same thing, yet his request—wanting to hear the words from me—hit me in a way that I never expected.

Sterling cupped my cheeks. "Because that would be a very accurate assumption. I don't recall the last time I did." His eyes closed before they opened. "No, there was once, but that time it was too late." Letting go of my cheeks, Sterling softly kissed my lips. "Will you tell me it's not too late?"

My cheeks rose as a smile curled my lips. "*Will* I? Yes, Sterling, I can and will forgive you. I'm not fragile. As a matter of fact, I'm strong. You push me in ways I..." I searched for the right words. "...in ways I find exasperating and also energizing. I have no idea nor could I try to explain the changes that have occurred over the last few weeks, not only in my external world, but inside me—my thoughts, my concerns, my everything.

"That said, I have lines that can't be crossed. If I say stop, you have to stop. I need to know in my mind and in my heart that you will."

"Your safety—"

I lifted my finger to his lips. "I get that this world is dangerous and it's new to me. I'll try to listen and do my best to follow your requests. Please listen to me when I say that the way to make your point with me is not by manhandling. It's by talking and explaining things to me. I will listen. I am listening." I laid my palm against his cheek. "Sterling Sparrow, you have my full attention." *You have since the first time I saw you.*

I didn't say that last part though it was true.

"You'll work on following *requests*," he emphasized the word. "I'll work on talking." His lips quirked upward. "And no manhandling."

My head tilted. "We can work on the definition of that word. There may be some room for negotiation."

His smile faded. "I'm also capable of listening. Your *no* will be respected." He shook his head. "The thing is that I despised my father for violating that same line with my mother." The vein I'd seen earlier in his forehead was back. "I swore that I'd never..."

I flexed my fingers on his cheek. "Sterling, I believe you. I forgive you."

After a kiss, I turned, settling back between his legs with my back on his chest. "Now, while we're in this sharing conversation, tell me about that woman—my mother."

Saying those words aloud should give me hope and excitement for the possibility of a family; however, every time she entered my mind it seemed as though I was dishonoring Josey. The two didn't go together. A mother was more than the woman who gave me life because from all that I could assess, that woman who looked alarmingly like me had abandoned me.

I laid back my head onto Sterling's shoulder. His chest rose and fell a few times.

"Part of me hoped you wouldn't remember her."

Reaching for his hand, I intertwined our fingers. "From what you know, was she telling the truth?"

"Yes, Araneae. Annabelle Landers is your biological mother."

I gripped his hand tighter. "My father—McCrie."

"Is gone."

I nodded. "I think I knew that. Weren't they married? Or did she change her name?"

"Yes, they were married. She never changed her name. They were both attorneys and later she became a judge."

"A judge?"

"Circuit court...when you were born. Today she's a federal judge."

That should impress me. It made me wonder if part of the reason she didn't want me was because of her career. I loved Sinful Threads. So did Louisa, yet I'd never give up a child for it. I'd make it work. At least, I thought I would. "She's the one who gave me to the Marshes. Do you know why?" I believe I wanted confirmation that it was altruistic and not selfish.

"I'll be honest," Sterling replied, "we've been working on this puzzle for years, and we don't know."

"Josey told me that she and my biological mother were friends a long time ago. My biological—Annabelle." I shook my head. "It's strange to have a name. Anyway, she told Josey that I'd be safe with her. It had to do with my father —McCrie."

"This all happened when I was young, too. Many of the original players are gone. We can explain more of what happened in time. From what is believed, your father had some incriminating evidence. McCrie tried to leverage that evidence to gain power that didn't belong to him. It backfired.

As for a connection between Annabelle and the Marshes, we've found none."

My mind spun. "I think they went to school together...I can't recall. Why doesn't she—Annabelle—want me with you?" *And why did Josey warn me against you?*

"Wait," Sterling said, before I could add the second part, "I just remembered what Annabelle said before we entered the elevator. She asked why you were marrying me. Why would she say that? I'd told the men in that room you were mine. I never mentioned marriage, not since the helicopter."

I took a deep breath. "No...it wasn't the pilot that gave her that idea. It was me."

"You?"

"In the ladies' room, she approached me. It made me nervous. *She* made me nervous. I said I had to leave, to get to my fiancé."

Sterling's chest flexed as his head nodded. Letting go of my hand, he lifted warm lavender water, raining it over my shoulders. "You know..." He kissed my neck. "...I think you've found the perfect answer."

"What is that?"

He lifted my chin until my neck was craned backward his direction. "We should get married."

What?

That wasn't the way I imagined a proposal. I thought it may start with the word will.

Sterling wasn't serious

I scoffed. "Right. First, let's concentrate on uncovering the veil of lies that I've been told my entire life, and while we're at it, you can work on the request thing."

ANNABELLE

Twenty-six years ago

"*D*aniel, talk to me. Where are we going?" My tone was no longer calm. It hadn't been for the last hour. This wasn't right. "You know the doctor said I shouldn't be more than two hours from home. For God's sake, we're in Wisconsin."

I rubbed my growing midsection. It wasn't growing, but grown. At thirty-six and a half weeks, I could go into labor at any time. I'd been so distressed after my last doctor's appointment—after being blindsided the way I'd been—that the obstetrician for high-risk pregnancies ordered me on bed rest.

I had been.

All of my court cases were reassigned. I was home.

That was, until now.

Currently, I was in a rental car, riding on refreezing spring-time roads, winding our way toward Madison, Wisconsin. Yet for some reason we weren't even on Interstate 90 anymore.

Daniel had exited onto smaller two-lane roads winding us through the Wisconsin wilderness.

"We're on a drive," my husband said, his head shaking back and forth. "We're not in Wisconsin, dear. You're mistaken."

I wasn't. We'd been headed north and had left Illinois a while ago. I was capable of reading signs. On top of that, the forecast was calling for snow. Daniel was lying, as if he could gaslight me into believing him instead of the evidence.

Whenever I started to speak, my husband shook his head. He didn't want me speaking or asking questions. He knew me better than that, and yet with each mile my anxiety grew. The angst wasn't helping our baby.

As my analytical mind processed our situation, it made sense that whatever was happening was connected to the FBI raid last week. There had been two: one of our home and one of Daniel's office. The agents seized our private phones and boxes of papers as well as our home computers and not only ours, but his assistants' too. For the next four days, Daniel had been MIA. I didn't know if he was alive or dead, and I didn't even know who to ask.

Two days ago, he returned a different man.

He was acting strangely. His usual confidence shaken, he was paranoid of everyone and everything, and he'd also been drinking more than usual. This morning, a Sunday, he woke and announced we had plans. I thought it might be with his sister, Pauline, and her husband, Rubio. They were our only family since both of us lost our parents. While they didn't have children, Pauline has been very helpful and supportive of my pregnancy. A few weeks ago, she'd thrown me a baby shower.

At forty-one and financially secure, a baby shower seemed unnecessary, but it was greatly appreciated. The symbolism meant more than the gifts. It had been like a dream come true, surrounded by friends and colleagues with pink gift bags and wrapping paper. At that moment it seemed like Daniel's and my dream was finally coming to fruition.

That was one week before our world fell apart.

The man who intruded upon my obstetrician appointment was Agent Bane, from the Criminal Investigative Division of the Federal Bureau of Investigation. He informed me of the occurring raid and offered me immunity if I agreed to be questioned and testify.

I didn't have a clue as to what he was talking about.

Question me about what?

Testify about what?

I was a judge.

Agent Bane said I hadn't answered his requests.

I hadn't received his requests.

None of it made sense.

What would I possibly know about crimes, other than the ones in cases over which I presided and ones with statutes I researched?

The tires of the rental car bounced as Daniel pulled onto the gravel parking lot of a small motel. Surrounded mostly by forest, the one-story building sprawled out both directions from the center where the office appeared to be, only four units on either side. The dilapidated business was directly off the two-lane road and basically in the middle of nowhere.

The darkening spring sky didn't help the run-down appearance. With one of the lights out on the sign, instead of motel it said 'mot-l.'

As I started to speak Daniel put his finger to his lips.

My head shook in frustration as my midsection contracted.

"I'll be right back," he mouthed.

A cold chill filled the car as Daniel opened the door and quickly slammed it shut.

No, just no.

I pulled my coat up over my shoulders as I wrapped it tightly around me.

Peering through the windows up to the sky, an ominous feeling settled in my stomach. I'd lived in Illinois since law school. I recognized the billowing dark-gray clouds. They contained snow—a lot of snow. We were over three hours north of Chicago. Even in late March this area could get significant snowfall. A few years ago, there had been over two feet of accumulation in less than twenty-four hours.

I wouldn't stay here. I couldn't.

Unfortunately, I didn't have a new cellular phone, as I'd been promised the FBI would soon return mine. However, common sense said there would be a telephone in the motel's office. Daniel was crazy if he thought I'd stay in this flea-infested establishment.

This was ridiculous.

I shouldn't have left the house with Daniel. I should have known better. Then again, he was my husband and I trusted him. I had or I did. I wasn't sure anymore.

Tears came to my eyes as I quietly spoke to our unborn daughter. "Spider-girl, it will be all right. I promise."

I'd come up with the name Araneae by accident. Since my name began with an A and my mother had been Amelia, I had been searching for something unique, strong, and resilient that also began with the letter A.

It was during the time we'd learned our child was a girl that I was presiding over a horrific case of accused child abuse. The public defender was young and inexperienced. He'd asked the appropriate questions of his clients, but the research wasn't all there. What should have been a simple judgment denying the parents custody ended up being reconvened, as evidence began pointing to a growing problem especially evident in larger cities: child exploitation and trafficking.

The evidence kept me awake at night as I wrestled with photographic proof that we were bringing a child into a world where things like that could occur. Girls weren't the only victims of these crimes, yet in most instances, they outnumbered boys. While our court kept the young man in the dispute away from his parents who were associated with the crimes, our one case did little to infiltrate the bigger ring.

Nevertheless, it pleased me to see the young man leave with his grandparents, as later his parents were both taken into custody.

That case confirmed my desire to take time away from the bench and raise Araneae. Like a spider, Araneae would be fierce, a survivor, and hardy. Daniel wasn't sure of my choice and only agreed if I'd pronounce it differently than the spider: *uh-rain-ā*. I agreed, yet in my head and once she was born, she'd be my *uh-ron-e-eye*.

The car door beside me opened. In Daniel's hand was a hard-plastic keychain with a number four and a dangling key.

As I got out of the car, I looked his way.

Unlocking the door, he said, "It's time I tell you everything."

The door opened inward to a one-room standard motel room. Within seconds, we were met with the offending odor of stale cigarette smoke combined with harsh cleaners. Bringing my gloved hand to my nose, I asked, "Everything?" I wasn't sure I could listen, not to my husband. "And why here?"

"There's no place in the city I trust. There are bugs everywhere: in our home, our cars, our telephones, even our cellular phones. That's why the FBI was there, planting devices that overhear everything. It's why I rented the last-minute rental car with cash. No record. But I had to show them my license, so we still couldn't trust it. I just hope we weren't tracked. I need time to explain."

Did I want him to explain?

Wasn't it easier to plead ignorance?

I couldn't be forced to testify against my husband. I knew the law, but that was the problem. I believed in the law.

What had he done? What did he know?

The threadbare carpet under my boots held a stained path from the entrance past the bed to the vanity. Leaving the outside door ajar, Daniel stepped forward toward a partially opened door to the right of the vanity. He pushed the lavatory door inward. Next, I heard the jingle of hooks on a rod as the sound of a moving shower curtain filled the small room.

"Close the door," he called.

When I did, he asked if it was locked. "Daniel, I'm nervous. You're scaring me. We need to get back to the city. The baby."

He pulled out one of the chairs to the small table. The cracked vinyl of the seat matched the chipped surface of the laminated table. Leaning down, he lifted a metal panel and turned a knob, bringing the large heating unit under the window to life. The offending odors blended with warmth as the unit roared.

"There. It should warm up," he said, as if the temperature were my only concern. "Annabelle, I'm so sorry. This is going to take some time."

My head shook. "No, Daniel. I need to get back to Chicago."

"Sit down. Let me tell you why we aren't going back—ever."

ARANEAE

The stubborn side of me wanted to wear clothes I brought from Boulder for my first day back to Sinful Threads. However, the part of me that loved fashion and quality and had run the luxurious material through her fingers, found it difficult to not try on the clothes from the collection within the closet, including soft and sexy underclothes. That wasn't usually a consideration of my morning routine.

Sterling had a way of infiltrating my thoughts even when I was dressing. I'd never before dressed for work thinking about undressing after work, and now I was.

Unlike the underclothes, the choice in clothing wasn't based on Sterling. I doubted he would care about whatever I chose to wear over the sexy lace bra and thong. He'd never voiced an opinion about my attire except with evening clothes for his special occasions—the red and black dresses came to mind.

After our talk last night, we both fell sound asleep. There was something comforting about clearing at least some of the air, acknowledging that we both had strides to make, and knowing that we were safe behind the infrared protection of his apartment. With each nugget of information on Annabelle —I wasn't ready to call her my mother—my indecision grew. Did I want to know more about her? Did I want to know her?

I couldn't answer those questions right now.

I had too much new in my life to give her the thought she probably deserved.

Between Sinful Threads and Sterling Sparrow I had enough monopolizing my mind.

Sterling didn't mention what happened yesterday while he was gone, what he'd done or what he'd ordered done. My mind had created scenarios I didn't want to believe were possible. I wasn't sure how he could confirm my safety, yet there was too much conviction in his declaration to not believe him.

When I awoke this morning, there was a note, in his swirling handwriting, wishing me a good day back to work, letting me know that Patrick would be waiting with my phone, and that he wanted to hear all about it tonight.

I'd never had anyone other than Louisa who was interested in my work or my day. It didn't seem fair that I couldn't ask him about his. Nevertheless, that didn't quell my excitement to tell him about mine.

After all that had happened the last few days, the idea of having Patrick with me throughout my day wasn't upsetting. In a strange new way—in my new strange life—it was reassuring. Dressed mostly in clothes from the closet, including a blue pencil-style skirt, cream silk blouse, blue closed-toe pumps—because I planned to visit the warehouse and open-toed shoes were against warehouse policy—and a Sinful Threads brooch and bracelet, I made my way downstairs.

As I descended the stairs I heard the chatter coming from the kitchen. Turning the corner, the amazing aroma of coffee and sizzling bacon beckoned me closer. My steps stilled at the doorway for a moment as I watched Lorna, Reid, and Patrick talk, joke, and eat.

Lorna said she worked to make this place a home, a place where the men could relax from the stress of what went on in their day. Watching them interact, she'd succeeded.

Lorna turned my way first. "You're looking even better today."

Looking down at the outfit I'd chosen, pink came to my cheeks as thoughts of the sexy lace bra and panties beneath came to mind. Oh, that wasn't what she meant. She meant me —my health. "Thank you, I'm feeling better. Whatever it was, it must be gone."

A few minutes later, with a mug of coffee within the grasp of both of my hands, a plate of fruit, eggs, and toast in front of me, I asked, "So since you're all here, does Sterling get to drive himself?"

Reid and Patrick scoffed.

"He doesn't mind driving. He likes it, if he can get away," Patrick began, "but no, we have someone else with him."

"Is it usually you?"

Patrick nodded.

My lip went below my teeth. "Then why don't I get the other person and you can stay with Sterling?" I'd been thinking about everything Sterling had told me. Combine that with what Lorna said about each time Reid left, and I was a bit concerned about him being out there—in his world—without Patrick. It wasn't that I doubted Sterling's ability to handle himself. It was that he'd left before I woke, before I had a chance to tell him...

What did I want to tell him?

Surely it wasn't that I loved him.

Maybe it was that I cared.

Yes. That was it. I cared.

Patrick's lips quirked. "You're my job."

"So you've been demoted?" I asked with a grin.

"No, not at all. Sparrow has his priorities. Ms. McCrie, you're number one. Being entrusted with you is about as far from a demotion as possible."

I shook my head. "While you're all here, let's get this out in the open."

They all looked my way. "Would you please all stop with the *Ms. McCrie?*"

"Ms. Hawkins?" Patrick said with a grin.

I shrugged. "Well, according to you, that's still my name at Sinful Threads. While we're h-here..." I almost said at home. "...it seems too formal. How about Araneae? I need some help getting used to it, and I think you might be the ones for the job."

Everyone nodded. Patrick eyed my nearly empty plate. "Your new assistant is due in at ten." It was only seven-thirty. "We thought you'd like to take a look around the new office space first. It's not very large, but traffic is unpredictable."

"Since I was planning an office or a closet at the distribution center or maybe a cubicle at the warehouse facility, I'm certain this will be an upgrade from there."

"When you're ready?" Patrick said standing and lifting my

satchel, the one that now contained my laptop as well as other items I'd brought from Boulder.

As I reached for my purse, Patrick handed me my phone. For a moment I stared at the screen. It was a strange sensation having it again in my possession. Even though I'd missed it, being without it gave me a sense of freedom from responsibility that I hadn't enjoyed since...well, I couldn't remember when.

Now with the phone within my grasp, I didn't have the urge to call a million people or check emails or social media. I wasn't even tempted. Somehow over the past days and weeks, Sterling as well as everyone in the kitchen with me had convinced me that listening to them was my safest course of action.

As I put the phone into my purse, I realized something I hadn't been willing to admit to myself. I trusted them...all of them. That didn't mean I distrusted those I loved: Louisa, Jason, the Nelsons, and Winnie. It meant that the circle of people for whom I cared and trusted had grown.

Turning toward Lorna now standing at the counter, I asked, "Do you ever get out of here?"

She laughed. "I do. Truth be told, I like it here."

My head moved from side to side. "It might not be so bad."

"Well, that's a step in the right direction."

"This way, ma'am," Patrick said.

"Araneae," I corrected.

"We're headed to Sinful Threads, Ms. Hawkins."

"But we're still here."

"Yes, Araneae, we are."

My steps stuttered as Patrick turned away from the front

doors, the ones Mrs. Sparrow had passed through and continued down the hallway near Sterling's office. "I thought we were leaving."

"Yes, this is the way to our private elevator that will take us to our garage."

"Our garage. We have to be at least fifty floors up. I'm sure there are a lot of people who need a garage."

This was part of the apartment I hadn't explored. Taking a turn away from Sterling's office, we came to a stop by an elevator hidden behind a pocket door within the white wood-work of a doorframe. If I'd seen it last night, I wouldn't have realized what it was. At its side was a scanner. Patrick placed his palm over the sensor and the lights flashed. "This is the 96th floor." He tilted his chin up. "Your second floor is ninety-seven, one floor more than another tower you may have heard about in Chicago. Only the building previously called the Sears or Willis Tower is taller. And it's mostly the spires."

The doors to the elevator opened and we stepped in. The panel before us only had a few options: P, A, 2, and G. "It seems a little limited in our choices."

"It's safer that way. This garage is private."

As we descended, I gave it all more consideration. "Patrick, if I asked you something, would you tell me?"

He didn't verbally answer, but his lips quirked.

"Okay, I know you can't tell me some things. I want to know, if I looked at this building from the sidewalk, would I see the top floors?"

Patrick shrugged. "It depends on the cloud deck."

That didn't really answer my question.

The elevator came to a stop and the doors opened to what

he called a private garage. From the number of vehicles within, it seemed to be private for many people. "Who drives all of these cars?"

"People within the Sparrow organization."

"You mean Sparrow Enterprises."

"Yes, that's what I mean," Patrick said.

If these were based on Sterling's preference, it appeared he had none. The models were mostly recent with a few classic muscle cars. American and foreign manufacturers were represented. There were Audi, Mercedes-Benz, Lexus, and BMW. Styles varied. There were SUVs like the one I'd seen him with in the parking lot of my warehouse. There were sedans like Patrick had driven me in on my first trip back to Chicago. There were also crossovers and hybrids. Along the far wall were sports cars and Jeeps.

"This is like a dealership," I said in amazement. "It's too bad that I left my Honda Accord in Boulder."

Patrick pointed the opposite direction of the sports cars. "There it is."

My eyes widened as I followed his indication and saw my car. "How?"

"Ma'am, your apartment caught fire. It seemed best to get your car away from there."

"Then I can drive myself."

He didn't answer—not verbally—yet the small shake of his head told me that I probably wouldn't be driving myself to work, the grocery store, or the bakery.

As he opened the back door of a sedan much like, if not the same as, the one we drove before, I sat. Before bringing my heeled feet into the car, I asked, "Can you tell me if Louisa, Winnie, and Sinful Threads are safe?"

"That is something I can tell you. Yes. Sparrow is making sure of that."

I sighed. "What you all did for my neighbor...it meant a lot."

"It may be difficult to believe him sometimes, but when he says that if it's important to you, it's important to him, Sparrow's shooting straight. Ma'am, he doesn't lie."

I lifted my heeled shoes into the car as Patrick's words resonated. Before the door shut I said, "Still, thank you."

"You can thank him."

Once Patrick was in the car, our eyes met in the rearview mirror. "I will, but I'm thanking you, too. I mean it. Sterling told me that you were the one who remembered to text Louisa and Winnie while I was ill."

"I've watched you with Sinful Threads," he said. "It's important to you. I sincerely hope you'll be able to manage both."

The car was moving, slowly passing through a tunnel-like structure that had multiple gates.

"Both?"

"Sinful Threads and Araneae McCrie."

I thought about what he was saying. "Do you mean Araneae or Sterling?"

"I believe they're a package deal."

Were they?

Abruptly, the tunnel's road angled sharply upward. After one more gate, we were thrust into the morning sun, easing into rush-hour traffic. I tried to look up, out of the darkened windows to the buildings around us.

"The garage entrance and exit is two city blocks from the building," Patrick offered.

Taking my phone from my purse and opening my satchel, I reviewed a few notes I'd made last night on the phone with Louisa as I scanned new emails. Within minutes, I forgot that I was being driven, falling back into Kennedy Hawkins, co-owner and founder of Sinful Threads.

"Patrick," I said as I looked around, realizing I hadn't even tried to see where we were going. His eyes were covered by sunglasses, but by the tilt of his face, I knew he was seeing me in the mirror. "After the assistant arrives and we get her set up on phone calls, I'd like to make a visit to the warehouse, unless you've been given instructions to keep me in the office." I hated that those thoughts occurred, but that didn't stop them. "There are more than a few things that concern me about Franco Francesca."

He nodded. "My instructions are to keep you safe and let you do what you need to do. If Kennedy Hawkins needs or thinks she wants to go to her warehouse or distribution center, then that's where we'll go."

My cheeks rose. Sterling said he wasn't trying to take away my dream. "Thank you."

"There is one thing," Patrick said.

"What?"

"I'd like to enter the warehouse with you."

He'd said the same thing the first time we went there. That time I wanted him to enter with me because the man in the parking lot made me feel uneasy. Now, it could be the same reasoning. Having Patrick with me would be what that dark-eyed man from the parking lot would want; however, this time, it was more than that. It was more than Sterling's desire; Patrick's reassuring presence was what I wanted.

"I think that would be a good idea."

ARANEAE

"I'm in the office now," I said into my phone. "It's going to be perfect while I'm here."

"I'm excited. Hopefully after Kennedy is born, I can come see it. I get the feeling you have decided you want to keep Chicago."

I let out a sigh as I leaned back in my new office chair. The office around me was simple yet professional. Six rooms on the twenty-second floor of a building on South Wacker, complete with Sinful Threads etched in glass on the door. Computer equipment was new and connected to the Sinful Threads network in Boulder. My new assistant would be in the front office. That room connected to five others: my office with my own bathroom, a conference room, a supply room, another office, and another bathroom. Attached to my office was also another room—my new chaos room. That wasn't what Patrick called it, but that was what it would be.

From my office space, I had a spectacular view of other buildings.

Though it hadn't been confirmed, I doubted Sinful Threads was paying the current market rate for this little piece of real estate. The contract that I—actually, Patrick—sent Louisa over the past weekend was in my emails and according to that, the deal had been negotiated through Sparrow Enterprises. While it was a legal document—other than my forged signature—when I saw the monthly rent we were set to pay, I was certain this acquisition by Sinful Threads, if investigated, would be found to be way below market value.

"Of course not," I said, knowing how much Chicago has meant to Louisa. "You set up this market here. It's yours."

"I've been thinking about it and talking to Winnie and Jason. At first, I was upset. I'm just being honest with you."

I nodded as I pictured my best friend. There had been too many things happening in my life. I hadn't taken the time to consider how she felt about them, not really.

"But I've changed my mind," Louisa went on.

"You have?"

"Yes. With Little Kennedy coming, I think we should recognize that you'll need to do more of the traveling for a while. I'll be here. You know I would never leave Sinful Threads. I've decided to add a few furnishings to your office down the hall."

"What?" I asked.

"A crib."

That made me smile. "I can't wait to be back and have her or him sleeping while I'm working."

"Her."

My heart jolted. "Oh my goodness, you found out?"

"We weren't going to, but it was pretty obvious on the ultrasound yesterday."

"Yesterday? You didn't tell me last night."

"We weren't sure if we wanted to tell, but I can't keep a secret from my best friend."

Her words filled me with guilt. There were so many secrets I was now keeping, but I tried to keep my voice light. "I'm so happy for you and Jason."

"So when you're back for Kennedy's birth, we can talk about it more. I'm thinking that since you've rented this space, you plan on being in Chicago longer than we discussed —which is okay," she added. "Logistically, Chicago is a great place because we get most of our silk at the Port of Chicago. Besides that, there are more flights out of Chicago for you to jump over to New York or down to Atlanta. I'll keep things going here and fly west when needed."

I shook my head. "You've given this some thought."

"I have. I hate not having you here, but you were right. I've been a bit emotional and to be honest, my decisions have been based on hormones. Thankfully, I have Jason and Winnie. They helped me see that what you said made sense: divide and conquer. Together we've made Sinful Threads. Distance isn't going to keep us from making it bigger and better. If anything, it will help it."

"I miss you," I said honestly.

"Then call more or answer my damn calls."

"Yes, ma'am. You can be bossy."

Louisa laughed. "You need someone to tell you what to do."

That position was definitely taken.

"You think so?"

"Sometimes," Louisa said, "you can act a tad impulsively, like renting office space."

"It was a great deal."

"It was. But, Kenni, you also make great decisions. You're smart and I know we wouldn't have taken the chances we did without your confidence. Just because I might not agree at first, it doesn't mean I can't be convinced."

"Hey, thanks, Lou."

Patrick stuck his head into my office. "She's here."

"I need to go."

"Okay. Talk to you later. Winnie is ready to talk to whomever you hire. She's cleared time in her schedule. Oh, and she's over the moon about being in Chicago next week. It's all she's talked about and seeing her friend."

"I'm excited to see her too. I'll talk to you tonight."

"Bye."

Hanging up the phone, I walked around the desk as Patrick brought a young woman down the hall toward me. "Jana?"

"Ms. Hawkins."

"You already have a job," I said, puzzled.

"I do. I also have a husband and son here in Chicago. I would never leave Mr. Sparrow, but the opportunity to not have to travel was too good to pass up. I promise I'm a fast learner."

My eyes went to Patrick as his smile grew.

"Jana," I said, "please have a seat." I gestured to the chair grouping in the outer office. "Could you excuse us a moment while I have a word with Patrick?"

When Patrick followed me back to my office, I closed the

door. "I'm confused and a little upset."

"Why? You know her. Isn't that better than a stranger?"

I turned a small circle. "Does Sterling know about this?"

"I told him I'd hire from within."

My head shook back and forth. "Listen, I appreciate this..." I gestured around the room. "...all of this, such as the office space. I do. I know Sterling is renting this to us for a ridiculously low price. But you *and he* are both overstepping your bounds."

Patrick didn't speak, waiting for me to finish.

"Sinful Threads is mine and Louisa's. I'll be more than happy to talk to him about it at the end of the day, like...a couple talks to one another. I do not want his employee working for me and reporting to him. That's a hard no. And besides, when I mentioned her to him in Ontario, he blew a gasket."

I leaned my backside against the front edge of my desk and crossed my arms over my chest.

"A gasket?"

"I got the *whom to trust* lecture."

Patrick nodded. "Ms. Mc—Hawkins, I'll tell her to go or you can, if that's your decision. Sparrow has a lot on his plate. The daily running of Sinful Threads isn't one of them. Right now, he thinks it would be best to keep Araneae and Kennedy separate. We both know that won't last long." He shrugged. "I stepped in. I'm the one who's overstepped your bounds, not him. May I tell you why?"

I let out a long breath. At least Patrick had manners on his side. "Go on."

"I thought that when your two worlds came crashing together—which they are going to do—that it would be best to have as much of a buffer zone as possible around you, one that understands the importance of confidentiality and discretion."

Patrick was wrong. My two worlds had already collided. The public side of it would simply be residual tremors of the earthquake Sterling Sparrow had caused.

"Also," Patrick went on, "Jana's being forthright about her husband and son." Something Patrick and I knew wasn't legally part of an interview. "Her son is nearly ten years old and when Sparrow makes last-minute travel plans or changes his plans, it's difficult on her as well as her family."

"Yet," I said, "she could have just quit working for him."

"She wouldn't do that."

I thought more about what he'd just said. "Ten-year-old son? She looks to be close to my age."

"A year younger."

My eyes widened. "Okay. Will she still be working for Sterling?"

"Unofficially, as in she's doing something she knows he'll support. Officially, she'll be working for Sinful Threads. She'll be on your payroll."

"What if I can't pay her what he did?" I didn't let Patrick answer. "Then you'll be sure that she's compensated for the difference."

He didn't need to respond, but he did. "To her, not traveling is compensation. Would you like me to send her home?"

"Does she want the job? Is she capable?"

Patrick opened the folder he'd been holding and handed me two papers—Jana's résumé.

I quickly scanned the information. "It appears she's been employed by Sparrow Enterprises for the last six years." She was hired when she would have been only nineteen. "No employment before that. How does that qualify her for this position?"

"She had prior employment before that also wouldn't qualify her for this position. My opinion would be that what she lacks in personal-assistant experience, she'll make up for in enthusiasm and eagerness to learn. How will you explain to an outsider when Sparrow decides to whisk you away at a moment's notice or even my constant presence?"

I laid her résumé on my desk. "I can't be whisked away. I have a company—"

"Wouldn't it be nice," he interrupted, "to have someone who could see both of your worlds and keep this one under control?"

I had to admit, Patrick was making sense.

"Fine. Send her in and I'll interview her. Then *I'll* make my decision."

Patrick nodded and turned toward the door.

"Patrick." He looked my way. "My company. The final decision on everything is mine and Louisa's. I told you that I appreciated your help but no more unilateral decisions by you or Sterling."

"Yes, Ms. Hawkins."

My brow furrowed. "That goes for Araneae too."

He smiled. "I'll remember that. Are you ready for me to bring her in?"

"Yes."

As he disappeared, I let out a deep breath. It seemed like I was having identical conversations with both Patrick and Sterling. Maybe I should give Reid a call and let him know the same applied for him.

Oh, no, I couldn't. He was busy beefing up Sinful Threads' security.

Gah!

"Ms. Hawkins?" Jana said, standing at my doorway.

Without her flight attendant outfit, wearing a skirt, blouse, and flat sandals, she looked more relaxed than she had on Sterling's plane. Maybe it wasn't the change in clothes but the fact that Sterling wasn't present. He had a way of stressing people out.

Her dark hair was pulled back on the sides with long, soft waves hanging in the back. The style helped her appear younger.

"Please." I gestured toward the two chairs before my desk.

It wasn't nice to judge a person's age, and I wouldn't have known hers if it weren't for Patrick. Another violation of personal information on an interview. However, knowing it, I decided that even with her hair down, she didn't appear younger than me. The realization saddened me. My gut told me there was more to her story, more than being a young mother.

Though that made me want to help her, I didn't like the idea of a Sparrow spy within my company.

Really? What was Patrick?

If Sterling Sparrow wanted information, he wouldn't need to get it from Jana. And although she'd been the subject of my *whom I could trust* lecture, Patrick must trust her or she wouldn't be here.

How would Sterling feel about this?

Why did that matter?

I looked her in the eye. "Jana, tell me why you want this job?"

ARANEAE

After my round of questions, I explained the structure of Sinful Threads to Jana, including a brief telephone conversation with Louisa. I later told Louisa the truth: I trusted Jana as a member of our team.

As much as I disliked Patrick's meddling in this hiring, I had a good feeling about her. I'd liked her on the plane before I knew anything about her. She had excellent keyboarding skills and passed the few tasks I asked her to perform on data entry with ease.

"Jana, the job is yours if you are sure you want it."

"I do," she replied, her smile growing.

"You can start immediately or if that won't work, we'll look at a calendar."

"No, if you want me, I'll start today."

"Then, here we go. Here in the office, I'm Kennedy Hawkins."

Jana nodded.

"With Mr. Sparrow, I'm Araneae McCrie."

"I heard that name on the flight. I was a little confused but didn't ask." She shrugged. "I still am confused, but at least now I know both names are you."

"Don't worry. I'm confused too. There's no one other than Mr. Sparrow or Patrick or Reid Murray," I added, "who should call for me as McCrie. If anyone else does, please inform them that there's no one here by that name."

"Ms. Toney?"

I shook my head. "No, to Louisa and Winnie Douglas, I'm Kennedy Hawkins."

Jana nodded as if it were common practice that the woman who was flown on Sterling Sparrow's plane would have two completely different names.

"We have scheduled shipments of silk coming in today. They don't go to our warehouse here. They're shipped directly from the port to Boulder. Call Winnie at the Boulder office and get the manifests. Next contact the port. I want the order confirmed upon its arrival and the shipment confirmed that's headed to Boulder."

Her eyes widened. "I'll call her."

"She'll help you. She's going to be here next week. I would like her to know you're willing to jump in and be a part of our team."

Jana's smile widened. "Thank you. I'll do my best."

"Patrick, let's make our unexpected visit."

He looked to Jana. "If we're not back by lunch, there are sandwich shops and cafes on the first floor. Remember to lock the office if you step out."

She was almost giddy with enthusiasm. "I won't let you down."

"Ms. Hawkins." He gestured toward the door.

On our way to the warehouse, I recalled the first time I saw Sterling. "Why was he at my warehouse the first time you brought me here?" I asked.

"He?"

"Don't do that. The omnipotent *he*."

Patrick's eyes met mine in the mirror. "All of the Sinful Threads properties in the greater Chicago area, your warehouse and your distribution center, are leased through Sparrow Enterprises."

My gut twisted. "No. I would have known that, recognized the name."

"Ma'am, Ms. Toney made the deals."

"Why? Does she know..." I didn't even know for sure what to ask if she knew.

"No one knows."

"Then why? It doesn't make sense."

"She never met with Sparrow," Patrick said. "He has contractors and agents. Dealing directly with small customers is not where his time is best utilized. Sparrow Enterprises made Ms. Toney the best deal."

Small customers.

To Sterling, Sinful Threads was small.

Why did that hurt?

My scrabbled mind did math. "That was years ago, over four years."

"Yes, ma'am."

Oh my God. How far back did this all go?

"Not only in Chicago," Patrick said, as he continued steering the car toward the warehouse district. "I'm telling you this so you won't freak out when you start digging, which I'm sure you will."

Too late.

"What do you mean?"

"Most of your properties were bought or contracted through Sparrow Enterprises. It's based in Chicago but deals with real estate worldwide."

"I negotiated many of those deals myself. I don't recall the name Sparrow."

"The deals you negotiated were with subsidiaries of Sparrow. He wasn't ready to take a chance on your making connections."

"How the hell would I?" My tone revealed that exasperation was getting the better of me. "And why did he do that?"

"Sinful Threads is important to you."

I shook the ominous feeling away before my mind could explode with the revelations. Sterling had been watching me for years. In a way, he'd told me that. It just seemed more real hearing it from Patrick.

Like before, the wheels bounced as Patrick entered the parking lot of Sinful Threads warehouse. This time, there was no SUV with a dark-haired, dark-eyed, incredibly handsome, and very annoying man. The thought made me smile in a way it shouldn't.

After stopping the car, Patrick opened my door.

"Since you had my phone, I'm going to assume you know about the blip on the security footage."

Patrick nodded. "Reid's been working on things. Your man Jason is too. I don't think he realizes that he's being led by Reid."

"Why can't we just tell him?"

"Because Sparrow—"

I lifted my hand. "My company."

"Reid is Sparrow's. How will you explain it?"

My head shook. I couldn't even explain it to myself. "Never mind. Let's see what we find in here."

Patrick followed me as he had the first time I was here.

Twenty-five minutes later we were on our way out. Even though it was painfully clear to me that Patrick knew everything that was happening with Sinful Threads, I appreciated that while I was in the warehouse and talking to employees, he took a step back and simply watched. This was my show.

Now that we were out, I was curious about his observation.

Once we were both in the car, I asked, "What's your gut telling you?"

"First, Francesca better learn to keep his observations of your appearance to himself or Sparrow may..."

"May what?" I asked, wanting the end of his sentence.

"The man's a pig."

I scoffed. "Well, that goes without saying. Louisa hired him. She's always liked him. I think he was one of her first big hires for someone outside of Boulder. Maybe that's the problem. She likes him, and when you like someone, you don't notice their faults. I'd only met him a few times in Boulder and was never impressed. Now he gives me the creeps. He was the one to bring up the discrepancy to Louisa, but with me he acts like it's nothing—a technical malfunction."

"If you approve, Reid could do some more digging."

"You're asking me?"

Patrick's sunglass-covered eyes moved upward. His grin

reflected in the rearview mirror. "It's your company, Ms. Hawkins."

My cheeks rose. "You could teach your boss a thing or two about diplomacy."

Patrick didn't respond.

Picking up lunch, we made our way back to the office. Jana was busy looking between two screens when we entered.

"How are you doing?" I asked.

"I'm good. Winnie said she'll transfer calls to me tomorrow. Today she wanted me to concentrate on some of the things she sent."

I nodded, setting the bag of food on her desk. "We didn't know for sure what you ate. We have salads, soup, and wraps."

"I eat anything," Jana said with a grin. "I was too nervous to eat this morning. Thank you for the food. I'm now famished."

"I'll take it to the conference room," Patrick volunteered.

As we sat, I looked around the conference table. The artwork on the wall was standard office fare. The room didn't have a window, but as we ate and chatted about the things Winnie sent, I realized that this entire situation may work. Maybe I was ready to branch out with Sinful Threads.

By dividing and conquering we would grow.

Our Sinful Threads dresses were already a hit. The production team in Boulder was looking to hire a second shift to keep up with orders. Louisa and I discussed if it were better to keep production limited. The more merchandise available, the less demand. If we restricted the number of each style we could raise the price and keep the merchandise in demand.

I hadn't yet mentioned my idea of Sinful Threads bedding

to Louisa, but it was on my list to discuss. Perhaps instead of increasing production on one item, we should continue to increase the number of items.

By five-thirty in the evening I was joyfully exhausted. "Jana, it's time to call it a day."

With her continual smile she nodded, turning off her computer.

"How did you like it?" I asked.

"I can't tell you how much it means to me to stay in Chicago and be able to go home to my family every night."

"Why didn't you tell Mr. Sparrow your misgivings?"

Her head shook back and forth. "I couldn't. He's done so much for me."

"What did he do?"

As if cued by a stagehand, Patrick entered the office. He'd spent a good part of his day in the conference room with his laptop. He may be babysitting me, but I was certain he wasn't missing a beat when it came to Sparrow's business.

"More than I could ever say," Jana answered as she reached for her purse.

In the car on the way home—it was odd to think of Sterling's apartment that way, but I did—I asked Patrick about Jana's answer to my question. "I'm sure you heard our conversation. What did Sterling do for Jana?"

"No more than he's done for others."

"She made it sound like it was more."

Patrick shrugged. "More to one person is nothing to another. Quantity is subjective."

"No, quantity is measured in numbers. Numbers aren't subjective."

"Ma'am, I agree to disagree."

"Then explain," I said.

"If you were walking on the sidewalk and you saw a twenty-dollar bill, would you bend down and pick it up?"

I thought about it. "Yes."

"What if it were in a sewer drain?"

I didn't hesitate. "No."

"Why?"

"Twenty dollars isn't enough for me to reach into a sewer drain. I'm not sure about Chicago, but in New York, I'd probably find a rat."

"When I was a kid, I would have climbed down in that drain for one dollar. The numbers twenty and one aren't subjective. What's subjective is what those numbers represent to each person. A dollar would have meant a bag of chips and maybe a coke. I would have had dinner."

"I'm sorry."

"Don't be," Patrick said. "A twenty could have fed me for days. It may not seem like much to one person, but to another it could be life changing."

I leaned my head against the seat and watched the buildings pass by as Patrick navigated the traffic. "You're right."

Patrick didn't answer, but in my mind, I heard Sterling's voice telling me that *he* usually was.

Before too long, we turned into the parking tunnel, disappearing behind a metal door. When Patrick finally parked, I again took in all of the cars, wondering if Sterling was home. I didn't know who had been with him today or where he'd gone.

"Is Sterling home?" I asked as Patrick opened my door.

"Yes, ma'am."

"Araneae," I corrected. We were done for the day at Sinful Threads.

"He is," Patrick said as he placed his palm on the sensor near the elevator.

It seemed like going up to the 96th floor would take longer, but it didn't. As the elevator came to a stop on what the control panel said was P, Patrick held the doors open.

"Good night, Araneae. I'll be in the kitchen in the morning."

"Aren't you coming in?"

"No, I believe Sparrow is waiting for you."

That news shouldn't make me smile or my stomach do flip-flops as I stepped out of the elevator, but it did. "Good night, Patrick."

Upon the marble floor was a trail of red rose petals.

Who knew Sterling Sparrow could be romantic?

Step by step, I followed. They didn't lead me upstairs; instead they took me past the stairway into the kitchen. Still carrying my satchel and purse, I stopped at the entrance. The room before me was colored in a golden glow, illuminated by the evening sun. A wonderful aroma filled the space, yet food was out of sight.

Leaning against the breakfast bar with his arms crossed over his broad chest was the man who stole my breath and made my heart beat faster. As if choreographed by a photographer, the evening sun added to his wickedly handsome features. Sterling Sparrow could be a model in a magazine.

The suit he wore to Michigan Avenue was gone, replaced by the low-riding jeans and the gray t-shirt I preferred. Scanning down his long legs, I saw his feet were bare, reminding me of last night, yet as I scanned upward, his dark hair was dry and wavy. As our eyes met, his grin did things to me I couldn't describe.

"Good evening, sunshine."

The deep tenor added to the twisting of my insides.

"Good evening," I replied warily as my lip momentarily went beneath my upper teeth. "What's this about?"

He stepped forward, his large hands coming to my waist as he pulled me closer. "This is what it's like to have someone to come home to."

My cheeks rose.

"This," he went on, "is the beginning of my attempt to rectify what didn't happen last night."

"What you didn't allow to happen," I corrected.

"Will you give me another chance?"

My smile bloomed wider as I lowered the satchel and my purse to the floor. "You're getting better with the requests."

He shrugged. "I'm trying."

He could be trying, but I definitely favored this kind of trying.

Sterling's finger traced from my ear down my neck as I leaned my head, granting him access. Slowly, his touch moved lower, teasing the edge of my scooped neckline. Each inch burnt a trail, setting my skin ablaze and hardening my nipples.

"Second chance or dinner?" he asked. "Lorna left us something in the oven that smells delicious."

I lifted my arms up and around Sterling's neck. "Dinner can wait."

STERLING

*A*s I awakened Sunday morning in a cold sweat, I was hit with the realization that today was the one-week anniversary of the incident in the club. Staring up at the ceiling, the memory burned within me, bubbling like a poisonous concoction in my gut.

I rarely knew fear. That night I did—an overwhelming fright of losing the woman who was now asleep beside me. That dread festered and then combined with a savage need for retaliation. Together they became a dangerous combination.

Lying next to Araneae, I had no regret for feeding the retaliatory hunger. I'd do it again.

The newscasters on the local news programs called the double homicide gang-related, another tragic statistic hidden in the shadows. The easy excuse helped fuel the perception of safety. Stay in the right places, avoid the wrong ones—the illusion was enhanced.

Bad things happened, just not in my world. It was the lie that kept Chicago alive.

No one wanted to believe that a man wearing designer suits and thousand-dollar shoes, one who walked in and out of downtown offices, employed thousands of people, and made billions of dollars could murder in cold blood. It was easier to blame it on nameless people lurking in the dark.

A man who walked in the light of day surely couldn't take the life of two twenty-something-year-olds with his bare hands after orchestrating horrifying torture—no that was unspeakable.

In reality, I could consider myself a savior. By the time McBride and his slut of a girlfriend breathed their last, they were begging for the agony to end. I did them a favor by granting them their final wish.

Blaming crime on those who hadn't committed it wasn't new.

Just as I'd told Araneae, the average citizen believed the fairy tale that Chicago was safe. People in high-rise buildings fortifying the economy weren't killers because that everyday person placed those people—people like me—on pedestals. The stories of organized crime were lore and folk tales of the past. This was a new day.

That had all passed away with Al Capone.

They didn't want to know the truth, that it was alive and well and included politicians and tycoons as well as all the men getting their hands dirty on the dark web, on the street, in the gambling establishments, brothels, private clubs, and on the stock exchange.

Chicago police, politicians, and the news media helped perpetuate the illusion. It was for the greater good. The evidence of evil could be staring people in the face, yet they couldn't comprehend what they refused to recognize. They saw what they wanted to see. Rose-colored glasses were distributed at birth, and only a few of us chose not to wear them.

By the time the lifeless, bloody bodies of McBride and his girlfriend were left on display, my statements had been made —loud and clear. All of the underworld got my message: Araneae McCrie was off-limits. No one touched her but me.

The more time I spent with her, the clearer it has become that for once in his life, my father had been right. She belonged to me.

As Araneae slept beside me, I fought the urge to touch her. Reaching out, I gently ran her blonde hair through my fingers, careful not to wake her.

In the dimness of the bedroom, I stared at my own hand. For the first time, the reality became alarmingly clear. Araneae brought out something in me that I'd never nurtured, never cared to cultivate. Tenderness and caring didn't work in my world, now her world too.

The same hand that could caress and hold her also killed.

The darker side of me was what I never wanted her to know. I didn't want her to understand the depths I would go to or what I was capable of doing. I wanted her to see the man she'd been with last night, the man who watched her smile. I wanted her to see a man who was devoted to her and her safety, a man who planned on keeping her and never letting her go.

I wanted her to wear the rose-colored glasses.

Twisting and untwisting the strand of her silky hair, I let it slip through my fingers. The long tresses were now sprawled over her pillow. Last night, that same soft mane had created a tunnel from her to me, blocking out the rest of the world as her fingers gripped my shoulders and she rode my cock.

While I was content to take her any way or anyplace, she shared that never before me had she been on top. Such a simple statement that filled me with pride.

My new goal was to do as many firsts as possible with her.

The spectacular sight of her tits bouncing above me was second only to the greatest possible friction that brought us both to climax. Once she was relaxed, I rolled her over and her golden locks became a halo behind her beautiful face and wide, velvety eyes.

Through the years, I'd searched those eyes in photos and videos. It astonished me that now they were here—that she was here. Last night, she'd come to bed in a long, sexy blue satin nightgown with thin straps that went over her slender shoulders and crisscrossed in the back. While the gown reached the floor, on each side were slits that revealed she wore nothing underneath.

Needless to say, the nightgown didn't last long. It was currently somewhere on the floor, where it landed after I'd moved the straps and watched the material slide from her body.

Though I'd been told since I was thirteen that Araneae belonged to me, nothing could have prepared me for what it was like to have her in my life. She was all I ever wanted and more: intelligent, motivated, resilient, sexy, sensual, sassy, opinionated, and outspoken. Being with her was what I'd never known was possible. Granted, my examples of relationships were pretty fucked up. In that department, Reid and Lorna were the best representation of what it should be.

Maybe in some way being a part of their lives opened a door to the idea that a relationship was possible.

It was no wonder when I fought Reid for wanting to bring Lorna into our lives that he didn't back down.

Knowing that Araneae belonged to me and enjoying having her with me were not synonymous. I now understood why Reid wouldn't and didn't give up. I couldn't and wouldn't leave Araneae or allow her to leave no matter who demanded it.

Up until a moment ago, her warm, sexy body had been curled against my side, her soft breath blowing against my skin. It wasn't until I moved that she did too.

Though my dick was ready for another round, it was too early in the morning to wake her.

Sleeping had never been my thing, but with her in my bed, I wished I could convince myself to stay by her side for another hour or two. Leaving her was one of the hardest things I'd done, whether I left her in bed or knowing she was out in the city.

Thankfully, according to Patrick, there had been no new threats, not on her physically.

And to make it better, Jana was working out well.

While Jana may not have been my first choice for Araneae's personal assistant, Patrick made a convincing case. Since I trusted him with Araneae, it only made sense to trust him with that decision too.

Reid was also on the job watching over my woman. In the process, he'd discovered a few attempts of cyber infiltration into Kennedy Hawkins and Sinful Threads. It wasn't possible to look into Araneae McCrie—officially she didn't exist any longer. She'd died at birth. He'd recently mentioned a trail he was following regarding Franco Francesca. We weren't jumping to conclusions, yet in my opinion that man was on borrowed time.

Beefing up the security at Sinful Threads had been a no-brainer. Araneae may not appreciate my making decisions when it came to her company, but there were some aspects of their incorporation that she and Louisa had overlooked for too long.

From my observations, both Araneae and Louisa were fantastic with merchandise. Their quality was the best. Managing the day-to-day operations as well as creative decisions was their thing. I couldn't come close to imagining the things they created. What I could do was ensure the safety of their data.

We had eyes on McFadden.

I didn't trust him with anything, nor could I accurately predict his thinking. It seemed to me that the longer Araneae was with me, her presence known, without her going after McFadden, the better it was for her.

Or that may be wishful thinking.

If I were in McFadden's shoes, I'd say there were two possible options. One, he could believe that Araneae didn't possess the secrets to her father's evidence and that the rumors from years ago were inaccurate. Or, two, he could think that she was sitting on the evidence and still a threat to his future.

The second option was why I refused to let her out of my or Patrick's sight.

Other than work, I'd kept her here, in my apartment. Though she hadn't complained, I knew it was time to get her out. A beautiful, vivacious woman like her didn't deserve to be held prisoner between work and home.

The reality that came with exposing her to the public with me meant that the rumors from last week at the club would be confirmed. There would be more sightings.

Since she'd told me more than once to stop making unilateral decisions, that probably meant I should ask her if she was ready to be seen with me again in Chicago.

What were the words she said I should use?

Will?

Would?

It was probably evident that the asking process was new for me. It wasn't an area where I particularly excelled. Yet I'd told her that I would make an effort—and for her, I would.

Slipping out of bed, I stepped into the closet and eased into a pair of sweat pants and pulled a t-shirt over my head. With a rake of my hair with my fingers, I was ready to go down to two—the heart of our operation. At only four in the morning, I never knew for sure who would be present.

When it came to sleep, Reid and Patrick shared my insomnia.

Perhaps it was because of the things we'd seen and done. Those thoughts could be compartmentalized while awake. While sleeping...that was another story.

Locking the bedroom door, I made my way through the darkened apartment. With the key to the bedroom in my pocket, I recalled how Araneae had locked the same door prior to her bath a few nights ago. When the knob didn't move, a bit of my displeasure—caused by her disobeying my order to stay in the room—lessened. By locking the door, she'd done as I'd said, securing that no one saw her sexy, naked body but me—ever.

Reaching the bottom of the stairs, there was no need to turn on the lights to navigate my dwelling. My life was formed in the dark. It was where I thrived.

The panel by the elevator flashed as my palm contacted the surface. A short elevator ride and one more panel outside the metal door and that door slid open. The room before me was filled with light.

"Patrick, why the hell are you awake?"

"I could ask you the same thing, Sparrow. At least you and Reid have someone in your beds to keep you there."

"If I work now, I'm able to spend more time with her when she's awake." I tilted my head up at the screens. "What's going on?"

Patrick shook his head as his fingers tapped on the keyboard. We weren't as phenomenal as Reid, but all three of us had skill.

"I woke up with a thought," he said, "one we haven't explored. At least I don't think we have. Since Walsh still hasn't resurfaced since Wichita and Reid can't find evidence of his untimely demise, I began thinking about the Marshes and how they disappeared off the radar. We've talked witness protection, yet we can't find anything to support that either."

"I'm not sure I'm following," I said, pulling out a chair, spinning it, and straddling the back.

"When Araneae's plane made the emergency landing in Wichita, we were so focused on her and on Walsh's connection to McFadden, I never took the time to learn exactly why the plane was stopped."

"She told us. A passenger ostensibly had an issue."

"I think it's more." Patrick pointed to the screen with a quick lift of his chin. "This was the man who had the incident that required the stop. This is from the Wichita airport security cameras. He doesn't appear ill. The airline is required to report the cause of an unplanned landing and they stated illness. What they didn't report was that this man is an air marshal."

"He's a fed?"

Patrick nodded.

My mind started clicking like a damn puzzle, the pieces falling into place. "We blamed McFadden but how would he have known that Kennedy was Araneae that fast?" I stood quickly, the chair rolling as I began to pace. "He wouldn't have," I said, answering my own question. "Fuck. He'd just sat with her for dinner at the damn Sinful Threads event. Our plan was to get her out of Chicago before he heard the rumors that she'd been sighted."

My fingers fisted and unfisted. "I've been beating myself up that we screwed up."

"But if it wasn't him that stopped that plane..." Patrick said, allowing his sentence to trail away.

His words sank in.

"What if we *did* get her out before he knew?" he asked. "What if someone else was watching her or watching for her?"

Fucking feds stopped that plane for a reason.

Why not let her get back to Boulder?

Because if they got wind of her being with me, they would expect me to have reinforcements in Boulder. Stopping the plane was their best option.

"Find out if Walsh was a plant." I said. "Could it fucking be possible that he's a fed infiltrating McFadden's inner circle and he'd been there for over a year?" The idea gave me hope. I wanted to stand back and watch the flames as McFadden and his illegal activities were brought into the light—leaving his presidential ambition in ashes.

In my mind, I'd been the one to do it—to bring him down.

I imagined that I'd have been the one who found Araneae, made sure she was safe, and then exposed the evidence she was supposed to have. The rumors had been whispered between the old guard of my father's capos. I'd heard them since before I could remember. At first their murmurings meant nothing...until that one day when I saw her picture. The day my father said she was mine. After that, I listened. I eavesdropped. I even snuck into his office and snooped.

It was my first hacking job.

It got my ass kicked more than once, but I didn't give up.

There wasn't an altruistic bone in my father's body. Allister Sparrow was a selfish bastard: women, money, and power were his motivators. He believed that Araneae possessed—or had the means to possess—whatever McCrie knew. It seemed as though my father believed that uncovering that information would rid him of McFadden for once and for all.

That was why the McFaddens were the danger.

Why then had Josey Marsh warned Araneae against us?

I didn't know the answer. I had believed the lies too, until now.

Araneae knew nothing of her biological family.

My father had been fed a lie, the same lie as McFadden. He'd fed it to me.

"Sparrow," Patrick said, pulling me from my cyclone of

thoughts, "Walsh is a fucking long shot with even further-reaching repercussions if it's true."

"Have Reid do a triple check on everyone in Sparrow. The feds want to infiltrate McFadden, great. Fucker's a senator with dirty hands. Make sure everyone in Sparrow is legitimate. Any question, any doubt, get rid of them. There's no way we're going down or Sparrow Enterprises is going down in some FBI raid."

ARANEAE

"**I**s it safe?" That was my answer on Sunday afternoon while Sterling and I were in his office, when he asked if I wanted to go out to dinner—out of the apartment.

"Sunshine, I wouldn't ask you if it weren't."

My cheeks rose. "You did ask."

His finger landed on my nose. "So observant. I did."

I'd been answering emails for Sinful Threads at the table while Sterling had been at his desk doing whatever he did. Now he was standing right in front of me, and focusing on the screen of my laptop was no longer my priority.

I stood to meet him. "Then does that mean I can say no?"

"You can say whatever you want. I thought you might want to get out of here."

My lips came together as I thought about his proposal.

Over the last week, I tried not to give it much thought. Each day, I left the apartment to go to Sinful Threads. While there, I came and went as I pleased and saw fit, with one stipulation: Patrick was at my side. I reminded myself of what happened upon our return from Canada.

The poisoning affected me mentally as well as physically. While a bit of claustrophobia was setting in, there was also a sense of safety behind the infrared protection of Sterling's apartment. Having Lorna, Reid, and Patrick nearby provided an occasion for camaraderie. At the office, I had Patrick and Jana. Daily, I spoke with Louisa and Winnie. Somehow, I'd accepted this new life, and yet when faced with the opportunity to go out and see more of the world than my office, warehouse, distribution center, or Port of Chicago, I couldn't quell my anticipation.

There was a world out there. I wanted to reenter it.

"Is this like a date—like our first one?" I asked.

Sterling's gaze simmered as he reached for my waist and pulled me toward him. The connection was no longer foreign as our hips came together. "Tell me, Araneae..." His deep voice reverberated from him to me. "... do you fuck on a first date?"

I tried to swallow, yet my mouth was suddenly dry. Shaking my head, I replied, "No, never."

What the hell did that sound like?

Sterling and I hadn't been on a date and nevertheless, we'd made love, fucked, or whatever I wanted to call it so many times that I'd lost count.

His large hand lowered to my behind, his fingers splaying as he pulled me tighter against him. "How about *before* a first date?"

Warmth filled my cheeks. "Not as a rule."

His eyes widened. "Tell me how many times you've broken this self-proclaimed rule."

There was something in his tone, the darkening of his gaze, and the pressure of his body against mine that tightened the muscles of my core in an inappropriate way. "Why?" I asked, my chin rising to keep his gaze. "That information is shared on a need-to-know basis, and I don't believe you, Sterling, need to know."

"That's where you're mistaken. I need to know because remember you're mine, and as mine, I am entitled to know everything about you."

"You're saying that this information wasn't something that came up in all of your spying?"

His hand swatted my ass.

"Hey," I yelped.

"Answer my question."

"What if I said that the rule has been broken many times?"

"Then before our first date, I'd have to spank your ass more than one slap because even self-imposed rules are rules. And it's my job to make sure you learn to follow them."

I lifted my hands to his shoulders. "What if I also told you that those many times were with the same man?"

"Are you telling the truth or trying to save your ass?"

"Both," I said with a grin. "The same man, many times, most of them great. He can be a real asshole sometimes, but that doesn't mean I don't want to go on a first date with him."

"Most of them?"

"Yeah, when he's not being that asshole."

"Would you consider breaking the after-first-date fucking rule?" he asked.

One shoulder moved up, then down. "I don't know. Will that get me another great orgasm or will it get me punished for breaking a rule?"

"Those aren't necessarily mutually exclusive."

"Then I guess it depends on how the date goes," I answered noncommittally.

His lips brushed mine. "Seven o'clock. Be ready. I will officially pick you up for our first date at the front door."

"Front door? Won't we leave through the secret elevator?"

"Sunshine, don't ask questions. Tonight is our first official date. You and the date are in my hands. You're about to learn what it's like to be wined and dined by Sterling Sparrow."

My cheeks rose. "How formal?"

He tilted his head. "That's a question."

"Yes, but I need to know."

"What you need to know is to wear that fucking fantastic Sinful Threads dress you had on the first night in the distribution center. No bra. I want to watch your nipples turn hard, knowing that this time when I get you home, I'll be the one to peel that silk from your sexy body and enjoy everything underneath."

His words tightened my core. "Sterling..."

"Also, if you're wondering," he continued, "no panties unless after dinner you want to start with that spanking. I saw how pink your cheeks turned when I mentioned it."

My nose scrunched. "That's kind of..." I searched for the right words. "...uncomfortable."

"The spanking? Yes, it's meant to be."

"No, the panty thing. It makes me self-conscious."

His lips quirked. "I don't usually suggest this on a first

date, but since we've broken your fucking rule, I'll give you another option."

Tilting my head, I watched his eyes, uncertain if this were a good thing or not. "What kind of option?"

"An option is when someone has the choice between two things."

"Stop being an asshole. I know the definition of an option. What choices are you proposing?"

"Number one: what I already said, Sinful Threads dress, no bra, no panties, thigh-high stockings—those are fucking sexy—and some great fuck-me heels."

I took a deep breath. "Or?"

"Number two: same attire, but to keep your mind off the lack of panties, before we leave, I insert a custom-constructed vibrator into your tight pussy."

"What—?"

His finger touched my lips. "What did I say about questions? Option number two was self-explanatory: vibrator in your pussy. It has a specially designed lip that also tantalizes your clit and multiple speeds."

This man was crazy—certifiable.

My mouth opened yet nothing came out.

His finger gently pushed on my chin, closing my mouth. "Your job, sunshine..." He spoke near my ear, his warm breath on my sensitive skin as his deep voice thundered through me. "...is that throughout our date you'll hold it tight and keep it in place because if it starts to slip, I'll be the one to put it back and while I won't let anyone see, they'll all know what I'm doing."

"You...want...wait...no..." I couldn't construct a sentence. There was no comeback for what he was suggesting.

"My job," he went on, "will be to press the button that will be on the remote in my suit coat pocket." He trailed his finger over my cheek. "I guarantee that you won't be overthinking the lack of panties. Your mind will be fully consumed by the multiple sensations in your pussy and against your clit. By the time we make it back here, you'll be begging me to remove it and replace it with my cock."

My head was shaking. "You're joking. You can't be serious."

"Options, sunshine, you have two."

"You wouldn't..." I couldn't even process what he was saying—or was he threatening? "H-how did you even think of that?"

"I'd offer you a vibrating butt plug instead, but I said there'd only be two options. If the idea intrigues you, you can ask for that for our second date."

"Yeah, right," I said with all the sarcasm I could muster. "Butt plugs should definitely be reserved for at least the second date. I usually say third, but who knows?"

"If you think I'm not serious—"

It was my turn to silence Sterling. I did it with my lips.

My mind was clearing.

If he thinks he can shock me into compliance, he had a lesson or two to learn about me. Leaning back, I gave him my most seductive smile. "You drive a hard bargain, Mr. Sparrow."

"The decision is...?"

I shrugged. "Not two."

"Then one," he said with a bit too much satisfaction.

"We'll see. Whether you realized it or not, you offered me a third alternative earlier—which would make the two you just said numbers two and three. In that case, three is off the table. Between the first two, I guess you'll need to find out." Lifting myself up on my tiptoes, I kissed his cheek. "I'll see you at seven. No coming into the bedroom."

"Then how am I supposed to get ready?"

"You're Sterling Sparrow. I know you have your ways."

Turning my back to him, I closed my laptop and secured it in my satchel with some notes I'd taken. Though earlier I'd been thinking about Sinful Threads, those thoughts were gone. All the way to the bedroom, his final two options played on repeat in my head.

How did he come up with that?

And the butt plug—no.

Hard no.

Hell no.

I'd never...

Then again, it could be worth trying at home, alone in our bedroom. Not only had I never considered anything anal, I'd also never had a vibrator *inserted*. I had my own vibrator in Boulder and even in college. However, it wasn't as he described. And when I'd used it, I was alone in my bedroom—in my bed.

Never in public.

I tried to imagine what it would be like to be among strangers and having something moving inside me.

What would that be like? Why was I even curious...?

My core clenched at the thought.

Stop it, Araneae. Don't even think about it.

It was too late. I was thinking about it.

While I couldn't predict the future when it came to Sterling Sparrow, I could say with one hundred percent certainty that nothing would be *inserted* before we left on our first date. This was what Sterling did to me. He pushed me out of my comfort zone, making me desire things I should never want— things that I'd never before considered.

I meant what I'd said. The option was off the table. Yet he'd planted a seed.

Damn you, Sterling.

When I entered our large closet, I found the dress Sterling requested. It was clean and steamed and hanging in a clear dry-cleaning bag from Boulder. It was the Sinful Threads dress with the black onyx-like neckline, the one I'd worn to the party on the Riverwalk, and the one I'd worn most of the night on the plane back to Boulder. It was the one I'd changed out of in the Wichita airport and thrown into my carry-on.

The clock near the bed read a little after five.

With the hanger in my hand, I gave my attire for the evening more thought.

With a smile, I walked back and forth from the closet to the bed. Systematically, I put together my strategy. Laying the dress on the bed, I added the accessories: the thigh-high stockings, the pair of crystal-adorned black peep-toe pumps I'd worn to the club, and lastly, a black satin thong.

Walking to the bathroom, a grin came to my lips as I imagined Sterling coming into the bedroom to fetch his clothes for our date. It wouldn't matter that I'd locked the door. That wouldn't stop him.

I wasn't certain he remembered the first option he'd given me: *"...no panties unless after dinner you want to start with that spanking."*

The idea of him turning my ass red before bringing me

pleasure shouldn't twist my insides in knots. I shouldn't desire his hands on me in that way. I knew that.

There were many things about Sterling Sparrow I *shouldn't* desire.

My brain comprehended.

That was part of the problem. I'd stopped listening to my brain the first day I saw him in the parking lot.

Now when it came to Sterling, my body was in charge.

Get ready, Mr. Sparrow.

You like to push me?

My smile grew. I'm going to push back.

ARANEAE

For a confident woman, I was indecisive. Freshly showered with my hair styled into long curls hanging onto my back and dressed in the black Sinful Threads dress, the stockings, and shoes, I'd put on and taken off the damn thong about eight times.

Sterling pushed me, and I wanted to push back.

And then my decision would waver. Touching up my lipstick, my hand trembled. I was as nervous as I'd ever been on a first date.

You're being silly, I told myself. Yet it didn't ease the full-blown case of nerves.

What was I afraid of?

That he wouldn't like me?

That he'd not call tomorrow or the next day?

Taking a deep breath and staring at myself in the mirror, I reached for the thong now on the vanity counter. I was due at the front door in only a few minutes. I needed to decide once and for all.

To be pushed or to push back...

As I rounded the corner to the landing, my steps stuttered. Standing at the front door one story down was my date, his dark eyes peering upward to the second floor. Even from a distance, I could see that the dark gray suit he wore was custom made, accentuating what I now knew was underneath. The unbuttoned tapered jacket highlighted his broad shoulders. The button-up shirt beneath was black with an open collar and tucked into his trousers. His shoes were also black as was his belt. My gaze stilled on the silver buckle causing my heart to beat faster.

The temperature of the room increased.

My neck straightened as I walked. With my hand on the banister and my charm bracelet dangling from my wrist, I took in Sterling's growing smile.

Did he know what I'd done, that I'd decided to play with fire?

Though I'd made the choice, as I studied the man waiting for me, I realized that I hadn't truly considered the ramifications of being burnt.

With each step I took down the stairs, Sterling's gaze darkened, scanning me from head to toe as I'd done him. My skin grew warmer as his eyes lingered. The way he stared was as if I weren't dressed as he'd requested, as if I weren't dressed at all. By the time I reached the final step, my body was doing exactly as he'd asked. His lips quirked noticing my reaction as the lush satin of my bodice tented above my hardening nipples.

"You are exquisite," he said as his compliment washed through me.

Stepping down onto the marble floor, I replied, "You're very handsome yourself."

With a quick turn, Sterling reached for something that had been out of sight.

Flowers.

In his grip, Sterling now held a bouquet of red roses.

"Sterling?"

He handed them my way. "For our first date."

With the roses now in my grasp, I inhaled. The scent of the flowers was lost in the fog of his spicy cologne. It wasn't overpowering as in too much, but overpowering as in consuming my thoughts. Looking up, I smiled. "If this is what it's like to be wined and dined by the great Sterling Sparrow, I may like it."

"The night is young."

After finding a ready and waiting vase in the kitchen and leaving the roses there, we made our way toward the secret elevator. As Sterling placed his palm on the sensor, I asked, "When will I be able to do that?"

The doors opened and he placed his hand in the small of my back. "Never."

"What?"

He pushed the G button for the garage. "There's no need."

The magic of the date evaporated with each floor we descended. "Yes, there is a need."

Sterling's fingers splayed on the skin of my back as his tone deepened. "Could we postpone this conversation until after our date?"

"What if there was a fire?"

"There won't be."

The doors opened to an idling large black SUV, similar to

the one I'd seen in the parking lot of the Sinful Threads distribution center, and our driver at the waiting.

"Your carriage," Patrick said with a grin, opening the door to the back seat.

It seemed as though I'd have both of my bodyguards along on this date. "Thank you, Patrick."

Sterling and I both scooted into the back seat. While Patrick was walking back to the driver's side, I whispered, "Postponed, not settled."

Sterling's hand rested on my knee as he turned my way. "Currently, we have more pressing matters."

My painted lip disappeared beneath my front teeth. "We do?"

"We do." His voice was low as Patrick entered the car, and we began to move toward the tunnel. Bit by bit, Sterling bunched the skirt of my dress until the silk stockings were almost completely exposed. His lips came to my ear. "Tell me what I'll find?"

My eyes opened and closed as his warm breath tickled my skin. I didn't expect him to question my attire this early and not in the seat behind Patrick. "Please, can we postpone this too?" His hand inched higher until I placed mine on top. "No."

I don't know what I was expecting, perhaps an argument. Instead, the tips of his lips curled upward. "All right, sunshine. You're right. That's a bit forward for a first date, but after..."

Sterling turned his hand so we were now palm to palm; our fingers intertwined.

"Where are we going?" I asked.

"To one of the most exclusive restaurants in the city."

I tried to come up with a name. "I'm not that familiar with Chicago...not anymore."

"Alinea."

"I have heard of that. I also remember hearing that they're booked months in advance. Is this another case of my taking another woman's date?"

Sterling laughed. "The dress you're referring to was obviously not another woman's. It was for you from Sinful Threads, and the restaurant, sunshine, was confirmed a few hours ago after you accepted my offer of a date."

"How do you do that? How can you get into a restaurant that's booked?"

"That is only one of my superpowers." He lifted my hand and kissed my knuckles. "I'll show you more later."

As his warm lips brushed over my skin, my thighs clenched, suspecting what *later* would bring.

Patrick wound our way through the city, first heading north on Lake Shore Drive. As we rode, Sterling pointed out Chicago landmarks. "Since this is where you live, you should be familiar."

"So I can drive myself?" I meant it as a statement, but its inflection made it sound more like a question.

"How about we agree that you should always know where you are?"

I nodded. I could live with that reasoning.

"You're familiar with Navy Pier," Sterling said.

When we reached Lincoln Park, Patrick pulled the SUV into a parking area. "This isn't our restaurant."

Sterling's grin grew. "Your powers of observation never cease to amaze me."

As the door opened, Sterling scooted out and offered me

his hand. "Our reservations aren't until eight. I thought you might enjoy a walk through the park."

"This really is like a date."

"No, Araneae. It is a date."

With our hands joined and Patrick a fair distance behind us, Sterling and I walked along the concrete path toward the water. When we came to stop, he turned me around. The skyline from this area was stunning. "Sterling, the city is beautiful."

"I'm glad that's how you see it."

"I do." I scanned the tall buildings, seeing the spires on one, I looked for the second tallest. "That building there..." I pointed. "...the one that looks like glass." There were many that looked like glass. "It's where we live."

He nodded. "It is."

"I can see how tall it is."

His head was shaking.

With my free hand, I slapped his shoulder. "Stop that. This isn't about observation. I had in my mind that the top floors were invisible to the world."

Sterling's laugh rumbled through me. "Not invisible—impenetrable. This is yours, Araneae."

"What's mine?"

"The city—Chicago. It's mine. You're mine. That makes the city yours, too."

"What does that even mean?" I asked.

"It means that when we arrive at one of the most exclusive restaurants with two hours' notice, we have a private room ready and waiting. It means there's nothing you desire that can't happen. It means if I'm the king, you're my queen."

Letting go of his hand, I turned toward the water. "What about that direction?"

Sterling turned also and curled his arm around my back. "What about it?"

"I don't want to be trapped in the city. I want the whole world." I wasn't being ungrateful or selfish, and I probably wasn't expressing myself well, what I truly desired.

"The world is yours, Araneae. Whatever is in my reach is yours."

Except freedom to wander. I didn't say that. I didn't want to ruin the mood of his gesture. However, it was what I was asking—not for the world or possession of any particular place or thing.

It was that the more he offered, the more trapped I felt.

What Sterling Sparrow was presenting to me took great power. With that came greater responsibility. I looked up at his handsome face. As he scanned the skyline, his granite features had returned. He wasn't seeing the beauty that I did. He was seeing the darkness he'd told me about.

I lifted my hand to his cheek. "I don't know what to say other than I don't know why I'm here. I don't understand how I got here or why you think I deserve to share what you've worked hard to secure."

"Because you were promised to me. The blending of the families will make us unstoppable."

My hand dropped. "What families? Your mother obviously doesn't care for me. I don't have a family. I saw my mother once, and I'm not sure I want to do it again."

"None of that matters," Sterling said, "none of it, Araneae. What matters is that you're finally where you belong." I started to speak, to again ask why, when he continued. "Think of what this will do for Sinful Threads. That's also your family."

"Sterling, I still don't understand."

"It's going to take time."

In time. His words from our first meeting came back to me.

Letting go of my waist, Sterling reached for my hand. "I need one thing from you."

"What?"

"A promise. One where you agree to give me the time that's needed to help you understand and the time to expose the secrets and lies that have hidden your true identity."

"How can I say no? You've already shown me much more than I otherwise would have ever known."

His head shook from side to side. "There are parts that will be difficult to face. I hate that those parts are there. If I could keep them hidden, I would, but that wouldn't be fair to you. It's all or nothing."

Nothing.

Could I walk away now if Sterling gave me the option?

Could I forget what I'd already learned and go back to living Kennedy Hawkins's life?

I knew the answer. "Will you make me a promise?" I asked.

His stare penetrated mine, searching for what I may ask of him, probably knowing there were secrets he'd never share. Finally, he said, "I'll try."

"Two promises, I guess."

Sterling nodded.

"Be honest with me. Never lie about things you think will hurt me."

"And," Sterling encouraged.

"And stay with me. Don't let me learn the good or the bad alone. I've been alone for too much of my life. I've had friends —great friends—but still, there's been a void I didn't understand. I didn't try. Over the last few weeks, that's disappeared. I don't know how to explain it..."

He ran the tip of his finger over my cheek. "Sunshine, you don't need to explain it. I know exactly what you're saying. Yes, I promise to do as you ask. And you..."

"I promise," I said, "to accept all that you tell me—the good and the bad because you won't leave me alone to figure it all out."

Our lips came together. In the evening Chicago sunlight with the skyline before us and the breeze coming off the water behind us, we kissed as if no one were watching.

When we pulled back, Sterling's grin returned. "Is it after the first date yet?"

"No, Sparrow, you promised me dinner."

"Then we should get back to the car."

ANNABELLE

Twenty-six years ago

*I*n the small, stale motel room, my knees gave out as my midsection contracted.

"Ever."

The word echoed off the smoke-stained walls.

I collapsed into the cracked vinyl chair. "Daniel, I don't know if I want to know your reasoning. I can't go anywhere else. I can't stay away from Chicago. I'm taking a leave of absence from the circuit court for Araneae's birth, but I can't walk away from our life." Before he could speak, I went on, "My doctor is there, too. With my age and history, this is a high-risk delivery." Tears pooled on my lids. "I can't."

Sitting on the edge of the bed facing me, Daniel let out a long sigh.

Although the scene was blurry through my tears and my emotions were all over the place, I tried to think like Daniel's wife. The man sitting near me with his knees spread and his elbows on his knees, holding his head, was about as far from the law student who made me fall in love with him as a man could be. Disheveled and distraught were two descriptors that came to mind.

"It began before I left Keller and Hawkins..." Daniel said dejectedly.

"Daniel, please. I'm a judge."

He sprang to his feet. "You're my fucking wife. You know the law. You can't be compelled to testify against me." He paced the small worn path to the vanity and back. "It's more than that. There's an even better reason why you can't testify."

I didn't ask, yet I couldn't look away.

"They'll kill you. They'll kill me." Red filled his face as he gestured toward me. "They'll kill her, probably before she ever takes her first breath. Annie, they won't hesitate. Fuck, prison would be safer, but they have people there too. They're everywhere. But if we leave the country..."

My skin prickled as the ice of his statements flowed through my veins. "We aren't leaving the country. We call the police. That's who helps people when they're threatened."

"They own the fucking police."

"Then we call the FBI," I said. "I know. We contact the ones who did the raid. Or Agent Bane. He gave me his card. We call him."

Daniel's head shook back and forth. "No."

My stomach twisted as nausea bubbled, and Araneae moved within me. "Tell me who," I demanded. "If my life— our daughter's life—is in jeopardy, I should know from whom."

"You know who my clients are."

"Rubio." Daniel's sister's husband. Rubio McFadden owned one of the biggest construction companies in Chicago and was serving his second term in the Illinois state senate.

"Yes, thanks to Pauline," Daniel said. "That client acquisition helped me branch out on my own. The McFadden account is the cornerstone to McCrie and Associates. Getting out of criminal defense and into finance and crisis management has made us very wealthy."

"Are you saying that your own family is threatening to kill us?"

Daniel sat back on the side of the bed. "The McFaddens aren't my only clients."

My head shook as I swallowed the churning bile that was burning my throat and chest. "You have many clients."

"Including..." he encouraged.

"Are we talking big or small?"

"Big, Annie, the biggest in Chicago."

"Sparrow," I said louder than before. "You're working for Allister Sparrow?"

I might be a judge, but I wasn't blind. I knew there was more to Allister Sparrow than Sparrow Enterprises. I'd heard the rumors, the whispers, and seen the headlines.

"In a way," Daniel said.

It was my turn to stand and pace. "We're in the middle of nowhere, and you're talking in riddles. Tell me what happened. Do you work for Sparrow Enterprises or not?"

"I can't say, not completely." He took another deep breath. "When my clients have an issue that needs fixing I help them. Pretend there's a mistress who needs an abortion or a girl-friend who needs incentive to keep her mouth shut. It's not always that kind of stuff. Sometimes it's finding people who have gone missing, when the parents can afford to keep the details away from the media. Most of the time, those cases are simple situations where a rich teenage kid goes rogue, borrows Mom or Dad's credit card, and hops a plane to the Caribbean.

"My firm finds them and brings them home. No one knows—no potential colleges or military programs—and the problem is fixed.

"Financially, I move money. I do what can be done to help people, even Rubio, from paying taxes on some of the income, especially if the income comes from less-than-legal sources."

I shook my head. "Stop, Daniel. I can't testify against you, but I could against your clients if I know what's happening."

"The money moving is especially lucrative and easy," he went on as if I hadn't spoken. "It's not complicated especially with shell companies."

"Dan—"

He lifted his hand. "I'm telling you this because if or when something happens to me, you need to know that I've hidden a great sum in a few different accounts—"

The bubbling won.

My boots slipped on the worn carpet as I regained my footing and ran toward the lavatory. Reaching for the toilet seat, I fell to my knees. I hadn't eaten much since breakfast. The bigger Araneae became, the less room I had for food. That didn't stop the dry heaves as I hung my head over the toilet and my body convulsed.

With my head pounding, they eventually stopped. Standing, I made my way to the sink. Cupping a handful of sulfur-scented water, I held my breath and rinsed my mouth. By the time I turned back around, Daniel was standing, his face red as tears descended his cheeks.

For a moment, I couldn't speak.

I'd never in our lives seen him cry. He'd been sad when I'd miscarried, but he never showed it. At the time, I thought it was his way of supporting me, letting me know he didn't blame me. What I was seeing now was different.

"Annie, I'm so sorry."

"Did you steal that money?" I asked. "From our family?"

He shrugged. "It came from multiple sources. Some here and some there."

"Is that why we're in danger?"

"No," Daniel said, "I haven't been caught."

"Then, dear God, what is this about?"

"About a year ago, a kid went missing. He was—"

"Please, don't use names," I said.

"Okay," Daniel replied. Sitting on the end of the bed, he patted the surface beside him. "Annabelle, have a seat, and I'll do my best to make this impersonal."

As I sat, he went to our coats that had been left on one of the vinyl chairs. When he turned, he was holding a small flask. "I'm sorry. I know how you feel about me drinking, but I can't get through this if I don't."

There was no fight left in me. "Impersonal," I reminded him.

The bed shifted as he sat. "This kid wasn't my normal type of client. His family didn't have money. The mother worked for one of my clients. That client came to me, knowing what I had done in the past and asked for my help. She offered to pay whatever expenses were incurred if I found the kid.

"It was a rabbit hole. The dark web..." He took a drink

from the flask, leaving the cap open. "...I started putting together bits and pieces. The trails were well hidden. I shouldn't have been able to follow them. But over the years, I've worked with and for some of the best. I started to uncover things that were strangely familiar." His eyes closed. "Once I saw, I couldn't unsee.

"I thought maybe I could leverage my newfound knowledge, save the kid and make money in the process."

"Blackmail?" I asked, flabbergasted. "You blackmailed—"

"Technically, it was *attempted*. It didn't work like I'd hoped."

"Was any of this on the computers or in the files that the FBI seized?" I asked.

"No. I played that part smart. The evidence is all hidden. The FBI will come up empty. That's why we're still alive. I swore on my own life—on all of our lives—that the evidence would never be seen.

"I gave Allister what he wanted, but it wasn't enough."

"Do we have to leave Chicago?" I asked. "Can't Rubio help us?"

Daniel's eyes closed and opened a few times. "He's my brother-in-law, but I'm already in debt to him. If I ask this..."

"Then I'll talk to Pauline. We'll work it out. If anyone can help us against Allister Sparrow, it's Rubio."

"I can't go back on my agreements. Leaving would be the safest."

My head pounded from the stress.

"Daniel, I want to go home. But I'm not sure I can make the car ride right now." I stood and walked toward the head of the bed. Pulling back the covers, I assessed the sheets. They were white. I said a little prayer that they'd been bleached since their last use. "I'm going to lie down. When I wake, we're going home."

"The evidence. Don't you want to know where it is?"

"No," I answered matter-of-factly.

"Annie, if something happens to me, it could be your saving grace, your bargaining chip."

I laid my head on the pillow and met my husband's gaze. "Then don't let anything happen. Stay safe."

Daniel didn't say another word as the heater roared to life. With nothing but white noise, I drifted to sleep.

I didn't know the time when I'd lain down or for how long I'd been asleep, but when I awoke, I was alone. In the chair was my coat. Daniel's was gone. With my heart beating faster, I slipped on my boots and made my way to the old ratty drapes covering the window. More stale odors filled the air as I moved the drapery. Beyond the glass, the sky was dark, yet the yellow beams from the lamp posts in the parking area reflected new accumulating snowfall.

A tear fell from my eye. Pushing it away, I made a vow to be strong.

"For you, spider-girl," I said aloud.

She and I were alone. Daniel's rental car was gone. Based upon the level of snow in the spot where he'd been parked, he'd been gone for a while.

ARANEAE

*S*terling had been right about our private dining area. Much like the club last week, the hostess greeted us with excessive enthusiasm, forgoing other customers as she personally escorted us up the modern-looking stairs to our private dining area.

In shades of gray, the interior was chic and subtle. Through a larger dining area and off a hallway we were led to the private room. One wall was covered in gray tile as water flowed over the surface. The other walls were like the rest of the restaurant, shades of gray.

Beside our table was a silver ice bucket, complete with a bottle of champagne.

Sterling pulled out my chair with a grin as his stare bore into mine.

After the hostess promised us the best service possible, we were momentarily left alone.

Sitting in the chair beside mine, Sterling's hand disappeared under the black tablecloth, finding its way to my knee. His gaze teased as his fingers inched upward. Almost immediately, a gentleman dressed in all white appeared in the doorway. Sterling's lips quirked as his hand found mine and pulled our union to the top of the table.

"Mr. Sparrow," the man said. "It is a great honor to have you and your guest with us tonight."

Though his expression had lost its mischief, our connection remained unsevered. Sterling squeezed my hand. "Chef Nicholas, this is my very special guest, my girlfriend, Araneae McCrie."

Girlfriend.

It seemed strange for a man like Sterling to use the same term that teenagers used, yet unlike other descriptors he'd employed, this one seemed accurate. If it were, that made him my boyfriend.

No, Sterling Sparrow wasn't a boy.

According to Sterling's rules, my introduction to the chef meant I could speak.

Why did I remember that?

Chef Nicholas stepped forward and offered me his hand. With my right hand free, we shook. As we did, he said, "What a lovely and unusual name."

Sterling nodded. "For an extraordinary woman."

"Well, thank you," I replied.

"For you, tonight," the chef said, "the menu is yours to design. Tell me what you desire and you shall have it."

Sterling looked my way, his gaze telling me that what he desired was not on the menu. He turned back to Chef Nicholas. "We'll have the ten-course tasting with wine pairings. Surprise us."

As Sterling spoke, another gentleman entered the room.

"This is Anthony," the chef said. "He will be one of your servers this evening." He gestured toward the chilled bottle of champagne. "Once he opens your champagne, we will prepare your feast."

My eyes grew wider with each statement.

The pop of the cork echoed as Anthony, with a towel over his arm, poured a small amount of the bubbling liquid into one glass.

"Sir?" he said, offering Sterling the glass.

Sterling nodded my way. "Let the lady try it." He looked at me. "If it's not to your liking, we'll open bottles all night until we find the right one."

Anthony handed me the crystal flute. "Ma'am."

Letting go of Sterling's hand, I accepted the flute and brought the rim to my lips. The liquid bubbled, tickling my nose as the tart dry taste covered my tongue.

"Will it do?" Sterling asked.

"Yes," I said to both men, setting the flute down upon the black linen tablecloth. "It's delicious."

After filling both glasses, Anthony excused himself, leaving us alone.

Sterling lifted his glass and I did the same. "To our first date."

Our glasses came together to the clink of connecting crystal.

"I believe I chose our destination unwisely," he said after a sip of the champagne.

"Why?" I asked, looking around. "This place seems amazing."

"Wait until the food arrives. It's a production. Dry ice

makes smoke effects. LED lighting hidden in the plates and under ice. The various servers will explain every dish, and just wait for dessert."

"And why is that a problem?"

"Because, Araneae, I want nothing more than to finish what I started prior to Chef Nicholas's entrance; however, with Alinea's attention to service and detail, I'm afraid that will have to wait."

My muscles tightened. "Anticipation, Mr. Sparrow. This is our first date. And with ten courses, I'm afraid what you're wanting may have to wait for tomorrow. I may have a food coma."

"I would prefer to put you in another type of coma."

I didn't get the chance to answer; we were joined again by another server.

The courses and wine continued until I wasn't sure I could eat or drink another mouthful.

A balloon.

That was what came with the dessert. The entire evening was truly a unique experience. As we stood to leave, I mentioned to Sterling that I needed to make a stop in the restroom.

"I'm not comfortable letting you out of my sight."

"Then you're going to need to get me a female bodyguard because I don't have a choice, and I don't think even the great Mr. Sparrow should be seen entering a ladies' room."

Placing his hand on my back, he replied, "I'll escort you, sunshine. I'll be right outside the door."

The truth was that I had an alternate reason for going in the restroom. Locking the door of the stall, I did what I should have done back at the apartment. I removed the satin thong. Yes, it made me uncomfortable to walk to the car, and down the stairs.

Oh jeez.

However, our first date had been—well, everything.

Maybe it was the multiple tastes of wine. All I knew for sure was that I was ready to get back to the apartment, but the fire I wanted to play with was the heat that had been smoldering all night long in Sterling's eyes, not what would happen to my ass if he knew I'd defied him.

When I opened the door, Sterling was waiting. "Are we all set to go home or would you like another stroll down by the lake?"

"Home sounds good."

"It does when you say it. Patrick is waiting outside."

As we climbed into the back seat, I turned to Sterling. "Thank you, this was the best first date I've had—ever."

"It's not over. Remember, we have unfinished business."

"I think you've forgotten my first-date rule."

"No, I didn't," he said. "I plan to break it and then punish you for doing so."

My head tilted. "That doesn't seem fair."

He leaned closer, his whisper low. "I'll let you come."

My cheeks grew warmer as they rose. "Maybe I won't let you."

Without warning he tugged my leg closer to him and walked his fingers near my core.

"Oh," I moaned before I could bite my lip. "Sterling."

His lips were at my neck. "Shh. I'm just checking, doing what I've wanted to do since you walked down those stairs."

Willingly, I opened myself to him as my eyes closed.

A simple sweep of his finger and a lingering roll of my clit was all it took to string me higher. My fingers splayed over his thigh as I tried to ignore that Patrick was right in front of us.

Removing his hand, Sterling brought his finger to my lips. Without hesitation I sucked his digit, not stopping when it was clean, but instead reaching for his hand and taking his entire finger into my mouth.

The control in his gaze changed before my eyes, melting into molten desire. "Sunshine, you're playing with fire."

I liked fire.

"I have an idea," I said as he retrieved his hand.

"You do?"

"I do. A way to not break my rule, not technically."

His head tilted.

It wasn't until we were back in our bedroom that my idea was made clear, yet by Sterling's actions, I was relatively certain we were on the same wavelength.

"First," he said after our door was closed and locked, "that dress needs to go."

I reached for the zipper at the side of the bodice.

"No, sunshine, I'm peeling it off of you."

My hands stilled as he walked toward me, each step more predatory than the last. A further tug of the zipper and a pull of the golden scarf that had been my sash and Sterling lifted the hem, pulling the dress up and over my head. He teased a strand of my hair back over my shoulders. The cool air-conditioned air contrasted with the fire in his eyes as he scanned me from my high heels to my blonde hair.

"Araneae, you're so fucking perfect."

I took a step closer and pushed his suit coat from his shoulders. As my pulse surged faster and without a word, I did what I'd once told him I wouldn't do. Dropping to my knees,

I reached up to his belt and undid the buckle. A threading of the button out of its secure place and his erection was already tenting his slacks.

Sterling reached for my chin and pulled my gaze to his. "You're gorgeous on your knees."

"I want to do this."

His chest heaved with heavy breaths as he ripped open the front of his shirt and buttons littered the floor, allowing me the view of his toned torso. Dark hair trailed from his belly button to below his trousers. Lowering the zipper, I freed his hard, angry cock. The tip glistened as veins bulged to the surface.

"Suck me."

It had been my plan, but hearing the words that rumbled through me, deep and demanding, heightened my desire.

Opening my mouth, I held on to his steel rod, the surface velvety under my grasp as I lapped the moisture from the tip, its salty taste like nothing I could describe.

This wasn't my first rodeo, yet everything with Sterling Sparrow was unique.

At first slowly, I took him in, my hands servicing what my mouth couldn't handle.

"Fuck yeah," Sterling said as his hands came to my hair. "More, you can do it."

He was guiding but not overpowering me, allowing me to take this at my own speed. Pushing up on my toes, I did as he said, taking more of him from a better angle. The deeper he went, the more my senses filled with everything Sterling Sparrow. The aroma of musk and the coarseness of his hair both combined with the tightening of his balls below my chin.

The room filled with our sounds, primal and raw. A quick

glance upward and I was greeted with the vision of his handsome features, contorted as he was lost in what I was doing.

Though I was the one on my knees, there was power in my position.

Sterling Sparrow was somehow in control of Chicago. His name had clout, his word authority, and yet in this moment, the man before me was completely under my spell.

My jaw ached, but I wouldn't stop. The room filled with the loud pop as I came all the way off and immediately went back down, rolling his tight balls between my fingers. His stance widened as his hips began to rock.

Reaching for his firm ass, I held on, refusing to leave him unsatisfied.

"Fucking...goddamn...Araneae..."

I moaned as his cock throbbed and warm liquid filled my mouth, spilling down my throat. Swallow after swallow I drank, as Sterling cradled my head against him. When I was finally content that he was satisfied, I eased off and peered upward.

The stare looking down at me was one of wonderment and adoration.

Sterling reached for my hand and helped me stand. Though he'd been the one to come, my knees were weak as I leaned against his broad chest and his strong arms surrounded me. "Our date is officially over," he said.

"It is? Well, it was a pretty nice date."

Sterling lifted my chin. "After what just happened, I don't want to break your rules, but sunshine, you're getting fucked."

I squealed as he lifted me from the ground, my legs covered in the stockings and high heels going over one arm as he cradled and carried me toward the bed.

"Then," I said after a kiss to his cheek. "I'm glad the date is over."

"Not as glad as you'll be in a bit."

"Kind of cocky, aren't you?"

"I'm about to remind you."

ARANEAE

I was almost giddy with anticipation as Jana and I prepared the second, smaller office for Winnie. With Patrick's help it was all set up, including the computer equipment connected to our Sinful Threads network.

"I'm excited to meet her in person," Jana said.

My cheeks rose. "Winnie's been with Louisa and me for over three years. She was our third assistant. There was something about the ones before her that didn't really click." I smiled at the memory. "I remember when Winnie walked in. You've seen her on video, but she's like five feet, three inches and one hundred and ten pounds dripping wet of kick-ass woman." I had a flash of Josey Marsh. I used to say my mom was a pit bull in a toy poodle body. Winnie could also fit that description. "She's a straight shooter," I went on, "not afraid to voice her opinion or objection. She's from Colorado but apparently has a friend here she's excited to reconnect with."

"On the phone and video chats she's been great."

"Yeah, Sinful Threads has been successful because we all work as a team. There's no competition. Everyone's job is secure as long as each individual does it. We all want to help one another."

Jana turned my way. "I know I've barely been here a week, but I don't feel like I've properly thanked you. This is one of the best opportunities of my life. My son, Bailey, is ecstatic to have me home every night." Her cheeks pinkened. "And my husband is happy too."

"I'm glad it's working out."

Part of me wanted to pry more into what Sterling had done to make Jana such a devoted employee, but I'd decided that she'd share if and when she was ready. Simple math told me that when Sterling hired her, she was only nineteen and her son would have been four. Patrick said she was employed before Sparrow Enterprises, but he hadn't elaborated greater.

Knocking on the doorframe, Patrick entered the office that would be Winnie's—or Louisa's if she ever came to Chicago for any length of time. With a glance to his phone, he said, "Winifred's plane has landed."

As I turned his way, my gaze narrowed. "Tell me she didn't fly on Sterling's plane."

How in the world would I explain that?

"No, Ms. Hawkins, she flew commercial, the flight that she booked herself. She did hire a car service."

"It can't be the same one she hired for me because you're here."

Patrick's smile quirked. "In a way it's the same one, different driver."

I shook my head.

"Important to you. Important to..." He let the final word go unsaid.

Jana's eyes were wide as she followed our conversation.

"Jana," I said, "it's better if Winnie thinks she has some random car service. I couldn't even begin to explain to her the intricacies of Mr. Sparrow. Sometimes I'm not certain how to explain them to me."

Memories of our first date warmed my skin.

Jana nodded.

Patrick had been right about Jana. It helped having someone close who could see both of my worlds and help me keep them separate.

In the late morning, as I was talking on the telephone with the manager from the distribution center in New York, I heard the commotion in the front office. Immediately, I recognized her voice.

"Jana," I heard Winnie exclaim. "It's good to finally meet you."

"Robert," I said into the telephone, "I'm going to need to call you back about those numbers. Something's come up."

"Sure thing, Ms. Hawkins. I have things that need to get done too."

I looked at the clock in the corner of my screen. "Will two o'clock work for a callback?"

"I'll be here."

"Thank you, Robert."

As I began to hang the phone receiver on its cradle, there was a knock on my mostly closed door. Hurrying around my desk, I pulled it open. Winnie's bright blue eyes shone. Her auburn hair was shorter than before, cut just above her shoulders and tapering even shorter in the back. I'd always thought of her hair as red, but compared to Lorna's which was bright strawberry red, Winnie's had more vibrant shades of auburn and brown.

Other than her haircut, she was exactly the same.

"Hi!" we both squealed in unison as we hugged.

"I feel like it's been forever," I said, fluffing her hair. "I love the cut."

"Thanks. I was ready for something new. I know it's only been around two and a half weeks, but it does seem like it's been forever." She looked around. "Goodness, Kennedy, you weren't kidding. This place is great."

"Come in and look at my lovely view of buildings and rooftops."

As we stood at the window, Winnie spoke low. "Louisa and I have been worried about you."

"You have? Why?"

"This is all so...out of character." Before I could respond, she went on, "But now, seeing you...I can't describe it. Kenni, you look different, in a really good way. I think Jason and I were right to encourage Louisa to go along with this change. Whatever you're doing looks fantastic on you." She eyed me up and down. "And damn, even your clothes. You're really stepping up the fashion."

I looked down at the sleeveless blue and black wool-blend sheath dress I was currently wearing. Suddenly self-conscious, I wondered if instead of Sterling's provided wardrobe that I should have worn something that I'd brought from Boulder. I ran my hands over my exposed arms. The bruise on my right arm was mostly faded, yet now that also had me uneasy.

Turning toward my desk, I eyed the light sweater on the back of my chair.

How odd would it look to put it on right now?

"Not that you didn't know fashion before," Winnie continued, paying more attention to my clothes than my arm. "It is what you do. I just mean..." She stared down toward the floor. "...are those shoes Louboutin?"

"They're closed-toed, you know, in case I need to visit a warehouse."

Winnie leaned closer. "You're not skimming from Sinful Threads, are you?"

"What? No."

"Sugar daddy?"

"Winnie," I said, "your and Louisa's imaginations go wild sometimes." I gave her another squeeze. "I've missed you."

"Hey," she continued her whisper, "who's the handsome yet kind of scary Hulk-like guy in the designer suit in the other room?"

Was Patrick handsome? Was he scary?

Maybe he was. Even with his short blond hair and light blue eyes, there was something reassuring about him that others might see as intimidating. The aura he gave off didn't come only from his sometimes-unapproachable appearance, but also from his presence and actions.

It was something that he, Sterling, and Reid had in common—confidence and fortitude. Other than the one time when Patrick had taken me to Sterling—which I now realized was beyond his control—he'd never ceased to put my safety first.

"His name is Patrick Kelly. He's my driver and..." I shrugged. "...kind of assistant. He's been very helpful. I don't know if you remember, but initially you hired him."

"And you are still using him? Why? You sent for your car.

I'd assume you'd be driving yourself. Are you still worried about whatever that was your mom told you about regarding returning to Chicago—that old wives' tale you never really filled us in about?" She eyed me questionably. "If you are, why are you here?"

Jeez, this was more difficult than I realized.

"The driving company made me a great deal," I said in my most carefree voice, "and I've learned that I hate Chicago traffic—they're as crazy here as in New York. And when I'm driven, I can work during my commute."

Winnie's head shook. "Okay, fine. Show me around this joint. Then let's get to work and sell some freakin' fantastic silken fashions. It looks like we need to support your new lavish lifestyle."

I laid my hand on her arm. "I promise, Sinful Threads is not doing that."

Her eyebrows danced. "Then the only other option is a sugar daddy. Does he have a friend?"

Forcing a laugh, I looped my arm through hers. "Let me show you around."

Throughout the day, the sound of Jana and Winnie chatting filled me with both excitement and anxiety. I was thrilled to have my friend with me in Chicago but also a bit nervous. Winnie's questions were grating on me. I wanted to be honest with her and Louisa, yet there were some things that couldn't be said.

Around three o'clock, Patrick stuck his head into my office. "Ms. Hawkins?"

I looked up with a grin. "That's me, right?"

"Yes, ma'am, right now it is. May I come in?"

I nodded and leaned back in my chair. After Patrick

closed the door, he sat in one of the chairs opposite me. "Jana is good."

"Okay, thank you. Tell me why you felt the need to come in here and say that."

His broad shoulder shrugged. "You're worried. I could tell at lunch, and throughout the day it's getting worse."

I let out a sigh. "Is it that obvious?"

Patrick shook his head. "No, it isn't. Not to others. To me—yes. I read people. It's part of what I do; it's how I learn things. There are simple tells. At lunch, you tapped your foot under the table and bobbed your knee—which you don't usually do. You keep wrapping your arms around yourself, yet you're wearing that sweater, so there's no way you're cold. When Winifred asks questions, you bite your lip."

I stood from my chair and paced a small trek behind my desk. "You were right...about the two worlds. I never realized how difficult this would be." My arm went toward the door. "And the two of them have been talking all day. What if Jana slips up?"

"I'm less worried about Jana than I am you."

My feet stilled as my eyes grew wide. "Me? Why me?"

"Jana has been in our employ for six years. She was in our world even before that. Discretion is essential. It's how we survive. She wouldn't still be here—she wouldn't be with you —if she didn't understand that implicitly. I also know that you get it, but it's new to you. I'm confident Sparrow has mentioned it."

I cocked my head to the side. "You think?"

Yes, that came out bitchier than I intended.

Patrick lowered his voice. "Araneae, when you're here,

when you're around people for Sinful Threads, be Kennedy Hawkins."

"I can when I'm talking in person to Franco, Vanessa, or Ricardo. It's easier on the phone, even with Winnie and Louisa. I can pretend that nothing has changed. This is different. Winnie *knows* me." I emphasized the word.

"Show her the woman she knows."

I placed my hands on my desk and leaned forward. Tears prickled the back of my eyes. "I'm not sure I know who she is anymore."

He took a deep breath. "May I make a suggestion?"

"My company," I reminded him.

"Noted. Did I hear Jana and Winifred—?"

I raised my hand. "Now that she's here, I'm warning you. If you call her that name to her face, she's going to rip you a new one. It's her name, but she very much prefers Winnie."

Patrick's grin grew. "I'll keep that in mind. As I was saying, I heard Jana and Winnie discuss a new silk shipment arriving today. Perhaps you—the cofounder of Sinful Threads—would like to go to the Port of Chicago?"

"To get away from here?"

"Start again fresh tomorrow."

I let out a long sigh. "That feels like running away."

"No, it's doing what you do. It's emphasizing one of the reasons you've relocated to Chicago."

"But it's her first day and night. I feel like I should ask her to dinner or do something with her after work."

His eyes narrowed.

"I know," I said, shaking my head, "I can't."

"No, you can't. No one comes into the apartment without Sparrow's approval. I know she's your friend, and you've known her for a while. That doesn't give her a pass. Very few people ever receive that pass."

"Genevieve Sparrow does."

"She's Sparrow's mother, and I'm relatively certain he'd revoke the pass if he could."

"Dinner and/or drinks," I said again, "somewhere around here?"

"Will that make you more comfortable?" Patrick asked. "What might you say over a glass of wine?"

I collapsed back into my chair. "I feel trapped."

"I can't comment on the way you feel. I can say that Sparrow is doing everything he can to keep you safe while at the same time granting you as much freedom as possible. I'm certain you realize that there's a part of him who would be content to keep you in the apartment twenty-four seven."

"So I've been granted a leash or a tether?" I asked.

"Ms. McCrie..."

I sighed, holding tightly to the armrests of my chair and refusing to cross my arms over my chest and pout though it was what I wanted to do.

"We could go straight to the apartment," Patrick offered, "if you'd rather. Araneae, the choice is yours, not his."

I shook my head. "Take me to the port. I need to get out of here. I also need to tell Winnie something about tonight."

"I'm sure you'll come up with a plausible excuse."

Retrieving my purse from a desk drawer, I handed Patrick my satchel. When he opened the door, Jana and Winnie turned our way.

"Ladies, it's great hearing the two of you working together." I forced a smile. "This is going to work better than I imagined. I'll be back in the morning. Patrick and I are headed to the Port of Chicago to check on our silk shipment."

"Is there a problem?" Winnie asked.

"That's what we're going to find out," Patrick responded.

Her face tilted up, searching him as if wheels were turning in her head. "Why do I get the feeling you're more than a driver?"

"Winnie."

"Because I am, Ms. Douglas," Patrick responded. "I have experience as well as education in merchandising and finance. I understand distribution channels and exploiting the most profitable means. Ms. Hawkins has been kind enough to allow me to utilize that knowledge and help her navigate the city at the same time."

Winnie's arms crossed over her chest. "Well, damn. You are more than a pretty face connected to a rock-hard body."

Holy shit.

We needed to get out of here.

"I'm sorry," Winnie continued. "Louisa has me making up all kinds of stories on why Kennedy made this move." She turned my way. "She really does have an active imagination."

Shaking my head, I replied, "Overactive, I'd say. Hopefully after their little girl is born and her hormones get back to normal, she'll give up some of her conspiracy theories."

"Kennedy," Winnie said, "it's official. That's what Jason and Louisa are naming her."

My lip went under my teeth until I realized that was my *tell* as Patrick would say. "I thought she was teasing."

"Maybe at first, but now they both want to do it. Kennedy Lucille."

"After her mom and me."

"Yep," Winnie said with a smile.

I reached for her hand. "I'm sorry I can't be more of a hostess tonight. I have plans that are difficult to break."

Impossible was a better word.

"No. Don't worry about it. I've been trying to reach that friend of mine I told you about. I talked to her not too long ago. I'm going to stop by her place. I mean, if she won't answer her calls, texts, or emails, then she's getting me on her doorstep."

I loved her confidence.

"Have a great time."

"Oh, I will," she said. "And I'll be back here bright and early in the morning."

Nodding to both Winnie and Jana, Patrick and I passed through the doorway, stepping out of Sinful Threads.

On the way to the car, I asked, "Was what you told Winnie true...about your experience and education."

"It was."

"May I ask about the education part? It's not that I don't believe you..."

Patrick's grin curled upward. "Business and finance at University of Chicago, Booth."

"Damn. Impressive."

"While I appreciate my education, I would say that the experience has been the most beneficial."

I shook my head as he opened the back door. "And you're babysitting me."

"Not a demotion, Araneae. I promise."

ARANEAE

$\mathcal{E}$verything was fine at the dock. Truly, it was quite the production watching the lifts raise the shipping containers from the cargo ships and line them like blocks in rows. After a quick discussion with the overseer at the port and confirming the arrival of our order, I told Patrick I wanted to go home.

I did, and yet I didn't.

It was summer in Chicago, and the lake beyond the shipping yard was beautiful. The breeze blew my hair in a way that reminded me of the breeze in the mountains in Colorado. It's the sensation of the warm air contrasting with a cooler wind.

Now that I was back behind the infrared barrier, I could see the blue sky and the lake. However, I couldn't feel the breeze or the warmth of the sun.

Impenetrable also meant isolated.

When I first arrived home, I'd changed into jeans and a

light sweater. It may be summer, but as I'd mentioned, the sun's heat didn't make its way into the apartment. Sitting in the living room with my legs curled on the sofa beneath me, I tossed my Kindle onto the cushion to my side. Reading wasn't going to work. My concentration was shit. My mind was all over the place.

Patrick's words came back to me: *I'm less worried about Jana than I am you.*

I hated to admit that he was probably right. I needed to talk to Sterling about what I could and couldn't say. I sure as hell didn't want Louisa or Winnie—or anyone—thinking I was stealing from Sinful Threads.

I wasn't.

I wouldn't.

The twisting in my stomach and pounding of my temples led me to believe that I wasn't cut out for a double life.

Instead, I concentrated on the colors in the sky. The sun was slowly moving toward the horizon, yet at a little after seven in the evening, it still had a way to go.

I tried to distract myself from loneliness as I gazed around the large living room. Though I'd been home for over two hours, there was still no Sterling.

I could call him to find out where he was, but that felt like nagging. He never called when I was late—well, to my knowledge. I always had Patrick, which more than likely meant that Sterling was always aware of my location.

I didn't even know the name of his new driver.

Inhaling, I laid my head against the soft cushion. The first floor was filled with the aroma of whatever Lorna had prepared and was waiting in the kitchen for us to eat. It seemed that since my arrival, a routine of sorts had been established. All five us—or whoever was home—ate together at breakfast. At dinner, Lorna, Reid, and Patrick disappeared. It was only Sterling and me who usually ate sitting at the breakfast bar.

The atmosphere was informal. With all of Sterling's obvious money, I liked that he didn't feel the need to flaunt it, that he was comfortable with casual.

Dinners with just the two of us were as if for a little while we were a normal couple, eating and talking.

I'd told Lorna more than once that I would cook, but as of yet, whenever I arrived home, she was already in the process or done with some delicious concoction.

With my mind in a million places, I was gazing through the large windows out over the buildings to the lake beyond when my phone buzzed across the table before me. *WINNIE* appeared on the screen.

I tapped on the text message:

"MAY I CALL YOU?"

I started to text back when I decided it would be easier to hit the call button. She answered right away.

"What's up? Is everything all right with your hotel?"

"I-I haven't checked in yet."

I glanced at the screen of my phone. "Winnie, it's getting late. You need to check in."

"I will," she said. "I'm worried about my friend. I talked to her... gosh, it was over a week ago, and she was excited about us catching up."

"You said you were going to her place. Was she there?"

"No." Her voice lowered. "And the whole thing was strange, like out-of-a-bad-movie weird. Her apartment complex is in Gage Park. It has security, you know, where you buzz a box before you can get in the building?"

"Yes," I said.

"I buzzed and buzzed. Finally, this woman came out and asked me what I wanted. I told her that I was a friend of Leslie Milton's and that I was there to see her. Kenni, the woman's face turned white, like she'd seen a ghost or something. She told me to go to the front office and talk to them."

As Winnie's voice became more concerned, I sat forward, placing my feet on the floor. "Did you go talk to them?"

"Yes, but they said they couldn't release information. It all gave me a weird feeling."

"Oh, honey..." I stood and paced along the tall windows. "...I know how excited you were to see her."

"I was, but it's more than that. I'm worried. I want to be sure she's all right."

My lip momentarily disappeared as I thought of the praises I'd heard from everyone regarding Reid's technological ability. "Hey, no promises, but if you'd like, I can ask someone to look her up. I know this person who's pretty good with that kind of stuff."

"A policeman?"

I almost chuckled. "No, not quite."

"Hell, I don't care who it is. I'd appreciate learning anything. I'm going to have the driver take me to the hotel, and then I'm cutting him loose. He creeps me out a bit, and well, I can just Uber to and from the office."

I'd probably been around Sterling and Patrick for too long,

but I didn't like the idea of her out around Chicago alone. "Really, the driver is no big deal. I mean, it's what they do. Why don't you let me ask my friend about your friend and you keep the driver for now?"

"Fine," she said. "After traveling, I'm too exhausted to argue. Once I'm checked in, it will be room service and bed."

"Maybe add wine," I said, trying to lighten the mood.

"Did you think that wasn't implied?"

"Hey, Winnie, I'm glad you're here."

"Me too. Please let me know if you learn anything about Leslie."

I'd made my way to the kitchen. On my fourth try, I found a drawer with tablets of paper and pens. "Before you go," I said, "can you give me her name again? I'm going to write it down."

"Yes. It's Leslie Milton. She's my age, twenty-five. Blonde and...I don't know... pretty. Not model pretty, but sweet. I can give you her phone number too, but it isn't getting me anywhere."

"Yeah, give me what you have. The more information my friend has, the better." I wrote down everything Winnie said.

"Oh," Winnie added, "lately, she'd mentioned a boyfriend."

"Do you remember his name?"

"Paxon or Praxton...maybe Preston. I didn't commit it to memory."

"Have you checked her social media?"

"Kenni, it's all gone. Everything. The more I look and don't find, the more nervous it's making me."

"I'll call you if my friend..." It was then I heard footsteps coming from the way of the elevator. "...can help. Call me when you get checked in."

"Thanks, I will."

As I disconnected the call with Winnie, Lorna and Reid came through the doorway talking together. The way they were smiling at one another made part of my long day disappear. In every way visually, they contrasted one another—tall, short, dark, light—and yet together they were perfect. There was a glow about them when they were together—truly a handsome couple.

"Oh, Araneae," Lorna said, "We're sorry to bother you. I wanted to check on the dinner and didn't realize you were in here. I figured you'd be upstairs."

"No," I said, waving my hand. "Sterling isn't home yet." I looked to Reid. "Will he be soon?"

Reid pulled his phone out of the pocket of his jeans. "I'm a little surprised he isn't already. He went to a job site late this afternoon..." He was texting as he spoke.

"Job site? Can I ask?"

Reid looked away from the screen to me. "Sparrow Enterprises is real estate. There are condos going up in Buena Park. There have been some issues with the National Register of Historic Places. It was supposed to be all settled. When another issue came up, Sparrow decided to handle it himself."

My lips curled upward. "Yeah, that's right. He does real work, too."

"I'd say all the work he does is real."

Reid looked down at his phone again as Lorna opened the oven and pulled out a rectangular baking dish. The wonderful aroma that had been seeping into the air multiplied exponentially as my stomach growled.

"Lorna," I said, "I know I keep telling you that I'd be glad to cook for all of us or just Sterling and myself, but damn, what is that? It smells fantastic."

"Chicken parmesan. It was my grandmother's recipe." She nudged Reid. "Someone here likes it so much that our helping is twice as big." She placed the dish back in the oven and reached for the controls over the stovetop. "I'm going to turn this down—"

"He should be here soon," Reid said, interrupting her. "They're on their way now. This time of evening, they're dealing with traffic."

I started to ask who *they* included. I presumed it was Sterling and whoever was now driving him. It eased my mind knowing he was safe, doing real work and not something in the darkness he spoke about.

"You two have a good night," I said. "I'll clean everything up after dinner."

Lorna reached for Reid's hand. "Come on, I want you to eat before the next five-alarm emergency hits and you're gone again."

It was then that I remembered Winnie and the paper on the counter. "Hey, before you two go, could I ask a favor of you, Reid?"

"As long as it won't instigate that emergency," Lorna said with a grin.

"No, I don't think so. It's for my assistant, the one here from Boulder. She's my friend too..." I handed Reid the piece of paper. "...and she has a friend who lives in Chicago, actually in Gage Park." Chicago had a plethora of smaller neighborhoods.

Reid stood taller as he looked down at the note I'd written. "This is your friend's friend?"

"Yes, Leslie Milton. Winnie can't find her. They were supposed to get together. She said the people at her friend's apartment complex were acting strangely."

His dark eyes stared my direction, and I would swear that his jaw clenched.

"Did she give you any more information?" he asked.

I shrugged. "Not really. I told her that I had a friend who might be able to help. Can you?"

"He can do anything," Lorna volunteered, "after dinner."

"That's fine with me," I said. "Just if you learn anything, please let me know."

Reid nodded. "I'll do that."

Their footsteps disappeared toward the secret elevator. Finding myself alone again, I went to the refrigerator and pulled out a bottle of moscato I'd opened a few days before. Winnie was right. After today, wine should be implied.

ANNABELLE

Twenty-six years ago

The bell on the front door of the motel's office jingled as the door opened, and frigid air and blowing snow entered with Daniel.

"Annie, what are you doing?"

I looked from my husband to the telephone in my hand. "Where have you been?"

"Come back to the room."

"No, I'm going home."

His features changed from curious to stern before me. "I said come back to the room."

My gaze went to the woman behind the desk. Maybe girl was a better description. She was petite and couldn't have been any older than early twenties. She was watching us with big eyes. I'd had to convince her to allow me to use the motel's telephone. At first, she told me in broken English that it was against their policy.

"Ma'am," she said, "you go back to the room. We don't want trouble."

I stood taller. "There isn't any trouble. I need to reach my sister-in-law. She'll help me."

Daniel came forward and took the phone out of my hand. "Annie, the roads are getting worse. There's no way we can go or anyone can get to us."

I closed my eyes as my midsection contracted. The doctor called them Braxton-Hicks. I'd been having them for the last few weeks, but since the FBI man and this impromptu trip, they were getting stronger. Their frequency was still all over the place. "Daniel, I need to get to the doctor."

He tilted his head. "Come to the room. We'll call her."

"How? We don't have a phone."

"There's a phone in your room," the young lady volunteered. "You go there."

"It doesn't work. That's why I came in here."

Daniel pulled a rectangular phone from his pocket, the bottom flipped outward to talk and the buttons to dial were hidden underneath. "Come to the room."

"Where did you get that?"

His eyes closed as he exhaled. "Come to the goddamned room."

I turned to the lady at the counter and reached for a piece of paper and a pencil. After scribbling on the paper, I handed it to her. "Please?"

She took the paper. "No trouble. Now, you go."

I looked back at Daniel. "You're going to get me home." It wasn't a question.

He again opened the door, pushing outward against the increasing winds. More snow and cold air filled the office as he gestured for us to leave. Bowing my head to the freezing mixture pelting my face, I stepped unsteadily onto the sidewalk.

"Let me help you," he said, reaching for my arm. "Everything is getting icy."

I wrapped my coat tighter as I held onto my husband's arm. With the wind and snow whipping around us, I gritted my teeth together as I asked, "Where were you?"

Opening the door to the room he'd rented, Daniel waited for me to enter. "What the hell did you give that girl?"

"My name and Pauline's name and number. I asked her to please call Pauline for me."

Daniel grunted as he locked the door.

"Why the hell don't you understand what's happening?"

"Well, mostly because I don't know what's happening. I'm scared to death that I'm going into labor, and you have me in some godforsaken place in the middle of a blizzard."

"Take off your coat," he said. "Let me try to explain more. There's no way Pauline or Rubio can get to you. No one can. Not on those roads."

Tears came to my eyes. "Damn you, Daniel. When I woke and you were gone..." I gasped for breath. "...I thought you'd left me here."

He came closer, but I flinched away. "Don't you dare touch me."

Retreating, he reached for my coat. "May I help you get this off?"

I nodded.

"Annie, I thought about what you said. How you can't know what I know for if you did, they could consider you an accomplice, charge you with conspiracy to commit the crimes."

I didn't want to hear anything he had to say about what he knew or what he'd done. I needed to know he'd help us get home. "Where did you go? Were you going to leave me? Us?"

"No," he said as he removed his own and shook the snow from both of our coats. Dejectedly, he sat on the end of the bed. "I went to Cambridge."

"Cambridge? Cambridge, Wisconsin?" My mind tried to process. "Where we were married?"

He nodded. "I guess I wanted to talk to someone. I talked to Minister Watkins."

"The man who married us is still there?"

Daniel nodded again. "The church isn't large, but it's on the National Register of Historic Places and a favorable posting. He said he's been offered bigger churches but doesn't want to leave."

"Why did you risk going there in this weather?"

He didn't answer; instead, he went on with his story. "Minister Watkins remembers us. He talked about how the rain stopped the day we wed. It had been forecast for an all-day downpour, but do you remember?" he asked hopefully. "Two hours before the ceremony the skies cleared. It was like God was telling us it would work out."

I sat in one of the vinyl chairs and leaned back. "I'm not sure it will. I'm scared."

"He gave me the phone and some cash."

"Why? We have money," I said.

"We can't access it or..." Daniel lowered his head to his hands. His elbows were perched on his outspread knees. "I won't tell you the players. Nevertheless, you need to understand the severity. The information I found on that kid I told you about...we saved him, we got him out." Daniel took a deep breath. "I know you don't and can't talk about your cases as they're happening, but a few months back you had one that upset you."

It was my turn to nod.

"When the news released about it, the stations said it brought to light the problem of child exploitation and trafficking."

I gasped. "That boy...was he?"

Daniel nodded slowly. "Yes. We got him out, but we couldn't...we couldn't help others. The ones who run it, who profit, who utilize it..." His eyes grew wide and glassy. "Annie, they'd kill me if I tried to rescue more. I shouldn't have found what I did: the evidence, the names, and the organizations involved. I have it all." He stood and began to pace. "I thought that maybe...it seemed like our golden ticket. Knowledge is power. Right?" He didn't let me answer. "I thought that knowledge could or would help me, give me the fucking power for once. I mean if I couldn't save the kids, then I could help us, right?"

"No," I said indubitably. "How could you even—?"

"It didn't work. My plan..." He shook his head. "...I had no choice. They made me give up my evidence."

"So it's over?"

"No, Annie, that's the problem. It will never be over. I'm a liability and that means we're always in danger. They don't believe that I gave all the evidence up. They're lowlifes and they assume I made copies."

"But you didn't, right?"

"What do you think?" he asked. "They threatened you and Araneae."

I tried to understand. "Does Rubio know?"

"Not all of it."

"Allister Sparrow?"

"Not all. I tried to leverage one—fuck, Annabelle, I screwed up."

"And I..." I said, thinking about my message to Pauline. "...I'm having that girl in the office call Pauline. Does she know?"

"I doubt it, but she'll tell Rubio. At this point, I'm not sure we can trust him with our safety."

"You'd trust Allister over your brother-in-law?"

"Hell no," Daniel said. "It's so screwed up now that the feds are involved. If they had what I have..."

He stood and walked to the window. Turning back around, he asked, "How are you feeling?" He pointed to my oversized midsection. "Is she all right?"

"I don't know. Those Braxton-Hicks contractions are stronger, but there's no rhythm yet."

He nodded. "I am sorry. This wasn't meant to hurt you or her. It was to give you what I never thought possible. The money involved is astronomical. I thought, if we could get a cut...." He shook his head. "I'll get you back to Dr. Jacobs and I'll..." His Adam's apple bobbed. "I'll try again. I'll give them whatever they want. I'll make this work."

I walked to the window and reached for my husband's hand. Though it was daytime, the visibility was minimal. "I can't see the road or traffic."

"That's because there isn't any traffic. On the radio in the car I heard that US 90 is closed. I saw a small diner about two miles away. The open sign was still lit. I can try to get there and bring us some food."

I held tighter to his hand. "I don't want you to leave me—again."

"Then come with me. We'll go slowly." He laid his hand over Araneae. "We'll keep you both safe."

"Okay."

A half an hour later, we were seated in a classic booth of a small mom-and-pop diner. The floor was alternating white and black tile that had seen its share of traffic. The walls were discolored from the grease emanating from the different meats sizzling on a large griddle. The front of the building that faced the road was all windows. Beyond them the snow continued to fall.

At the moment I was simply relieved that my husband hadn't left us alone, and there was food to be had.

The waitress who greeted us said that since she and the cook were stuck, they decided to keep the diner open for stranded travelers. Currently, it was minimally patronized.

Along the breakfast bar that faced a big griddle and the backside of a large man dressed in a greasy white cook's uniform were three men all sitting at least a stool away from one another. Across the restaurant from us was a family of four. The mother and father appeared exhausted; however, their two children were blessed with an abundance of energy.

"What can I get you folks?" the waitress asked. Her wrinkles showed her age while her slender body made me believe that the gum she was chewing was simply a substitute for the cigarettes she preferred.

"A coffee and burger," Daniel said, staring beyond the waitress to the large menu above the grill.

"I'll have a hot chocolate and a vegetable omelet."

"Would you like toast with that?" she asked.

"Yes, please, wheat if you have it."

When she walked away, Daniel reached across the table for my hand. "It may not make sense, but I'm going to do my best to protect us, all of us."

I nodded, unsure anymore of what to believe. How much of our life had been a lie? I wasn't sure I even wanted to know.

Letting go of my hand, he reached into the pocket of his coat and pulled out something gold in color. He opened his hand. In his palm was a gold-linked bracelet with two charms: a heart locket and a small old-fashioned key.

"What is that?" I asked. "Where did you get it?"

It obviously wasn't new, more of a cheap antique.

"Minister Watkins gave it to me. Do you remember his wife?"

I nodded, recalling how she fussed around before and during the wedding. "She was sweet."

"She passed away a few years ago," Daniel said. "When I told him about you and the baby, he asked me to give this to you—for Araneae."

Tears returned to my eyes.

"He said," Daniel went on, "that his wife always wore it. They never had children. He wanted to know it would be passed on."

I lifted the bracelet from his hand. "That was nice."

"He said it meant a lot to her. He hoped it could continue to be sentimental."

Handing him back the bracelet, I held out my arm. Daniel wound the golden links around my wrist and secured the clasp. Lifting my arm, I let the two charms dangle. "Is there anything in the locket?"

"A picture of the church."

I smiled. "The church where we were married. I like that."

"It's a little faded, but if you open it, you can tell."

With the nail of my thumb, I pried open the locket. The picture inside was tiny and faded, but I recognized the church. Next, I held the small key between my thumb and finger. "It almost looks like a real key instead of a charm."

Daniel shrugged. "The key to his heart, Minister Watkins said."

I sighed as I leaned back against the vinyl booth and wiggled my toes. Even in my boots they were cold. At least I hadn't had a contraction in a while. I looked up at my husband. "I'm glad you went and talked to him. You seem calmer."

"It was a good decision. He helped me more than I can say.

"Annie, we're going to make it."

ARANEAE

"Araneae."

My name came from a distance as the sofa bowed and warmth came to my side. Opening my eyes, the room around me was mostly dark. So too was the gaze staring down at me. Still dressed in his suit from Michigan Avenue, Sterling laid a hand on my hip.

"W-what time is it?" I asked, suddenly aware that I'd fallen asleep after finishing my glass of wine.

Moving upward, his large hand came to my cheek. "Did you eat?"

I pushed myself up to a sitting position. "It's dark."

The sky beyond the windows was a velvety black, the city below aglow with lights. Out on Lake Michigan, the surface was dotted with lights from various boats while higher up the darkness went on forever. Looking back to Sterling's handsome face, I could see his features were granite.

I shook my head. "What's the matter? Why are you so

late? Reid said you were on your way home around seven. Was there a problem with the condos?"

"Condos?" Sterling asked.

"Yes, something about the National Historical—"

"No," he interrupted, "that was resolved." Shaking off his suit coat and leaving it on the couch, Sterling reached for my hand and encouraged me to stand. "Have you eaten?"

Wakefulness was coming back. "No, I was waiting for you."

A long sigh filled the room as he loosened his tie and undid the top button of his shirt. "Then let's go eat."

"Sterling, you need to let me know what's going on. You keep constant tabs on me through Patrick. I don't even know your driver's name."

"Patrick does," he said as we walked toward the kitchen.

My steps halted. "Really? That's your answer? I don't give a fuck if Patrick knows."

Sterling stopped and turned my way. "Don't do this, Araneae, not tonight."

My ire grew as I resumed walking. "Do what? I'm trying to have a discussion with you." The clock on the microwave came into view. "It's after ten. After ten o'clock at night." Each statement was louder than the last. "When I wake tomorrow you'll be gone. You usually are. I waited to talk to you tonight, and you left me here alone until ten o'clock. I'm a fucking prisoner in this apartment. I should have been out with my friend, with Winnie, welcoming her to the city instead of being stuck in here."

"You're never alone."

"Did you hear me? I'm stuck in here."

As if ignoring me, Sterling went to the oven and with oven

mitts removed what was remaining of our chicken dinner. Apparently at some point, Lorna had turned off the heat because instead of being burnt, it now looked cold.

"We can warm this up," he offered.

Why was it so sexy to watch a man cook even if he hadn't done the cooking?

"Sterling."

Leaving the baking dish on top of the stovetop, he turned my way. "You're just going to have to accept that sometimes things happen. I deal with them. They take time. It's what I do. That can't stop."

"And you need to realize that I won't be held prisoner."

He took one long stride toward me.

I gasped as he seized my shoulders.

Sterling's grip tightened with each word as his jaw grew tighter and his words became more clipped. "Go ahead, Araneae, get upset. Get it out of your goddamned system, and then when you've said your piece, thrown your temper tantrum, we'll eat our fucking dinner."

How dare he diminish the way I was feeling like I'm a child.

"Let go of me. I'm going to bed."

His fingers held tighter. "You're going to eat. This is a fucking stupid argument, but since you chose to have it, I'm choosing to win it." His grip loosened. "Now sit the fuck down and I'll warm this up." When I only stared, he rephrased, "*Will* you sit the fuck down?"

Huffing and murmuring a few derogatory descriptors under my breath, I did as he asked—and only because he asked—sitting at one of the stools at the counter. My brain told me to let my concerns go, that the mood wasn't right, but if I only saw Sterling for an hour or two a day, what choice did I have?

I took a deep breath. "Sterling, I also want to talk about the sensor thing on the elevator."

He'd been spooning sauce over the chicken breasts now on the plates when he turned my way, his head shaking. "You have fucking impeccable timing."

"Why? Would this be better discussed at three in the morning or whatever godforsaken time you wake? Maybe at seven at night when you're supposed to be here? How about during lunch if you ever met me for lunch? I'm not sure, Sterling, when is a good time to tell you I want my damn handprint to open that fucking elevator?"

He placed the plates in the microwave and hit the appropriate buttons. "Araneae."

I waited for more. The microwave dinged.

"Tell me," I demanded.

Setting the two plates on the counter, he added silverware and napkins. Going to the refrigerator he returned with two water bottles. Placing them down by the plates, he then sat on the stool beside me and turned my way. "Are you done? Can we eat?"

My eyes closed in frustration. "At least answer me."

"Tell me why you want to open the elevator."

I'd picked up the fork, but now I let it drop, its clink against the plate echoing through the kitchen. "Why the hell do you think I want to be able to operate the elevator?"

"You're not a prisoner here. If you'd wanted to leave after work tonight or any night when I'm not here, the answer is as simple as a call to Patrick."

"What if he's busy? What if he's with you?"

"Then you don't need to leave," Sterling replied matter-of-factly.

"Do you even hear yourself? If I'm not a prisoner, then my coming and going shouldn't be contingent upon other people."

Sterling pushed his plate away on the counter. "I was fucking here at this apartment a little after seven, but something came up, something that required my input. I should have called, but by the time I checked on you, you were asleep. I left you there until we came to a conclusion."

"You came to a conclusion? Does this involve me?"

"Yes."

I crossed my arms over my chest. "Okay, great and powerful one, what is your decision?"

"You and I are leaving town in the morning."

My head shook. "What? No. Winnie just got here. I'm not leaving town. I have phone conferences scheduled with two big-name stores tomorrow. The dresses are a hit and they want to discuss future merchandise." My heart beat faster. "Sterling, I have a life and a business, in case you've forgotten."

His chin jutted higher. "You do. And what better time for you to get away—to lessen your feeling of being trapped—than when Winnie is here to help Jana? Together they'll be able to handle the Chicago office. If there's a situation that requires your input, they can call you."

Getting down from the stool, I walked to the windows and back. My reflection appeared the opposite of the man watching me with the dark stare. While his suit coat was gone and his tie loosened, he nonetheless held the air of fashion and authority. I looked disheveled, my hair askew and my sweater wrinkled, thanks to my impromptu nap.

I turned back to him until our gazes met. "You are not allowed to make decisions regarding my business. It's off-limits."

He scoffed. "This decision isn't about your business. It's about you and me leaving town because it's what's best. How it affects Sinful Threads is a byproduct. It's your business, you make the necessary arrangements. We're going."

"Not tomorrow. On top of all that, I have a special meeting with someone I met at the dinner the night you ambushed me. She has the potential to be a great spokesperson for Sinful Threads. She's interested in some exclusive designs. Sterling, that can't wait. And," I went on, "Winnie has something personal happening. I don't want to leave her."

Standing, he came my way and reached for my shoulders, gentler this time. "It can all wait. Patrick may have mentioned that you were feeling trapped. I get it. It's not my intention, but it's the reality of this..." Letting go with one hand, he motioned between us. "...this life, us, and me. I'm all for more dates. I'm for walks in the park and on the shoreline. Even those need to be planned and scouted. You only saw Patrick, but we had others watching us, protecting us. There's no running to a mall, the grocery store, or even a fucking bakery. Whatever you want, tell me, Patrick, Lorna, or even Jana. I won't apologize for the reality of how it is because the payoff is worth it."

"Is it?" I asked. "Are you sure?"

His hands moved to my waist. "Without a doubt. Having you here, having you safe, and having your fucking amazing body in my grasp." He lifted his finger to my lips. "Even hearing your sassy, smart mouth..." He kissed my forehead. "...it's worth it." He reached for my hand. "Now eat or watch me eat. Just come over here."

Step by step I followed as he led me back to the breakfast bar.

Before sitting, I said, "I'm having another glass of wine. Do you want one?"

His nose scrunched. "Not that sweet shit you like. I'll open a bottle of merlot."

"Okay. My glass is in the living room. I'll be right back."

As I retraced the path we'd taken, I mentally revisited the conversation.

While I'd lost a bit of my fight, I was adamant about tomorrow. I couldn't leave town in the morning. The meeting I'd mentioned was with Pauline McFadden. She asked to personally meet with me. If her husband pursued his bid for the White House, having her dressed in Sinful Threads would be a great marketing triumph.

Picking up my phone that I'd left lying beside my wineglass, I touched the screen and entered my code. I had one missed call and two text messages.

First text message from Louisa:

"WANTED TO LET YOU KNOW THAT I'M THREE CENTIMETERS DILATED. THE DOCTOR SAID THAT I COULD BE THIS WAY FOR THE NEXT TWO WEEKS, BUT THE BRAXTON-HICKS CONTRACTIONS ARE HAPPENING MORE FREQUENTLY. I'M GLAD WINNIE'S WITH YOU, BUT I'D LOVE TO HAVE YOU BOTH HOME."

I sighed. Yes, Sterling and I needed to talk, and if I were to take a trip, it should be to Boulder.

Call and second text message from Winnie:

"ALL CHECKED IN. YOU DIDN'T ANSWER. IS THERE ANY NEWS FROM YOUR FRIEND? IF I DON'T LEARN MORE BY MORNING, I'M THINKING OF CALLING THE POLICE. I WOULD TONIGHT, BUT AFTER TWO BOTTLES OF WINE, I'M PROBABLY NOT A GOOD CHARACTER WITNESS."

I replied to Winnie:

"GLAD YOU'RE SET. SORRY I MISSED YOUR CALL. NO NEWS YET. HOPEFULLY WE'LL HEAR BY MORNING. GET SOME SLEEP."

She replied immediately:

"THANK YOU FOR TRYING. SEE YOU IN THE MORNING."

When I reentered the kitchen, Sterling was standing near the bottle of merlot, the opener in place, partially in the cork, with his phone in his hand and a grim expression.

"If your phone bothers you that much, why don't you stop looking at it?" I asked.

His dark eyes met mine. "Do you have something to tell me?"

Shrugging, I retrieved the bottle of moscato from the refrigerator, pulled the stopper, and poured some of the cool, refreshing liquid into my glass. "Besides that I can't leave tomorrow, Winnie has personal things happening, and I want Reid to make my handprint activate the elevator, nothing else is coming to mind."

"How about Louisa?"

I held the rim of the wineglass at my lips, pursed and ready to drink, and then slowly I lowered the glass back to the counter. "What about Louisa?"

"When did you plan to tell me that she could go into labor at any time?"

"What the fuck?" I asked. "How do you know that?"

"I'm no expert on babies," he said, "but doesn't dilation mean that labor is imminent?"

I cocked my head to the side.

Fucker read my text messages.

"In most cases conception means labor is imminent. No one wants that shit to go on longer than nine months." My hand went to my hip. "Is there something you'd like to tell me, like why you're reading my text messages?"

"Araneae, there are things happening."

I picked up the wineglass and took a healthy swallow. My tone dripped of sarcasm. "I can be an asshole because it's all for your safety, blah, blah."

Instantly the wineglass I'd been holding was out of my hand. The room echoed with the shattering glass as the glass hit the backsplash. Crystal shards exploded while white wine splattered, dripping onto the granite countertop.

My eyes opened wide as my pulse raced. "What the actual fuck, Sterling?"

"Do I now have your goddamn attention?"

I took a step backward. "What is the matter with you?"

His jaw clenched as the tendons in his neck strung tighter. "Be ready tomorrow morning at seven. You'll be reachable by phone, mostly, and also by internet. I'm sure Winnie Douglas can handle your calls and your special meeting. When it comes to Louisa's baby, if you're allowed to go to Boulder, it will be with me or Patrick. Now either eat or don't. This conversation is done."

STERLING

*A*raneae's stare blistered through me as white wine continued to drip from the tile, pooling on the granite as crystal debris littered the counter and floor.

Fuck it.

Lorna could deal with it in the morning.

Araneae wanted to know what is wrong with me.

That was her question. My tongue was almost bitten in half as I forced myself to leave that question unanswered. In reality, there was a shit-ton of things wrong with me—right now the epicenter was the woman standing before me. Anyone else in the world would have said, "Yes, Mr. Sparrow." Even women. Fuck, they got off on the private planes and chartered yachts.

Not Araneae.

No, everything with her was a fucking fight.

"If I'm *allowed*," she said, emphasizing the word I'd used and bringing my attention to her pert lips and flushed complexion. "Fuck you, Sparrow. You are not my boss or ruler or whatever the hell you think you are. I'll go wherever I want and that includes *not* going somewhere such as to your secluded getaway tomorrow at seven in the damn morning."

I took a step closer, making a conscious effort to refrain from touching her. Right now my anger and worry were too volatile. I couldn't take the chance of not knowing my own strength, not again.

I wouldn't be my father.

"You still don't get it," I said. "Your first damn night in Chicago you were poisoned."

"You're the one who keeps telling me that I'm safe now."

"And you are when you follow the damn rules."

She took a deep breath. "So going to the birth of my best friend's baby or refusing to go with you tomorrow constitutes breaking your damn rules? What are you going to do, Sterling, because I plan to do both of those things? What is your plan, spank my ass? I'm not a child."

"I might believe you if you quit acting like one." Taking a breath, I reached for her chin bringing her velvety eyes to mine. Instead of soft suede, her orbs were filled with fire, a raging inferno. The glare directed at me let me know that I'd been the one to strike the match. My tone deepened. "Sunshine, if you disobey me on either of those things, while it goes without saying that sitting will be out of the question, you should trust me when I say that your ass will be the least of your worries."

Taking a step back from my grasp and without another word, Araneae turned on her heels, leaving her uneaten dinner on the counter, and walked out of the kitchen toward the stairs.

Fuck!

This wasn't how I planned my evening—our evening. It all went to hell after I'd made it home. I'd been on the way from the garage when Reid stopped the elevator on two. It was a code, our way to alert me that my presence was needed.

Two and a half hours ago...

As soon as the metal door opened, I was met with his and Patrick's expressions of gloom. Without a word, Reid handed me a note.

Leslie Milton.
25 years old.
Blonde/pretty – not model.
Lives in Gage Park.
Boyfriend – Praxton, Paxton, or Preston???
Phone: XXX-XXX-XXXX

"What the fuck?" I asked.

"Araneae gave that to me. It's her handwriting," Reid said.

"Why?"

How in the hell would she know anything about the woman responsible for slipping her the roofie?

How would she have this information?

Reid's nostrils flared. "Leslie was the friend of Winifred's, the one she planned to visit while here in Chicago."

"You're shitting me?"

Patrick's head shook. "Fucking small world."

I fell into one of the desk chairs, dumbfounded. The connection was a sucker punch to my gut. The incident was done. My statement had been made. The police and news-casters had done their part to make it disappear into the realm of unsolvable homicides. We'd moved on.

"I've met Winnie," Patrick said. "She's as bullheaded as some other women around this place. She's not going to let this go." He shook his head. "I know she won't. Due to the unidentifiable condition of the bodies, the names of the victims haven't been released. The Cook County Medical Examiner's Office is backlogged. Without a priority status, it could be months, if ever. Many get lost in the shuffle. But if she starts pushing..."

"It won't lead back to Sparrow, boss," Reid said.

It wouldn't.

"No," I said, "but if Araneae learns the details—not even knowing who did it—then she'll see the filth, the ugly truth of the underworld. I fucking want to keep that from her. Keep her rose-colored glasses in place."

"The most Winifred will learn," Reid said, "will be that Leslie Milton is a missing person. Praxton liked to flash cash around. Maybe he took her to some tropical island."

Patrick ran his hand over his barely visible blond five o'clock shadow as his jaw stretched. "I wasn't sure I was going to say anything, but today Winnie made Araneae uncomfort-able by asking a million questions. I didn't hear all of them, but she's inquisitive."

My eyes narrowed. "About what?"

"Everything. Ms. McCrie didn't waver, but the process was wearing on her. By midafternoon I convinced Araneae to take a trip to the docks and check on a silk shipment—get out of the office."

Shit, so her day's been as good as mine.

"Jana?" I asked.

Patrick shook his head. "Solid as a rock. After all that woman's been through, talking straight-faced to Winnie about Ms. Hawkins was as easy as telling her kid a bedtime story."

"You made the right call about her," I said. "Thanks. How long is Ms. Winifred Douglas planning to be in Chicago?"

"It was going to be until Wednesday, but they decided on the full week, so now it's until Friday," Patrick replied. "The more worked up she gets about Leslie, the more upset Araneae will become."

"I'll tell Araneae that I can't find anything," Reid suggested. "Or I'll lie and say Leslie and Praxton boarded a plane for Bora Bora."

I shook my head. "No. Would you lie to Lorna?"

"That's different. She lost her rose-colored glasses a long time ago."

"That part's different but not what matters," I said. "Araneae asked me not to lie, to tell her the truth no matter how upsetting."

"Was that about *everything?*" Reid asked.

Standing, I took a step one direction and spun, walking the other. "The promise was referring to her family, but if I lie about one thing, she'll never believe me about anything else. I won't...no." I turned toward Reid. "What happens when the bodies are identified? What happens when the authorities say that McBride and Milton were killed the beginning of last week?"

"Winnie said she talked to Leslie a while back," Patrick said. "Reid, if we can access her phone records and find out when that call occurred, we might make this work. If she spoke to Leslie prior to last Sunday night, then...I wouldn't suggest Bora Bora but who's to say that McBride and Milton didn't leave town before returning?"

"I'm not lying to Araneae," I said. They both looked at me. "I'm not telling her the truth either. I'm getting her out of town until Winnie leaves."

Patrick's head shook.

"Listen, I'm aware she won't like it. Having her here with Winnie will only make it worse."

"We'll get the plane ready," Patrick said. "Where do you want to go?"

I fucking didn't want to go anywhere. I had too many things happening. "I don't know." I looked at Patrick. "Do you have anything? She say anything around you?"

He tilted his head. "Today at the Port of Chicago, she was watching Lake Michigan. It was all sunny and breezy and shit."

I nodded. "Forget the plane. Charter a boat at the Columbia Yacht Club—something nice. Vet the crew. It's summer on Lake Michigan. Cruising now is a better idea than in the winter." That may be the only reason it was better because I was confident that being whisked away the day after her friend arrived wouldn't go over well with Araneae.

Present...

. . .

I reached for the key to the bedroom, certain it would be locked. Yet it wasn't. Pushing the door inward, I let my eyes adjust to the darkened room.

I'd waited before coming up to the room. Spending time in my office, I hoped that with time Araneae would realize that I was right. She may not understand it, but might accept that I knew what was best and that leaving town wouldn't be a big deal.

The darkened room came into view. I scanned the other doors. The closet and workout room doors were closed. The bathroom door was open and the room beyond dark.

I fucking wanted a shower, but I needed to touch her, to know she was sleeping.

As I moved closer to the bed, the slightly wrinkled covers came into view. The stacks of pillows near the headboard, the barely touched comforter. My heart beat faster as I reached for the switch on the lamp on the nearer bedside stand.

The room flooded with the soft golden light.

My pulse raced.

"Araneae."

Her name reverberated through the empty bedroom.

I rushed to the bathroom, the closet, and the workout room. Every place was dark and empty.

Damn it, Araneae, where the fuck are you?

ARANEAE

*T*ears clogged my nose and throat as I sat alone in the darkened kitchen staring out at the lights of the city through the tall windows. They were there, so was the kitchen around me, yet none of it registered. My entire body quaked with emotion as I worked to swallow the food and stop the tears. I wasn't certain if my bout of minor hysteria was caused by the cut on my finger, the fact that I was mad at Sterling, or because I was sad that the night had gone to hell.

All of the above was probably the correct answer.

Sitting at the table with a damn paper towel wrapped around my finger, I forced myself to eat. It was my growling stomach that had convinced me to come back down to the kitchen; my pride was why I snuck quietly.

I wasn't ready to face Sterling.

Not after what he'd done—the way he'd behaved.

He said I acted childishly.

Screw you, Sterling.

I didn't throw a damn glass of wine against the wall and leave the debris for someone else to deal with.

As soon as I reentered the kitchen, I was met with the visual evidence of his ridiculous behavior. You might think that the person who did the deed would have cleaned it up. He hadn't. Hell, he hadn't even put away the food or cleaned up his fucking dishes.

How hard was it to move a dish and glass from the counter to the dishwasher?

Apparently, if you possessed a Y chromosome, the answer was impossible.

Taking a deep breath, I forced myself to take another bite of the cold chicken parmesan.

How was it possible that I was hungry yet too upset to eat?

When I'd gone upstairs, I'd half expected Sterling to follow me. At the time I didn't want him to, but the fact that he didn't added to my myriad emotions. And now it was nearly midnight and he was still in his office. I'd heard him clicking away on the keyboard as I came down the stairs.

Since I was upset that he didn't come find me, I wasn't going to him. When I stepped onto the marble of the first floor in my socks, I made sure to stay quiet and keep lighting to a minimum.

I was fully aware that my way of thinking didn't make sense—I didn't want him to follow. I was mad he didn't. I wouldn't be the one to go to him. These weren't the thoughts of a rational woman.

Gah!

Sterling Sparrow had me all kinds of mixed up. Since he came into my life, I supposed that rational was the last word that could be used to describe me.

As I entered the kitchen, my sock-clad feet stopped when I saw the remains of the wineglass. With only the light from my phone, I worked to clean the broken glass and spilled wine. In my opinion, it wasn't fair to expect Lorna to do it. From the remains, that had appeared to be Sterling's plan.

It was as I was trying to collect all of the shards of crystal that a larger one became embedded in my finger. I'd been concerned about stepping on them, and instead, one of them stabbed my finger. It wasn't like I was going to bleed out or anything, but it was tender and still bleeding.

At this time of night, every sound was amplified.

I held the fork as steady as possible as my heart beat faster at the reverberating sound of Sterling's shoes in the foyer echoing throughout the kitchen. Holding my breath, I waited for him to find me or for the footsteps to move away. Step by step, I listened as he ascended the stairs until the footsteps disappeared.

Quietly, I stood and scraped the remaining food from the plate into the trash can and put my dishes in the dishwasher. Taking a deep breath, I looked up to the ceiling. Even though I wasn't sure what I'd find upstairs, the part of me that refused to be the bigger child in this argument knew that was where I needed to be. It was time to come to terms with this debacle of a night.

A quick peek under the paper towel told me that my finger was still bleeding. Holding the paper towel tighter, I wiped the tears from my cheeks and took another breath. As I rounded the corner to the foyer, his deep voice came into range as he called my name.

With my hand on the banister I took one step and then another. From the direction of his voice and the slamming of doors, he was moving around upstairs, going from room to room.

As I reached the top landing, Sterling rounded a corner, his phone at his ear, and our gazes locked.

"I found her," he said into the phone. Disconnecting the call, his voice rose. "Where the fuck were you?"

My hand went to my hip. "Oh, I'm sorry, Sterling. Is it not enough that I'm locked in the apartment, I also need to check with you before I leave the bedroom?"

His eyes closed as he turned. Even though he was still wearing his suit trousers, shoes, and white button-up shirt, he was more casual than before. The cuffs of his shirt were now rolled to below his elbows, his collar open, and tie completely gone. His hand went through his hair as he completed a full spin and our eyes again met.

The muscles of his forearm flexed as the buttons of his shirt strained at the depth of his inhale. "Araneae, come to bed. It's been a fucking long night."

I crossed my arms over my chest. "This might be one of those times you consider making an apology."

His focus went from my face to my hand and the paper towel wrapped around my finger. "What happened to your hand?"

I brought it down in front of me. "Nothing. It's fine. I just cut it."

Sterling took a step forward and seized the hand with the wounded finger. "On what?"

Biting my lip, I flinched as he unwrapped the paper towel.

"Have you cleaned this?" he asked.

"Sterling, it's fine. It's a little cut."

"It's still bleeding."

"And you say I'm perceptive."

He looked up from my wound. This time as our eyes met, both our lips curled upward, threatening a smile. The next second, he pulled me against him, my hand trapped between us.

"Wait," I said, mumbling against his chest and trying to pull away, "I don't want to get blood on your shirt."

Sighing, he didn't loosen his embrace. Beneath his starched shirt and against my ear, his heart beat in double time. "I don't give a fuck about the shirt. You were gone..." His chin came to rest on the top of my head. "It didn't make sense, yet...don't do that again."

Placing a hand on his chest, I pushed myself away and tried to peer upward. "I wasn't gone. I can't..." I sighed, refusing to go down that road again tonight. "I was downstairs eating. I noticed your plate wasn't touched."

"I lost my appetite."

Leaning back farther, I looked up at him. "I don't want to fight with you. I don't. But you need to listen to me. I have to be in the office tomorrow. The meeting I told you about is with Pauline McFadden. Her husband is a United States senator and is considering a bid for the White House. Having Pauline wear Sinful Threads would be a marketing opportunity that I can't pass up."

With each of my words, Sterling's jaw clenched tighter until the cords were once again visible in his neck.

"What is it? Why are you turning dark?"

"Dark?"

"It's what you do...your expression hardens and you...I don't know...your eyes..."

He took a deep breath, and as he did his chest pressed against me, causing my breasts to flatten. "Come to the bathroom and let me look at your finger. After all, if you cut it on the glass it's my fault. We need to talk."

Was admitting that it was his fault the same as an apology?

No, but I had the feeling that with Sterling, it was still a step in the right direction.

I didn't move. "There's more. Winnie has something going on. I don't want to leave her. I asked Reid to look into it."

"He told me." He reached for my uninjured hand. "Come this way."

Allowing Sterling to lead me, I followed as he tugged me through the bedroom and into the bathroom, hitting every switch as if he commanded the afternoon sun to shine.

I squinted, unaccustomed to so much light. "Jeez, Sterling. It's too bright."

"No, sunshine, I need to see that finger."

"It's only a cut," I said again as his hands came to my waist and he lifted me like a doll, setting me on the edge of the vanity. Then he gently reached for my wounded finger and removed the paper towel. My face scrunched as he squeezed the end of my finger, forcing out more droplets of blood. "Ouch."

His face lowered, inspecting the cut. "Let me get some tweezers. I think there's still glass in there."

I withdrew my hand. "Um, no. It's all right. Maybe I could just run it under the water more?"

"After I get the glass."

"Do you have any idea what you're doing?"

"The medics are overworked in wartime. We all did what we could." His dark gaze glistened as his lips quirked. "My superhero talents are broad and diverse. It will take years for you to witness them all."

Years?

With my lip once again between my teeth, Sterling searched through the drawers, setting out tweezers, antibiotic ointment, and a Band-Aid. Though I closed my eyes as he fished for the crystal, it didn't hurt as much as I'd thought it would. Instead, I was suddenly besieged by a new emotion.

I couldn't recall the last time someone had taken care of me—yes, there was Dr. Dixon, but she was a doctor. I then remembered Sterling's care the morning he helped me shower after the poisoning. As he tended to my finger, I was struck by the care and compassion he demonstrated. It was in stark contrast to how he behaved other times.

Perhaps he was right. It would take me years to learn all the sides of Sterling Sparrow.

When he looked up, his head tilted as his thumb came to my cheek. "I'm sorry if that hurt."

I hadn't realized that another tear had fallen until he'd wiped it away. I shook my head. "Thank you for doing it—for taking care of me."

"Someday you'll get it, Araneae. You're mine. I take care of what is mine." He lifted me from the counter allowing my feet to be back on the floor. "Wash it well, and then I'll put on the ointment and bandage."

"You're bossy," I said, looking at him in the large mirror over the vanity.

His lips came to my neck. "Get used to it."

I hated to admit it, but I was getting there—getting used to him.

Once the bandage was in place, Sterling kissed the Band-Aid.

I wrapped my arms around his toned torso and buried my face into his chest. His shirt had the lingering scent of his expensive cologne as my senses filled with musk and spice. "I meant it, Sterling, thank you. You can drive me crazy, make me angry, and then..." I looked up. "...you do something so unexpected." I sighed. "You're a complicated man."

Surrounding me in his strong arms, he rested his chin on my head. "I wish this could be the end of our night. Say we're sorry and have some great make-up sex."

Was that the apology?

I shrugged. "I'm exhausted, but I'm game."

He lifted my chin. "Sorry, we need to have that talk." He glanced at the shower stall. "I'm going to take a quick shower while you get ready for bed. I'll meet you there. Then we'll talk."

"What if I'm talked out?"

"Remember the night at the cabin when I told you there were more things to discuss and you said they could wait?"

My eyes opened wide. "Did another plane crash?"

"Not yet. That's what we need to discuss."

ARANEAE

Sterling kissed my hair before walking out of the bathroom. My mind wanted to know what he was going to say, what warranted discussion over make-up sex. My body was on the brink of not caring. After the evening we'd had, the mood wasn't exactly erotic. Tender would be a better description.

The anger and rage from downstairs had dissipated. The tenderness didn't forgive that the anger had occurred, yet the current climate counterbalanced it, much as in nature. Perhaps the night could be best equated to the calm following a storm. The atmosphere, having been volatile and explosive, rumbling with thunder as lightning strikes zigzagged through the sky, becomes quiet, the energy degenerating or becoming something else. Where there had once been clouds and flashes, the sky was now clear, the mood now peaceful and calm.

Storms served a purpose. Lightning contained nitrogen

needed in soil. Without the lightning, the soil would become unable to support the growth of plants. Man could add it chemically, yet there was nothing like a good storm to bring nature back to life.

Maybe with Sterling, they also served a purpose—a balance.

As I began to ready myself for the night, Sterling returned to the bathroom, his clothes now gone. From his reflection in the large mirror before me, I scanned him up and down— from his mussed hair to his day's worth of beard growth, down farther to his broad shoulders and defined abs. My vision halted as it scanned even lower.

Sterling may have said he wanted to talk, but his body was considering other things.

I turned around, my lip secured between my teeth as my smile grew, pulling my lip from its captivity. When our eyes met, I said, "If you want to talk, you're using the wrong technique."

His head shook. "You're killing me. But I'd bet you already knew that."

"What if I decide to join you for the shower?"

He reached for my hand. "Your Band-Aid would get wet, and all that hard work will be for nothing." After a chaste kiss to my finger, he turned away and stepped into the large shower. Steam floated through the air, rising above the glass.

Working to keep my bandage dry, I washed my face, brushed my teeth and hair, and smoothed lotion on my skin.

The humid bathroom filled with the scent of bodywash and shampoo until the hot water ceased and Sterling stepped from the enclosure. Even through the mirror, his skin glistened under the reflection of the lights upon the droplets of water slowly descending his toned body. Our eyes met in the foggy reflection.

"I hope you like what you see," he said with a grin.

I turned back to him as he wrapped a plush towel around his waist. "Was I drooling? Because I just might have been drooling."

Taking a step closer, he cupped my chin and ran his thumb under my lips. "Nope, I think you're good."

Leaving me alone, he went back to the bedroom while I finished smoothing lotion and changed into a long blue nightgown I'd left hanging on a hook.

A few minutes later, in bare feet, I padded back into the bedroom.

As the door opened, I stood for a moment and stared. Sitting in bed with his damp hair, eyes closed, and head leaned back against the headboard, was Sterling Sparrow. It almost appeared as though he was sleeping. In reality, I rarely saw him asleep. It seemed I usually fell asleep before him and woke after he'd left. Seeing him this way, for some reason, felt like a gift.

Yes, he infuriated me.

Yes, he was exasperating.

And yet in a moment like this, he was vulnerable—as vulnerable as he ever was. In the short time I'd known him, it seemed that Sterling was a man who was always on his game, always watching, always listening, and always calculating. Few people were given the ability to witness him when he wasn't *on*.

He'd told me over and over that I'd been promised to him, that I was his, and yet as I walked closer to the bed, I wondered what that really meant.

How had so much happened in the span of a few weeks?

As I climbed up the small footboard to the mattress, Sterling's eyes opened.

"I'm sorry, I was trying not to wake you," I said.

He pulled back the covers, revealing the basketball shorts that replaced the towel, as he made room for me to sit beside him. Admittedly, there was a bit of disappointment that he was wearing anything beneath the blankets.

Between that and the way he'd been in the bathroom, it seemed that he was serious about our talk.

I turned off the lamp on my side of the bed and scooted closer. The now-familiar aroma of Sterling calmed me, as spice and musk filled my senses.

He inhaled. "I love the scent of your lotions."

My smile grew. "I was thinking the same thing about you."

As he wrapped his arm around my shoulder, I laid my head on his.

"Araneae, this is one of those times we talked about."

At first, I didn't speak. We'd talked about too much to know to what he was referring and then I remembered.

Craning my neck his direction, I took in his profile as the cords in his neck tightened and his jaw clenched. I couldn't fathom what he was about to tell me, but from his mood, I knew it wasn't something that was easy for him to say.

Placing one hand on his chest, I said, "Remember your promise."

He didn't answer as he stared down at me, his eyes swirling with a battle of emotions. The fight we'd had was forgotten as I gazed back, longing to take the pain away from his eyes, to reassure him that no matter what he told me, it would be all right, but I couldn't. I didn't have that ability. I couldn't reassure him when I too was now feeling the same unease.

"You promised to be with me, to not let me learn bad things alone."

He hugged me tighter to his side. "Araneae, I'll never leave you alone, never again. You're mine. I'm yours and that means that through it all, the secrets, lies, and promises, we're a team. I hope that after you learn more about yourself and about me, you won't see me as the monster I'm capable of being."

"Sterling, you've already told me more about my life than I ever knew, then I ever would have known. I'm learning more about you every day. I can't promise the future. All I can say is for right now, this minute, though sometimes you can be overwhelming, I'm where I want to be. I'm where I feel safe and...cared for." I almost said loved.

Was that how I felt?

I lifted my chin until our lips met. The connection was a spark, a flash, a reassurance that together we were more than we could possibly be alone.

"Sunshine, you're the overwhelming one."

"Me?"

His finger tapped my nose. "You. I'm never nervous or at a loss for words. I've done things you couldn't understand and wouldn't condone. I've seen the worst of the worst. I've stared the devil in the face." He looked down at the gold ring he wore on his right hand. "And through it all, I was dead inside. Nothing is able to hurt you when you're without feelings. I've lived a large percentage of my life that way. There are few things and even fewer people whom I truly care about. Yet right now, my stomach is in knots."

"What are you going to tell me?"

"I'm going to tell you why you can't have that meeting with Pauline McFadden tomorrow."

I jumped back, away from his embrace. "No, you can tell me about my life. What you can't do is demand anything regarding Sinful Threads. I've told you that before."

He took a deep breath. "For the record, almost everyone else in the world would respond, 'Yes, Mr. Sparrow.'"

I sat taller as my head shook. "That's not my response."

His lips quirked, the tips moving upward. "I'm well aware." His hand ran through his still-damp hair. "Let me clarify. This isn't about Sinful Threads. It's about your life—your safety. You can't have that meeting with Pauline McFadden *until* you know who she is."

"She's Senator McFadden's wife."

"Will you listen to a broader biography, a deeper understanding?"

My head tilted. I didn't like that he was discussing Sinful Threads, yet he'd said the magic word that gave me hope—*will*.

"Yes," I said. "I will listen, but then the decision is mine."

Sterling nodded as I settled back against his side, fitting under his arm perfectly.

I sighed, inhaling his clean scent. "Then go on."

STERLING

*G*o on.

When she'd first come upstairs, the red patches and redness of her eyes told me that she'd been crying. I'd been the reason then, and with all of the nondormant part of my heart, I was afraid I would be again. The organ that until recently I wasn't sure existed now ached, leaving me wondering how much I could say and how Araneae would take it.

I'd been truthful about my stomach. Araneae McCrie scared me in an unfamiliar way. Though she'd been mine for nearly two decades, I was woefully unprepared for how she'd affect me, how much I would enjoy basking in her sunlight.

What will happen when she learns more of the truth?

"Sterling?" she asked, waiting for me to speak.

I swallowed. "You can't meet with Pauline McFadden."

Her body tensed in my embrace. I held her tighter. "Damn it, Araneae, listen. Just listen." I pulled her chin to me and covered her lips with mine. Damn, she tasted like toothpaste, and I wanted to eat her up, forget this conversation, and make love to her until we both fell sound asleep.

Make love?

What the fuck?

Where the hell did that come from?

I'd never used that phrase in my life. I fucked. That's what I did.

Pulling away, I looked into her eyes. "Please, listen. Like I said before, you can't meet with her *until* you know the truth about who she is."

"Then tell me because we're meeting tomorrow at eleven."

I took a deep breath. Tomorrow morning by eleven I wanted Araneae on the yacht we had chartered. I didn't want her back at Sinful Threads at all with Winnie there.

One battle at a time.

"Fuck," I began, running my free hand through my hair. "There's no easy way to say this, so I might as well jump in. You're right that Pauline McFadden is Senator Rubio McFadden's wife. You're also right that he has the exploratory committee and is currently raising campaign funds all in preparation for a presidential bid. Not that he doesn't have the funds himself, he does. Big donors attract other donors. It is a lot of smoke and mirrors."

"Normal politics. So what's the problem?"

I scoffed. "That's a loaded question. McFadden has been big in Chicago since I was a boy, even before that. He wasn't in that room with my father the first time that I saw your picture because those were all men from my father's outfit. They were all Sparrows—not genetically, but family bonds run beyond blood.

"He wasn't in that room because he has his own—his own outfit," I went on. "Do you know what I'm saying?"

Araneae laid her head on my chest as her finger traced circles on my exposed stomach. "Is that what you do?" she asked. "I mean, I suspected, but is what you're telling me like...the mob? Like Al Capone and the Godfather?"

A sad smile came to my lips. "Bad comparisons, but for the sake of understanding, yes. I never want to tell you the details, so never ask. Like I mentioned before, it's called the underground for a reason. It deserves to stay there. The old saying that crime doesn't pay was created by people who didn't do it right. With this life comes money and power...and secrets."

Sitting up, she laid her head on my shoulder as her small arm came over my chest and her fingers splayed. The soft brown of her eyes stared up at me.

"I don't want you to see me like that," I admitted.

"Sterling, I don't know what you're going to say, but the man I see right now is a man who bulldozed into my life, who turned it upside down, and who is now sharing part of his life with me, a man I doubt shares much of anything with anyone."

I closed my eyes and took another breath, saying a prayer that what she learned wouldn't change that view. "My father..." I swallowed. "...utilized his power in ways different than I. Some of the ways he chose to make money disgusted me. I'm not perfect and I oversee some shit—a lot of it. It's that his shit was worse. While I was in the army, I kept tabs on Chicago, as much as I could. I wanted to know what was happening so I'd be prepared for my return.

"I was older and stronger than the boy he'd bullied all of

my life. I saw things in the war that would either break me or make me stronger. I did things. Patrick, Reid, Mason, and I. We were unstoppable. We planned. Mason was from Chicago. He knew my family, my name."

I shook my head at the memories. "He hated me. I didn't know why. It wasn't like we grew up around one another. I figured he was jealous, but why? I came from money, but I was in the same shithole as him. At first, we butted heads about everything. If I said it was blue, he said it was black."

"It sounds like not everyone says 'Yes, Mr. Sparrow,'" Araneae said with a grin.

My cheeks rose as I scoffed. "I stand corrected." I could have told her that he was no longer alive, but it wasn't because of that. I could even say it wasn't my fault, but that would be a lie. It was better to move on.

"He and I came to blows more times than I remember. After we'd have it out, it wouldn't rid us of one another. We'd end up together on some shit punishment. Finally, one day while we were digging a hole that didn't need to be dug, covered in sweat and filth, he told me why he hated me."

Araneae's eyes began to glisten with unshed tears.

I brushed her cheek. "I'm here."

She nodded. "Go on."

"Mason's sister could have been one of those girls on my dad's computer. One day between school and home when she was nine years old, she disappeared. That would have made me about eleven. Just two years before I saw those pictures. Mason's family lived in South Chicago. It wasn't and isn't uncommon for kids to disappear. The difference was that when they went missing from certain neighborhoods no one noticed, at least no one who could help, especially if those kids weren't blonde haired and blue eyed.

"Mason was two years older than his sister. He did what he could. He searched and searched. As he got a little older, he heard rumors about different rings right here in Chicago: rich men with sick fantasies who will pay a fuck-ton of money to play them out."

"Why did he hate your name?"

I looked down at her. "Because Sparrow—my father and his men—did both. They made a fortune by supplying the means and opportunities for those sick fuckers' thrills, and when they wanted, they took their turns without giving it a second thought."

I heard one of my father's capos in my head. He was laughing and talking to my father in the dark of that office. *"...she's going to make us a fortune, that new little blonde one."*

"Did you try her out?"

Laughing.

"Hell yes. So fucking tight it made my dick hurt. Need to stretch her out and stop the bitch from bawling the whole time. It won't take long. My men will get her ready."

"We need some good pictures before she gets too used up. Once we get it online, her schedule will be too full for her to have time to cry. Work on her swallowing, too. Had a customer want a refund because one of them couldn't take him down his throat." More laughter. *"And my guess is that his dick wasn't that impressive."*

My stomach reeled at the memory.

Araneae's head was shaking as tears spilled over her lids. "Oh no. Sterling, tell me you don't—"

"No," I interrupted, wiping her cheek with my thumb. "I don't. When I was younger, there was nothing I could do about it. When I was older, I vowed I would. When I came back after the war and after Michigan, I took over Sparrow for the sole purpose of stopping it."

"So it's over? There aren't children—"

"Sparrow is no longer involved. While over in the desert, the four of us vowed to do what we could for Mason's sister, for all of them. It took time to work out the details."

Araneae sighed as she turned away, her cheek against my chest.

"As I was saying, Rubio McFadden wasn't in my father's office because the McFadden name was also well known. It still is. He's done his best to distance himself from those rumors now that his political aspirations have grown. Back then, when I was young, he was only a state senator, not a US senator. He worked the state laws to help him and his friends get richer and richer while working the local politicians and lawmakers to keep their horrors buried. Of course, there is also a legitimate front to McFadden—construction. There's a lot of money in construction. Back then, it was one of the best ways to cook the books." I shrugged. "Real estate wasn't bad either. It's harder now."

She turned her face back toward mine and sat up a little. "Wait, are you saying that this man who wants to run for the highest office in America was involved in child trafficking and exploitation?"

"That's part of what I'm saying. I'm no saint, and don't ever think I am," I said. "I run a legit company, one worth billions. I also do bad things. It's part of how I stay in power and that other life also pays well. I won't give it up or stop doing what I do. I stay in power because of Missy, Mason's sister, to exert my power to stop what happened to her."

"Is she okay now?"

I shook my head. "From my experience observing, the victims are never okay. They learn to survive, and if I can help that in any way, I do."

Araneae gasped as she sat all the way up. Her eyes opened wide as both of her hands covered her mouth.

"What is it?" I asked.

STERLING

"*J*ana...?" Araneae asked, more terror in her brown suede eyes than I wanted to see.

I was sure she was imagining horrible things —and more than likely they didn't even come close to the horror of the reality. I inhaled. "Not my story to tell."

"Oh my God, Sterling, that makes sense. She was so young when you employed her...Oh my."

I reached for Araneae's hand and pulled it to my lips, kissing the tip of her Band-Aid. "Sunshine, she doesn't like to talk about it..."

Her head was shaking. "No, I wouldn't. I never would. It's that the clues were all there and yet I never imagined."

I tilted my head. "Do you know why you never imagined, why the thought never occurred to you?"

More tears came to her eyes. "Because...how could I?"

My finger went to her cheek as I shook my head. "Because you are sunshine and light. What I'm discussing is hell and darkness. I wish you never had to know, never had to even imagine that this existed. I hate telling you about it."

"I just...I just feel so..."

"Does it change the way you feel about Jana?" I asked. "You told me you liked her."

Araneae swallowed as she collected her thoughts. "I mean, no, it doesn't change...Well, yes, I guess it does. If anything, I respect her even more. She's been through hell and now she's out. She's a great employee, a fast learner, and..." Her smile grew despite the tears. "...she loves Bailey and her husband Marcus. She brought some pictures into the office and asked if she could have them at her desk." Another tear slid down her cheek. "She's a survivor. That's fucking amazing."

I nodded. "It is. Not all the stories have happy endings and many ended way too soon like Missy." *And Mason.* I couldn't say that. I still had trouble facing it.

Araneae's head shook "McFadden can't be president. Fuck, Sterling, he shouldn't even be where he is. Oh! Does his wife know?"

"The particulars, I doubt it. My mother chose to turn a blind eye as long as her social status wasn't affected; I'd assume Pauline has done the same. The Sparrows and the McFaddens have never—in my lifetime—seen eye to eye."

"Expose him. You have power, you can do that."

"It's different today. Reid's good, but most of this shit is encrypted on the dark web and McFadden's stepped away from any direct connection. It's not like it was twenty-six years ago."

"Twenty-six years ago..." she said. "This is the information that my father knew."

"You're not asking."

Araneae shrugged. "Am I right?"

"Remember I said he—Daniel McCrie—was a fixer. I was too young to understand, but from overhearing things and research, we've put together that your father stumbled upon the trafficking rings. There was even a raid of his office by the FBI not long before you were born. He never was forced to testify, so he didn't have any evidence hidden there or at his home."

"We've been able to confirm some of this, like the raid, by scouring old records, newspapers, and public documents. Those sources don't tell the whole story. Other parts have been pieced together. Your father figured if he didn't tell the FBI, he would be able to leverage his knowledge as power over his biggest client, McFadden.

"The proof of involvement in the rings was believed to have been what he knew. He's gone now and the rumors were that somehow he left the evidence with you."

"Was his evidence against the McFaddens or the Sparrows?"

"No one knows for certain," I replied. "The way the story played out, I'd say for sure the McFaddens."

"Why would he go to them and tell them he had evidence that could hurt them?"

It was my turn to shrug. "Why do people do what they do? It's usually for money, power, or pussy," I answered honestly. "I would suspect McCrie's plan was to offer the evidence to Rubio in exchange for one or more of the above."

"And McFadden didn't take it?" she asked.

"Araneae, there's a lot we don't know. Things discussed in dark rooms are rarely recorded. All we can do is hypothesize and then meld that with the facts we've been able to unearth.

"I remember hearing my father say that McCrie owed him," I said. "My father and those men in that office knew that you were alive—they were confident. That was when you were with the Marshes. He had your picture—not just that one. He'd get them periodically. That first picture that I saw of you was why you were given to me—why you're here now. It would fit that somehow my father helped hide you and because of that debt, your father owed him."

Araneae shook her head. "My mom, I mean Josey Marsh, said that she was old friends with my birth mother— Annabelle. It's still strange to have a name. Josey told me to never come back to Chicago because of your father and you, not because of anyone named McFadden. And besides, you said my father worked for McFadden. Why would he go to a Sparrow for help?"

I wasn't ready to take the Marshes road with her yet, to tell her they only existed when she was with them, and now they're gone.

"Like I said," I went on, steering the conversation, "we don't know for sure. We've made some giant leaps in our theories. Sometimes they can be proven, other times they're left with nothing more than speculation. The intricacies of what my father knew died with him over six years ago. Most of the players from that time, those in the Sparrow outfit, are dead or reassigned. Some secrets stay hidden for a reason. If the information your father had included implications against the Sparrow outfit, it could affect Sparrow Enterprises. Nevertheless, time has passed. My father is gone. We would weather the storm better than McFadden. He was a key player. His political career would go up in smoke."

Her eyes narrowed. "Is that why you found me and

brought me here? Not for me but for evidence? If I had it and you found it, you'd be in complete control of what was disseminated. You could release the shit on him, but not on your father."

I exhaled. "That possibility was why I never gave up on the idea that you were mine. Those times when your fucking eyes looked so damn innocent, when my world was covered in crimson and I hated everyone, when I knew I didn't deserve to have sunshine in my life, I didn't stop watching and waiting for you, and yes, I'd be lying if I said it wasn't also because you were a possible means to bringing down McFadden."

Araneae's neck straightened. "I don't have it. I don't—and didn't—know anything. So let me go, forget about me. I'm not what you wanted."

I reached out, gently seizing both of her hands and pulling her closer. The scent of vanilla and gardenias surrounded us. "I couldn't let you go if I wanted to, and fuck, Araneae, I don't want to. I still don't deserve you—I never will. Stories like this are darkening your light, but I meant it when I said you're mine. I'm never letting you go."

"Even though I'm useless? I don't have what you need."

I ran my finger over her cheek, over her jaw, down her slender neck, and stopping at her collarbone. "*You* are exactly what I have wanted since I was thirteen years old. And from the moment I had you in my grasp, in that office in the fucking distribution center, I knew without a doubt that you, Araneae McCrie, were the only person on this earth who I needed."

She sighed and lay back down, again resting her cheek against my chest. "This is so much."

"Over the years McFadden heard the same rumors about

your existence. However, like everyone else, he'd been told you died after birth. My father and his trusted crew were the only ones who knew you were alive. McFadden only heard talk. We believe something happened on your father's end when you were sixteen, something that precipitated your hasty departure from Chicago."

"Why would they hide me here? That doesn't make sense."

"My guess was to make it easier for my father to keep an eye on you, assure that his hold over you remained solid."

Araneae shook her head.

I went on, "Now that you're confirmed alive and real, Reid, Patrick, and I believe that McFadden may think that you have the information. He no doubt believes what you just said, that I found you, raised you from the dead to bring him down. If that's the case, you're a threat to his future. Only someone with his power and money could crash-land a 737 full of passengers."

"But," she began, "I sat with him and his wife at that dinner?"

"That was a week before. At that point, he hadn't put it together that Kennedy Hawkins was also Araneae McCrie. He sure as hell didn't expect to meet you at an event for a fashion retailer. Later, with the plane crash and fire at your apartment, he'd learned in concept. Your name was being whispered. He was hedging his bet to stop you from coming forward. Then his suspicions became reality when you and I walked into the club and he saw you."

"Why was my mother with him instead of his wife?"

"The easy answer is that she's his sister-in-law."

Araneae sat back up. Damn, she was like a bobber tossed in the waves of Lake Michigan.

Her eyes stared my way as her complexion paled to a ghostly hue. "He's my...uncle?"

"Pauline McFadden's maiden name was McCrie."

"The woman who wants to meet with me tomorrow is my aunt, my father's sister?" When I didn't respond, she went on, "And my uncle wants me dead?"

"He wants you silenced. I'll never let him get close to you."

Araneae laid her head back down and pulled my arm over her like a shield. That was what I wanted to be, a shield to keep this world away from her.

"What's the hard answer?" she asked, looking up.

"What hard answer?"

"You said that my mother being his sister-in-law was the easy answer. What is the hard one?"

I stroked her yellow hair, moving silky strands away from her face. "Since your father has been...gone, Rubio and Judge Landers have spent more time together. A federal judge is appointed; the nomination usually comes from a government official. McFadden nominated your mother."

She nodded.

My chest expanded and contracted. "There's more." Her eyes opened wider. "They've spent more time together socially and privately."

"How privately?"

I shrugged.

"But that's his...he's her...that's...eww. It's disgusting."

I turned to the clock. "Sunshine, we have five hours until our getaway."

"Sterling, postpone it one day."

"You can't meet—"

Araneae scooted to her pillow and turned my way, reaching up and touching my lips with the tips of her fingers. "You can be at my office if you want. Patrick will be there. I don't care if you want the entire Chicago Police Department surrounding the building, but I'm meeting with Pauline McFadden. I want to know if this is really about Sinful Threads or if it's about a family reunion."

Damn, couldn't she for once say "Yes, Mr. Sparrow?"

One fucking time?

I slid down under the blankets until our faces were even. As much as she infuriated me with her stubbornness, as I looked at her angelic face, her golden halo of hair on her pillow, I was in awe of her strength. "You don't need to do that. You don't owe her a damn thing."

"You're right." Her hand cupped my cheek. "Sterling, I want to. When it comes to this getaway, I'm saying not yet. You promised that you'd listen to me. Give me one day."

Fuck promises.

"One day," I said, hating myself for agreeing to her demands while at the same time knowing that doing so was the best for us...yet also afraid it would be the worst for Araneae. "We're leaving Wednesday morning. No other delays."

Araneae leaned in and kissed my cheek. "One more thing."

My lips came together in a straight line. So help me, if she mentions the damn sensor...

"I need to tell Winnie and Louisa about you—something."

"We decided that keeping Sinful Threads—"

Her finger again came to my lips. "No, Sterling. You decided, or you and Patrick and Reid. My point is that I didn't decide." Before I could respond, she went on. "I agree that I can't do business as Araneae McCrie. In the eyes of the law, I don't exist. My birth certificate, according to what you've told me, says I'm deceased. Kennedy Hawkins will remain the cofounder of Sinful Threads. However, today, Winnie insinuated—and I understand why—that I was acting out of character and perhaps I was skimming—"

"Skimming? Are you fucking kidding me?"

"No. That's what friends do. They call you out when you suddenly move away and start wearing clothes that cost a month's salary. Real friends ask questions."

"Real friends would know that you wouldn't do that."

"You're right," she said. "That's why they're concerned." Araneae sighed. "I'm not sure how much to tell them now. The entire story is confusing and I'm in the damn middle of it. I think, just that I met you and we hit it off—you swept me off my feet."

A smile curled on my lips. "Is that what we did—hit it off?"

Her slender shoulder shrugged, causing the spaghetti strap to slide down. "I could tell them that you blackmailed me into moving to Chicago, kidnapped me over the border, and have kept me locked away in your glass tower when I'm not at work under the constant supervision of your henchman."

A small laugh resonated from my throat. "I think hit it off is currently the best option."

"So you approve?"

"Well, sunshine, since I'll be with my henchman tomorrow at your office, we need to say something."

She leaned in and kissed my lips. "Good night, Sterling."

I doubted I'd get much sleep.

ANNABELLE

Twenty-six years ago

*B*owing our heads against the wind and swirling snow, Daniel and I stepped from the warmth of the diner. The icy accumulation continued to fall around us as we trudged through the parking lot, our boots sliding, unstable within the frozen precipitation as we made our way to the rental car. Peering beyond the blowing and drifting snow, many more inches had accumulated since we entered the diner. Its heavy weight bowed the pine branches—a rather beautiful sight if I weren't so worried about getting back to Chicago.

The exit to the parking area was hidden, buried beneath the blanket of white. The only indication that the road back to the motel still existed were the quickly filling grooves of tire tracks.

As the car warmed, I fastened my seat belt around our

baby. "I need to get to Chicago, to Dr. Jacobs," I said as calmly as I could muster.

"What did she say when you called her from the diner's pay phone?"

"She said to try to relax. Officially, I'm not due for two and a half weeks, and the Braxton-Hicks contractions have been going on for a few weeks. They may be nothing to worry about. She said to try to walk through them. Braxton-Hicks fade where real ones grow stronger."

Daniel forced a smile my direction as he shifted the car into reverse. "Then that's what we'll do, Annie. We'll walk."

The tires spun, not finding traction.

"Around that tiny motel room?"

"Yes, if that's what we need to do."

"Maybe there's a doctor who can come to the hotel, or better yet, a hospital nearby?"

"When we get back to the motel..." The car was finally moving, albeit slowly and unsteadily. "...I'll ask in the office."

As my midsection contracted, I closed my eyes and counted. This one lasted longer than others, forcing me to tighten my muscles and exhale as I'd been taught in the classes at the hospital.

Relax.

That's what Dr. Jacobs said.

When my eyes opened, Daniel was staring out to the whiteness. "I'm sorry. This was a mistake. I'd take you home, but damn, I can't even see the road."

The trees lining the sides were a help. However, when we'd arrived, I recalled seeing ravines on either side of some of the roads. Covered now in snow, they were small valleys waiting to lure us into their depths. "Please stay on the road."

My labor began around two in the morning. Not that I'd been sleeping well, but the pain woke me. Crying out, I reached for Daniel.

He'd spent the better part of the evening and into the morning walking laps with me. Each time we did, the contraction lightened, just as Dr. Jacobs had promised.

"This one is different," I said with tears in my eyes. The pain wasn't concentrated to my midsection, but around my body to my lower back.

Daniel reached for the telephone on the bedside stand.

"It doesn't work," I reminded him as panic bubbled within me.

"I'm going back to the office," he replied. "That girl said there was a small hospital less than twenty miles away."

Tears bubbled in my throat and nose. "I don't want a small hospital. I want University Hospital. I want Dr. Jacobs. I want a NICU unit if we need one. Daniel, we have to get back to Chicago."

I threw back the cover. I wasn't sure how I hadn't realized what had happened. Perhaps my mind was too full to process. Nevertheless, the sight before me stilled my rapid heartbeat. The sheet and my nightgown were saturated. "Oh God. My water broke." A moment later I was doubled over, crying out as the biggest contraction yet pulled at my body, squeezing me and our daughter. "Go!" I screamed. "Get help."

Hurriedly pulling up his trousers while simultaneously pushing his feet in boots and wrapping a coat around his shoulders, Daniel nodded.

From my position, as he opened the door, the night sky was black beyond the lights of the parking area.

Thank God. The snow had stopped. "Daniel," I called before the door shut. He stopped and looked back. "Call Rubio, he could send a helicopter or something."

Daniel's Adam's apple bobbed as he nodded again.

"Araneae," I said, after the door closed, leaving us alone. "Baby..." Tears covered my cheeks. "Mommy's here. You're coming to see us soon. We love you."

My feet went to the dirty carpet as I tried to stand, but before I could, the next contraction dropped me to a squatting position. I tightly gripped the wet bedsheets. My fingers fisted as I suppressed a scream, instead groaning with the pain.

Perspiration coated my skin like an adhesive, gluing my nightgown against me as I exhaled and exhaled again. Panting, I tried to find the thoughts to help me through this, to transport me from a dirty motel room to a better place.

What came to mind weren't memories but visions of what was to come: a beautiful, healthy baby girl, wrapped in a pink blanket, lying in my arms. I envisioned a faint soft yellow crown of hair, taking after me, and while I loved Daniel's blue eyes, in my mind's eye, our daughter also had my eyes, soft brown like cream swirled into a cup of coffee. In my mind, I unwrapped the blanket as Araneae's gaze stayed fixed to my voice—the one she'd heard while inside me—and I counted her wiggling fingers and toes. Her fingers were tiny, yet long and slender with perfect little fingernails. True to her name, her grip was as strong as an infant vise.

When the pain subsided, I fell to the floor and cradled my hardened midsection. "We're going to be okay," I said aloud, "because you are strong. You are resilient. You are a fighter. Did you know," I asked my soon-to-be-born daughter, "that based on density, a spider's web is five times stronger than steel?" I rubbed my ballooning midsection. "That's right, Araneae, stronger than any man-made substance. That's what you can do, what you're capable of doing, baby girl. Whatever you create will be stronger than anyone else's creation."

The door behind me opened as Daniel and cool air rushed in. I peered over the bed.

"Annie, the local volunteer fire department is coming. They said they can get you to St. Michael's hospital. It's not too far."

"Dr. Jacobs?" I asked as my eyes overflowed with tears.

"I called her. She said she'll get there as soon as she can."

I screamed out again as the pain returned, scrambling to my feet, my knees bent, bearing down. "Oh please, she's coming."

They said that different people's bodies responded differently to pain. The agony of childbirth was a natural process, one that women have endured for ages. It wasn't that I couldn't or wouldn't. There was nothing I wouldn't do for our daughter. It was that as urgent and imminent as Araneae's birth had been at the motel, once we made it to the rural hospital, the labor continued and continued.

Daniel fed me ice chips between contractions and placed cold compresses on my forehead. A few minutes of sleep would provide the strength to endure the next intense contraction. Yet through it all, the dilation stalled. Even without pain medication, I wasn't progressing. I'd seen the concern in the nurse's eyes.

It was afternoon the next day, in a small hospital room

when Dr. Millstone, an older gentleman, came to my bedside.

"Mrs. McCrie, it's time. We need to make some decisions."

"What kind of decisions?"

"I've spoken to Dr. Jacobs. She told me that she mentioned that based on the baby's weight and your pelvis, a cesarean section may be necessary."

Though Dr. Millstone's face blurred with my tears, none fell. I had none left. "I want to do this. Please, I can keep going."

"You can," he said, his hand covering mine. "However, over the last hour, your daughter's vitals have declined."

"Declined?"

"She's not at a state of critical stress yet, but I feel that with your history, the baby's size, and what I've witnessed, she could be very soon. This is for her."

I turned toward Daniel with a mixture of emotions in my eyes. I wanted and needed his support. I wanted to be confident that whatever decision we made could be lived with by both of us. Within my gaze was also pain, not physical but emotional. I didn't want to blame him for this situation, but I did. He was the one that put greed before his family, ushering a dangerous chain reaction into our lives. He was the one who brought me to nowhere, to a hospital without a neonatal intensive care unit and thus had me away from Dr. Jacobs.

"May I speak to Dr. Jacobs?" I asked.

"Of course," Dr. Millstone said. "We'll get the call connected."

A few minutes later I heard her voice through the telephone receiver.

"Annabelle, tell me how you're feeling."

"Scared," I answered honestly. "I'm afraid for Araneae and..." I didn't want to sound selfish, but it was the truth. "...for me, too."

"Your blood pressure is high. It's much higher than what we want. The concern is that your water broke over twelve hours ago. Though we don't usually worry about sepsis until twenty-four hours, I'm not confident of the conditions you've been in since it broke. And more importantly, Araneae's heart rate has slowed significantly."

"I'm nervous. If this had to happen, I wish that you were here to do it." My tears were again flowing.

"Me too. The state of emergency is still in effect. The roads north of the state line remain closed until they can remove more snow. The temperature is rising, so it shouldn't be more than a day. Once I can get to both of you, you know I will."

I nodded, swallowing more tears. "Our daughter can't wait for that, can she?"

"No, Annabelle, I don't believe she can."

My sad eyes went to my husband as I nodded.

I'd heard stories about women being awake and alert during their C-section. That wasn't what happened. They explained that it was because of my blood pressure. Witnessing the procedure could cause it to spike. That would be bad for both Araneae and for me. The last thing I recalled after the medication going into my arm was changed was Daniel's voice as his hand squeezed mine.

"I'm going to be here, Annie. You're going to wake up to our daughter."

There were no preparations that could have been made for what greeted me as my eyes finally opened. As if waking from a bad nightmare, I had recollections: voices, a baby's cry, commotion, and beeps. They all blended together—a kaleidoscope of sounds and images, unable to find its true pattern.

My hands flew to my midsection, no longer enlarged, my flesh was tender.

I tried to sit upward to see the room and find the small bassinet containing our daughter. Yet nothing was different than when I'd been in labor other than that the trays of equipment were gone and I was now alone.

Other than the beeps from the machines behind me, the room was silent.

"Daniel?" I called out, repeating his name over and over, each time louder and more frantic than the last.

Finally, the door opened inward.

The world as I wanted it disappeared in a new shower of tears.

My husband didn't need to tell me what had happened. The grief was written on his face—a neon sign blinking with intensity. Not only was it written on his face, but telegraphed through his body language. My husband's usually broad, proud shoulders were bowed forward in defeat.

"No...no..." The word echoed through the room as he came to me, wrapping his arms around me.

"Annie, I'm so sorry. They tried everything—"

I fought back, slapping at his chest, his face, anywhere I could connect. "This is your fault. I hate you... I hate you... this is all your fault..."

He didn't stop me, taking all I gave him.

His decisions had led us here.

The *here*—life without our daughter—was not a place I was confident we could ever return from, not as a couple. Our dreams of a family were gone.

"I hate you..." My words and phrases lost steam as my entire body, wracked with sobs, collapsed against his chest. Daniel held me as I cried for the loss of our daughter, our marriage, and our life's dream. Wiping my tears and nose, I sat straighter. "I need to see her."

"Ann-ie..." He elongated my name.

"I have to say goodbye." I looked up to his eyes. "Did you hold her?"

Daniel nodded.

"Was she..." I had trouble forming the words. "...alive?"

His Adam's apple bobbed. "She was gone so fast. We all wanted her to stay, but..." He shook his head. "...it wasn't meant to be."

My chest ached, physically ached. I fought the urge to look down, to see if there was bodily evidence of my broken heart because the way it felt, the once-beating organ had been ripped from my chest.

"How can you say that?" I asked. "Of course, she was meant to be. She was conceived in love. She was who we wanted." My sobs returned. "Oh God...she was meant to be."

Daniel's head shook. "The things I've done. Maybe God knew she wouldn't be safe."

"She would have been!" My voice grew louder, a madwoman on the brink of a breakdown. "I would have done anything to keep her safe."

"So would I. I'm sorry."

"I want to see her," I repeated.

"I think it's better if you don't."

"I don't give a shit what you think." My body shook as the door opened inward.

"Ms. McCrie, you need to settle down." It was a nurse I didn't recognize, yet she was dressed in scrubs.

I reached out to her. "Please, let me see my daughter, my Araneae. I need to hold her. Let me hold her."

Daniel shook his head as he stood from the edge of the bed where he'd been seated. "I can't do this again."

Ignoring him, I kept my eyes on the woman beside the bed. "Please." Swallowing my tears, I forced a smile. "I named her after a spider. I-it..." I hiccupped my words. "...was to make her strong and resilient. Please..."

She squeezed my hand. "Let me see if we can."

I nodded.

Once I was alone in the room, Araneae was brought to me and placed in my arms.

I unwrapped the blanket as I'd imagined doing. However, instead of counting wiggling fingers and toes, I gazed down at the perfection of her. Proportionate and even plump, the only thing missing from her was life. I stroked her hair, darker than what I'd imagined. Though I couldn't see her eyes, I envisioned light brown. Tears streamed down my cheeks as I stroked her cold skin. "Baby, I'm sorry. You will always be my angel."

When the nurse returned I asked, "What will happen to her?"

"That's up to you. The county examiner will retrieve her, and then she can be taken by a funeral home to Chicago for a service.

I shook my head.

"Ma'am, your husband..."

My neck straightened. "This is *my* decision. There won't be a service in Chicago. I'd like to call Minister Watkins at the Methodist Church in Cambridge. They have a small graveyard there." *One I remembered from our wedding.* I didn't say that part.

The nurse nodded and smiled a sad smile as she took Araneae away.

When my phone rang, I answered, speaking with the minister. I wanted a small service, whatever provisions were best for Araneae's soul and nothing for show. I wasn't up to accepting the false condolences of others. There was no one —unless they'd experienced this devastation—who could understand.

As I hung up the phone, the nurse returned. Looking her in the eye, I asked, "May I ask you one favor? Please, this is special."

"Anything, Mrs. McCrie."

I'd never taken Daniel's name, yet at the moment, it wasn't a concern.

I reached for my wrist, the one still wearing the bracelet Minister Wilkens had given to Daniel for Araneae. Unclasping the latch, I let it fall into the palm of my hand. The small locket now held the place her earthly body would remain, and the key represented what the minister had said: Araneae McCrie would forever hold the key to my heart.

I handed the bracelet to the nurse. "If it's not too late, will you be sure this stays with Araneae?"

She looked down at the gold charm bracelet I'd placed in her hand. "Is it special?"

I looked for a name tag, but there was none. "I'm sorry. What's your name?"

"Josey."

"Yes, Josey, the bracelet is special. I would like it buried..." The word brought more tears. "...with my angel. I want her to have something to remember her mother."

ARANEAE

"How are you feeling?" I asked Louisa from my phone before Patrick and I left for my office.

When I woke, as per usual, I was alone with a note in Sterling's scrolling script, telling me that he would be to my office by ten thirty. If I was ever going to do as Lorna suggested and tell him how I felt about him before he left each day, it seemed I'd need to do it before I fell asleep.

"The same." Her voice was without its normal pep.

"You sound..."

Louisa feigned a laugh. "I know. Jason said the same thing. I think I'm tired."

I took a deep breath. "I needed to call you and talk about something."

"What is it?"

"I guess, first, it's an apology."

"For what, Kennedy?"

"I haven't been one hundred percent truthful with you or

Winnie." I kept speaking, afraid if I stopped I would chicken out. "There was another reason I chose to move to Chicago. It wasn't all for Sinful Threads."

"What's happening? What reason?"

Was she crying?

"Lou, please don't be upset. It's not a bad thing."

"I'm sorry, Kenni. I'm just so damn emotional. Commercials make me cry. I can't listen to music. Every song has me sobbing."

That made me chuckle. "When I was here for the dinner at the Riverwalk..."

"Yes?"

"I met someone."

"Was this a good or bad meeting? I'm thinking of your wives' tale."

Well, shit. That's a loaded question.

"It was a surprise meeting," I said. "I was intrigued and wanted to learn more about him."

"Him!" Louisa said excitedly. "Does this him have a name?"

"He does. His name is Sterling Sparrow."

Noises came through the receiver. "I think I may have misheard you. Can you repeat that name?"

"I know it's crazy. It's been a bit of a whirlwind." I recalled Sterling's and my conversation last night. "We hit it off, Lou. He swept me off my feet. I don't know what else to say. I was afraid to mention it. You know how I am with men."

"They're all assholes?" she said with a laugh.

At least I'm consistent.

"I do have a track record. However, yesterday, I knew it was time to come clean with you two. Winnie questioned me, asking about my clothes, and well, I knew it was wrong to keep this from you two, especially you. You're my best friend. I was...I don't know—scared. Besides, I figured you had enough on your plate."

A deep sigh resonated through the phone. "Kenni, I'm relieved. I'm thrilled. I need to process, and I definitely need to meet him because I don't care if he's some rich, handsome dude—yes, of course I've seen his picture in news and on TV —he needs to pass the Louisa test."

How did she recognize his name as someone newsworthy when initially I only thought of Josey's warning?

I laughed.

"That doesn't mean that I'm not mad that you kept this from us," she went on, "but I guess I understand. Are you seeing him now, like officially dating?"

My lips turned upward as I recalled our date the other night. "Yes, we're dating. I moved in with him."

"You what?"

"Like I said...swept me off my feet."

Louisa's tone softened. "Oh my God! Do you love him? Is that even possible this fast? Maybe love at first sight?"

I weighed her question. Louisa had been my best friend for nearly ten years since we met at St. Mary of the Forest. She deserved honesty. I was done with lies and half-truths. I wanted to be as straightforward as I could be. "I think I might. It wasn't love at first sight. Sterling is the kind of man who grows on you." My smile grew as I said aloud things I hadn't even admitted to myself. "I know I care about him. I worry about him. I want to spend time with him. I'm not used to having someone to come home to, not like you and

Jason, and I have to admit that I like it—a lot. He brings things out of me that I never imagined."

I meant emotions, not solely orgasms, although he does bring those too.

"Oh…" She said between gasps of breath. "I-I'm so happy for you."

"Babe, are you crying again?"

"Y-yes, sobbing actually. This is worse than the coffee commercial."

I shook my head with a smile. "Please don't tell Winnie. I'll tell her today at the office."

"I miss you," Louisa said. "But I feel better knowing you're not alone."

"I love you."

"Love you back," she said. "Thanks for finally telling me."

"I'm sorry it took me so long. It all happened very quickly. Give Jason my love and when Little Kennedy is ready to see us all, I better be the person you call after Jason and Lucy."

"You'll be first. They're closer."

When I disconnected the call, it was as if half the weight of the world had been lifted from my shoulders. The other half would be waiting for me at the office.

A half hour later, as I was talking with Lorna and finishing my breakfast, Patrick and Reid entered the kitchen.

"Are you ready, Araneae?" Patrick asked.

My cheeks rose higher at the use of my first name. "Almost." I turned to Reid. "Were you able to find out anything about Winnie's friend Leslie?"

His lips came together. "I'm usually very good at this. She seems to have gone off the radar. There's been no activity on her credit cards, and her cell phone is off. I can't even ping it."

"That's strange. Don't you think?"

Reid shrugged his wide shoulders. "Sometimes people decide to take a break from connectivity and go off the grid. It's hard to speculate their reasoning."

I nodded. "I'd forgotten, Winnie said that Leslie's social media accounts were also gone."

"I'm sorry, Araneae. I can keep looking."

"If my man can't find her," Lorna said, "that girl wants to be hidden."

"I wonder why?" I shook my head. "Well, thanks for trying. I'll tell Winnie. It does seem strange, but Leslie must have her reasons."

A collective hum filled the kitchen with everyone's agreement.

"One more thing, Reid," I said.

"Yes?" he answered as more of a question.

"I think it's time to make my hand do the elevator sensor."

His eyes opened wide as he and Patrick exchanged a sideways glance.

"Well..." Patrick said. "...Sparrow or I are usually with you."

"Seriously, it's like all three of you share a brain." I pointed my finger at both men. "This conversation is not over. I don't care what Sterling said. It will happen."

Both men's lips quirked. It was Patrick who spoke first. "For the record, and I'll deny this if you say a word, but if we're taking bets, my money's on you."

My cheeks rose. "Thank you. I'm glad someone has faith in me."

"I'll put ten on Araneae, too," Lorna chimed in.

"Shall we go?" Patrick asked.

"We shall," I answered, "since I can't operate the damn elevator."

As upsetting as the stupid sensor thing was, as Patrick and I walked to the hidden elevator and he placed his hand over the sensor, a smile tugged at my lips. It wasn't because of the lack of ability or that I had no choice but to need him.

It was because I genuinely enjoyed my new friends. There was a relaxed atmosphere that we shared. Once the doors shut and we began descending toward the garage, I thought about Louisa's test for Sterling. If I had to pass a test with Sterling's closest friends, as I looked up at Patrick, I'd say I'd passed.

The only one left to include in my newfound honesty was Winnie.

ARANEAE

I stared across my desk as the silence in my office grew. Seconds ago, I'd finished telling Winnie the same story I'd told Louisa. However, instead of excited, Winnie appeared to be in a state of shock, staring at me with her mouth agape as if I had grown bunny ears and a tail.

Okay, that description was because of her 'sugar daddy' comments yesterday. The longer she looked at me, the more I felt like I should be dressed like a 1960's Playboy Bunny. However, for the record, "Yes, Mr. Sparrow" was still not in my vocabulary. He was not old enough to be my daddy—and ever calling him that was just gross.

"So now you know," I said, trying to sound lighthearted and carefree, "the other reason why I moved to Chicago."

I looked down at the clothes I was wearing, a professional yet stylish two-tone beige dress with an asymmetrical neckline that rivaled yesterday's in quality and price. My stockings were thigh-high and sheer, and instead of Louboutin, I wore shoes from Gianvito Rossi—definitely out of Kennedy's price range. Hell, their price tag would probably pay my rent in Boulder.

Honestly, I'd chosen my attire with Pauline McFadden in mind, not Winnie.

"And also about my clothes," I added. "I promise, no skimming."

"S-Sterling Sparrow, the real estate mogul?" she asked as if she'd finally found her voice. "The one whose name is on a building here in Chicago as well as New York? The one who was on the Forbes list of wealthiest people in the United States? The one whose picture looks like he could be a model or movie star while at the same time a bit intimidating. The one who—"

"Yes," I interrupted. "The same one."

"You just met him?" Her questions were coming rapid-fire. "How did you happen to meet Sterling Sparrow? Was it at that dinner you went to? I saw the guest list. I don't recall his name on it...but then again, things were strange that day. My phone went missing and then I found it in my apartment, and I swear I'd had it with me. I thought I was losing my mind."

"Your phone went missing?" I asked, remembering the missed calls from her about the incident at the distribution center. Patrick had said she'd called him. "Did you call me that night, the night of the dinner to tell me or Patrick something?"

She shrugged. "I don't remember if I called you. I would remember if I called him."

My breasts pushed against the front of my dress as I sat taller and took a deep breath, my mind filling with thoughts about that first meeting with Sterling. I supposed I knew once it was over that the incident at the distribution center was all a ruse and Winnie wasn't involved in my arranged meeting with Sterling. In all the craziness, I hadn't confirmed it.

"Kenni, I'm...I'm happy for you. It's...I wasn't expecting it." She looked up, her bright blue eyes a kaleidoscope of questions and emotions and her complexion a bit pale. "Are you happy?"

My cheeks rose as my smile blossomed. "I am, most of the time. I'll be honest, he can be maddening and he can be incredible." I ran my thumb over my finger covered by a new Band-Aid.

"So," Winnie said, "you're saying that he can be a man?"

Yes, Sterling was all man. Of that, I was confident.

"Pretty much," I admitted. "I also wanted to let you know that my friend came up cold on Leslie. From what I understand, he's very good at this kind of thing. He said her cyber trail went cold. No use of credit cards. No cell phone. And you said her social media is gone."

"Hmm," she said as if in deep thought. "Okay...If I hadn't told her I was coming, I wouldn't think twice about this. Leslie can be flaky."

"My friend said sometimes people want off the grid."

Winnie nodded. "That seems like something she may do. Well, I'll be back. After this week, I'm commuting —remember?"

"Hopefully, the next time, she's back on the grid." I swallowed. "Also, I know I mentioned the meeting with Mrs. McFadden, but I've decided I want to feel her out on my own first. Then if she's interested, bring you and Louisa in on the next conversation."

Winnie nodded. "Jana did say the senator's wife wanted to speak directly to you."

"And," I added, "Sterling may be by the office this morning. He's trying to convince me to go away this week, saying that since you're here, I could let you handle Chicago."

"This must really be...real," Winnie said as she stood. "I mean, when has anyone convinced you to step away from work?" She twisted the Sinful Thread bangle on her wrist. "Kenni, I was wondering about that Franco Francesca guy."

"What about him?"

"Louisa has kept me up to date. She hired him, but she said you don't like him. I've met him before, but I thought maybe while I was in town, I could give him a surprise visit."

I scoffed. "He should be expecting us by now. I've given him a few." I thought about her offer. "It never hurts to get another opinion."

She looked at the watch on her wrist. "If I hurry, I might be able to meet with him and still make it back to meet your man...I mean, since you don't need me for Mrs. McFadden."

"Jana will be here. Everything should be fine."

"You're right about her. She's a fast learner."

Two hours later, after completing the second call with the buyers from both Saks Fifth Avenue and Neiman Marcus about Sinful Threads dresses, I leaned back in my chair as the energy of the office shifted. It was strange how discernible it was, as if a warm and cool front collided, the ripples reverberating through the air almost as tangibly as literal straight-line winds. I sat straighter as I heard, through the mostly closed door, the sound of Jana's voice welcoming Sterling.

"Hello, Mr. Sparrow."

"Jana..." His deep voice rumbled through me, reminding me of the question both of my friends asked: *Are you happy?*

If it were an all-or-nothing answer, I would have to choose yes. That didn't mean I didn't get mad and that last night, I wasn't sad. However, wasn't that the way a real relationship worked? Those moments made the good ones better.

Instead of getting up, I waited until Jana knocked.

"Yes."

"Ms. Hawkins, Mr. Sparrow is here to see you."

With my arms crossed over my chest and a Cheshire-cat grin, I replied, "Please let him know that I'll see him in a few minutes."

Her eyes opened wide.

Sterling's voice came from behind the door. "Thank you, Jana, I'll take it from here."

I was more accustomed to Sterling's casual dress at the apartment. Watching him walk through the doorway in his custom silk suit, suit coat unbuttoned, crisp white striped shirt and a dark blue tie matching the stripes, was as Winnie had described him. Sterling Sparrow could be a model. However, the gleam in his eyes was the opposite of his intimidating stare. It wasn't that he couldn't give one. It was that at the moment, he wasn't giving that to me.

The look shining my direction did things to my body, tightening recently overused muscles and causing them to beg for more.

"Ms. Hawkins." The name he'd never called me rolled off his tongue as he closed the door behind him.

"Mr. Sparrow," I replied, standing to meet him.

Reaching for my hand, he leaned away, scanning me from the tips of my shoes to my blonde hair. His burning gaze roamed painfully slowly, leaving a trail of ashes in its wake. "Ms. Hawkins, you're striking." Before I could answer, he went on, talking in a deep, breathy whisper as he looked around the office. "This feels a little like role playing, the use of your other name..." His eyebrows jumped. "...this office. I imagine you as my naughty secretary. And I'd like to bend you over this desk."

Heat filled my cheeks.

"You see," I said, taking a step closer. "This is *my* office. I'm the boss here. So if anyone is the naughty secretary, it would be you."

Sterling's smile widened. "This is why I could never work in the same office space as you. The only thing that would get done is turning your ass as red as your cheeks are right now and fucking you from nine to five."

"That's a lot of fucking."

"I am sure I'm up for it."

Don't look, Araneae.

I couldn't stop myself as my gaze went to his slacks. Shaking my head, I said, "Rein it in, big boy. I don't think I want to meet with my aunt freshly fucked."

"Then I'll take a rain check."

Lifting myself up to my toes, I offered him a kiss. "I'm nervous."

Sterling shook his head. "I don't know if she'll mention it. She may be looking to learn what you know."

I collapsed back into my chair. "What do you think I should do?"

"About letting her wear your fashions?"

"About everything." I knew I'd said more than once that Sterling's opinion was off-limits when it came to Sinful

Threads; however, he was obviously a successful businessman, among other things. He understood my familial relations better than I, and I genuinely wanted his advice. "Like I said before, having a potential first lady wear Sinful Threads would be great exposure, unless..." I looked up to Sterling's dark gaze. "...somehow the truth came out about her husband. Then Sinful Threads would be the designer to the wife of a disgraced politician."

"No decision needs to be made today regarding the exclusivity of designs. My advice is to play it cool. Be Kennedy Hawkins. However, if she mentions Araneae—since Rubio was at the club the night we were there and he knows you are one and the same—then you have to make a decision."

"I'm not sure what that should be."

"It's true I've never thought highly of the McFaddens, but, sunshine, she is your father's sister." He shrugged. "Keeping you safe and with me are my top priorities." He leaned against my desk, facing me, and reached down for my hands. "My next priority is your happiness. Like I said last night, there are holes in the facts. Patrick, Reid, and I have made some assumptions that fit based on those facts. That doesn't mean they're correct. There's always the possibility that Pauline could be a key to helping you learn more about yourself. This whole damn thing has become more complicated since I claimed you."

"You think?" I retorted with all the sarcasm I could muster.

Letting go of my hand, he encouraged me to stand and ran his finger over my cheek. "I do. Before you were here with me, it was about you and the evidence. Now, all I care about is you."

"Are you saying that you would support my having a relationship with my family?"

Damn, it sounded strange to hear myself use those words. I also didn't like that I was asking permission, yet it felt right.

Sterling's lips flattened. "One step at a time. Is that what you want?"

Moisture came to my eyes. "I don't know. I never thought I'd have that chance. I never imagined it." I laid my palm against Sterling's cheek. "Even having this choice is because of you."

He reached for my hand, the one with the Band-Aid and kissed my palm. "Araneae, my only desire is to keep you safe, with me, and happy—to give you your heart's desires. I don't trust Rubio. As for Pauline and Annabelle, my concern is that they'll hurt you, and I don't mean physically. I will never allow that. I don't want you to get your hopes up. Those women, including my mother, are where they are because of decisions and choices they've made. None of them are victims in this world. They survived because in the sea of influential women in this city, they are the piranhas. They chew others up and spit them out. Don't get me wrong. I'm no better. It's worth noting that my training came from both of my parents. The difference with the women is they do it with a smile painted on their faces.

"I can and will protect you from Rubio. Physically you're safe. If you choose to embark on an endeavor to know your family, it's your heart I'm worried about."

I tried to swallow the lump forming in my throat.

Sterling squeezed the one hand he was still holding. "This decision has to be yours. If you decide to go that way, then we'll do our best to make it work. Just don't expect me to sit down for Thanksgiving dinner with the McFaddens. I'm afraid it would not end well."

My lips quirked upward. "Noted and thank you for being here, for not letting me learn bad or good things alone."

Sterling looked around. "Where is Winnie? I thought I would meet her?"

"She went to check on things at the warehouse. I told her I didn't need her for the meeting with McFadden. She's making a surprise visit to the warehouse and promised to be back to meet you. I still don't have a good feeling about Franco Francesca. Even though the numbers are meshing, it's a gut feeling that something is off."

"Did she go alone?"

"No. I told her to keep her driver."

Sterling pulled his phone from his pocket and went to the door. "Patrick," he called, "come in here."

A moment later Patrick was with us, two mountains of men in suits standing before me. Suddenly, my office felt much smaller than it had.

"Who is Winnie's driver?" Sterling asked.

"Michelson."

"Make sure he has her."

"Why?" I asked.

Sterling turned my way, his expression from before replaced with the granite features. "You know how you said your gut has you uneasy about Francesca? Well, mine is telling me to be sure."

My pulse kicked up a notch. "Sterling, Pauline should be here soon."

"What do you mean she didn't call you?" Patrick said into his phone, his blue eyes opening wide. "She's been gone for nearly two hours. Go to the Sinful Threads warehouse. Let me get you the address..."

I looked up at Sterling. "She wanted to fire him—that Michelson guy. She said he gave her the creeps." I went around my desk and opened the drawer holding my purse and cell phone. "I'll call her."

Sterling's eyes never left me as he waited for my phone to contact Winnie's.

My trusted assistant and friend answered on the second ring. "Where are you?" I asked, the panic in my voice.

"The traffic is awful. Who knew stopping for coffee would be such a production. I'm almost to the warehouse."

"Who's driving you?"

"Some guy named David. Why?"

"David who? You didn't use the driver."

Winnie sighed. "Jeez, Kenni, you're acting like my mother instead of my friend. David is an Uber driver. His profile came up on my phone. Should I send it to you?"

"I'm only concerned. Is everything all right?"

"Yes, I'll call you once I'm done with Franco. I'll feel him out."

I looked up to Patrick who had just finished his conversation with Michelson. "Hey, Winnie, please humor me. The driver will meet you at the warehouse, the one from before. He'll drive you back here."

"Yes, Mom," she replied with an exasperated breath.

STERLING

I couldn't put my finger on what I was feeling. There was something out of place. We'd vetted Louisa and Jason Toney as well as Winifred Douglas. Araneae had been straightforward about her relationship with Louisa and her family. They'd stepped in pretty much as soon as Kennedy Hawkins moved to Colorado.

That sudden move still had me puzzled. Who were the Marshes and what exactly caused them to act so abruptly?

There was nothing we'd found to restrict Araneae's association with her Sinful Threads family. I wouldn't have encouraged Araneae's continued confidence in them if there had been. She may not want my input on her business, but her safety was another story. Whether she believed me or not, I wanted her continued success.

We were doing our best, but to say she hadn't had me distracted over the last few weeks would be a lie. Something today felt off-kilter, as if all of the avenues converging into our world were meeting resistance from every different direction. My nerves were probably shot. Besides the lack of sleep, I had been completely thrown by the Winifred and Leslie connection. Reid told me what he'd relayed to Araneae.

My directions to him had been not to lie. He'd followed them.

The information he presented was one hundred percent accurate. Leslie Milton had gone off the grid. That wasn't a lie. To add to my stress was the meeting beginning in minutes with Pauline McFadden.

I wanted to tell Araneae to cut her ties to them—to Pauline and to the mother who'd given her up at birth. I wanted to tell her that they didn't deserve to have her in their lives. Yet that nagging question remained.

What if Pauline and Annabelle too believed she had died?

Who besides my father knew the truth and why?

What about Daniel McCrie?

Currently, as I sat in the small room attached to Araneae's office, the walls were closing in on me. In the short time she'd been working out of Chicago, this room had filled with silk samples as well as prototypes, mostly miniature, sent from the designers in Boulder. Strewn across the table were scarves and accessories in all colors. Shelves held an array of boxes.

"Ms. Hawkins, Mrs. McFadden is here to see you."

I peered out the open door as Araneae came my way.

"Thank you, again, for being here," she said, her eyes veiled as she fought her own emotions

I reached for her shoulders. "If at any point you want me to make my presence known, I will."

"Only if I say I want your presence. Please respect my wishes, Sterling."

"Unless there's any concern as to your safety. Then all bets are off."

Araneae nodded as she took a step back and closed the door.

I hated the pallor of her complexion. If only we were sailing on the blue waters of Lake Michigan right now.

Twenty-four hours. I reminded myself.

My phone vibrated silently in my grasp.

PATRICK was on the screen.

"SHE'S NOT ALONE."

"WHO IS WITH HER?"

"ONE OF MCFADDEN'S MEN. I'D ASSUME HER DRIVER. REID IS WORKING ON FACIAL RECOG-INITION."

"MAKE YOUR PRESENCE KNOWN. HE ISN'T COMING IN HERE WITH ARANAEAE."

"ALREADY DONE."

"Send her in," Araneae said to Jana.

ARANEAE

Standing, I offered my hand as Mrs. McFadden entered my office. She was an attractive woman, as long as I worked hard not to imagine her as the sharp-toothed fish that inhabited South American waters.

A few inches shorter than I, with blonde hair short and styled to perfection, her face appeared smooth for her age. I had no doubt she'd had some surgical assistance, yet it wasn't overdone.

"Mrs. McFadden," I said with all the enthusiasm I could muster. "It is nice to see you again."

Her handshake was firm and fast.

"Ms. Hawkins, thank you for meeting with me."

A twinge of disappointment ran through my veins at the use of my legal name.

I gestured to the small table with four chairs in the corner of my office. "Please have a seat. May I get you some coffee or water?"

She declined, taking a seat at the end of the table.

"Then let's begin," I said. "We can start by discussing your hopes for a partnership with Sinful Threads and letting me know what you believe Sinful Threads can do for you."

Perhaps it was paranoia or maybe even hope, yet it seemed that Pauline had trouble taking her eyes off of me as I showed her sketches and prototypes that I'd had our designers put together based on Mrs. McFadden's body type.

After nearly twenty minutes into the presentation, she sat back and sighed.

"Is there a problem?" I asked.

Her head shook from side to side. "When we met a few weeks ago, I had no idea. I couldn't even begin to..." She began to reach for my hand and stopped. "May I...may I be honest?"

I sat straighter. "Why would you be otherwise?"

"I feel like I'm sitting here talking to a ghost."

No reply came to mind as her words twisted my already-knot-filled stomach.

Pauline swallowed. "My husband was at an exclusive club about a week ago." Her eyes widened. "Perhaps you saw him?"

I nodded.

"The woman with him, Annabelle Landers, was my sister-in-law. She was married to my brother. For many years she was my best friend." Pauline's gaze moved far away until her head shook. "I'm sorry, Kennedy, I'm an old woman reminiscing."

"Go on," I encouraged, my pulse beating faster by the second.

"I never had children. Annabelle and Daniel tried for a long time. Their daughter was to be the light of their lives, of all of our lives. And before she was born, there were problems, legal problems, for my brother. It was a difficult time—for all of us. What made it even more heartbreaking was the loss of their daughter."

I took a deep breath. "That's a sad story, Mrs. McFadden."

"It was. It was a dark time in our lives, especially for Annabelle. While we aren't as close as we once were...her pain was real. After that night at the club, she had difficulty dealing...understanding that after twenty-six years, after holding her deceased daughter and burying her in a small graveyard at a tiny church, that she could be alive." Pauline took a breath, turned her cold blue-eyed stare to me. "How could that be possible?"

"I can assure you, I don't know. You see, I was only an infant twenty-six years ago. There is no way for me to know or understand what happened."

Her wrinkled hand inched toward mine. "I had to see you again, look at you. I don't know if you're really who you claim to be. If by some strange sequence of events you are, I don't understand why you'd come back and open old wounds and to do so with an association with the Sparrows—going against your own family? It's almost more than Annabelle can take."

The door behind me opened. I knew without looking who was there. Without turning, I felt his dark, penetrating stare bearing down on the woman before me. Pauline's expression of shock accompanied by the sucking in of air confirmed my suspicion. And while I hadn't asked for his entrance, I welcomed it.

"Mr. Sparrow," Pauline said, standing, visibly shaken.

"Mrs. McFadden, I believe it's time for you to leave."

"I-I didn't..." She turned back to me. "Your fashions are stunning. The quality is beyond compare. I don't, however, believe this association will work in a mutually beneficial way."

I stood, utilizing my full height. "I would thank you for coming here today, and I will out of politeness. You see, I was raised by a good woman. The truth is that I wanted to see you too. My curiosity also got the better of me." I took a step back until Sterling was directly behind me. "Why would I associate with the Sparrows, you asked? I'll tell you. For twenty-six years I've lived in secrets and lies. Sterling Sparrow was the first person to offer me a promise of who I truly am. Sterling was right: our meeting is done. Goodbye, Mrs. McFadden." I tilted my head. "Or should I say Aunt Pauline? You see, I'd always prayed for a family." I reached for Sterling's hand as our fingers intertwined. "I'm more than content with the one that found me."

Pauline's gaze went to our hands and back to our faces as her chin rose higher and neck straightened. "The real Araneae McCrie would never betray her family like that. Your fabrication will never work. I don't know who you are or why you've allowed this man to convince you otherwise, but Araneae McCrie died. Some second-rate imposter who stole a bracelet won't get away with threatening our family." She turned to Sterling. "And Mr. Sparrow, you're never too old to listen to your mother. This was a mistake that you will regret."

"There's nothing about Araneae that I regret."

With Sterling's final statement she turned and left.

As the outer door to the office opened and closed, Sterling pulled me against him, wrapping me in his embrace, surrounding me with his strength and the magical scent of his spicy cologne.

"Sunshine," he whispered in his deep tenor near my ear, "I'm sorry. I didn't want this to go down like that."

Though my vision was blurry, I looked up to his granite features. "You kept your promise. That's all that matters. You were here. I wasn't alone."

"Never."

There was a knock on the doorframe. "Sparrow?" Patrick called.

I inhaled as we stepped back from one another.

"Come in," Sterling commanded.

Patrick's eyes were on Sterling. "It's Michelson. Winnie never made it to the warehouse."

ARANEAE

I didn't wait for Patrick or Sterling to make a decision as I raced back to the other side of my desk, opening the drawer and fishing out my purse. Removing my cell phone, I swiped the screen, bringing it to life.

WINNIE was on the screen. I opened the text message.

"KENNI, I'M SO SORRY. I HAD NO IDEA. LOUISA WAS WORRIED. SHE DOESN'T KNOW. I THOUGHT I WAS HELPING. WILL YOU EVER FORGIVE ME?"

I looked up from the screen and then turned it toward both men. As if they were one, their expressions darkened in unison.

"Have Reid find her," Sterling said. "Araneae, stay with me."

I shook my head. "I need to find her, find out what's wrong."

"Text her back. If her phone is on, Reid can find her."

Nodding, I typed back a message.

"WHAT IS HAPPENING? I'M SURE I CAN FORGIVE YOU. YOU FORGAVE ME FOR MY SECRET. WHERE ARE YOU? COME BACK TO THE OFFICE."

My phone pinged:

"I'M AT MY HOTEL ROOM."

I looked up. "She says she's at her hotel room."

Sterling's head shook. "This is wrong. Patrick, take her home."

"No," I protested. "Winnie's my friend."

"And we'll find her, Araneae," Patrick said. "It'll be easier if we're sure you're safe with Lorna."

"I won't be put away in the damn glass tower. I won't. I'll stay with either one of you, but I'm not going back to the apartment."

Sterling reached for my shoulders. "This is one of those '*Yes, Mr. Sparrow*' times."

I didn't respond, not in front of Patrick. Instead, my stare bore into his, silently saying all of the things I believed he could hear. Finally, I collected my thoughts and said, "She's my friend. She's here because of me, because of *you*."

"Then I'm going with you," he said. "You're not getting out of my sight." Sterling looked to Patrick. "You drive us. I'll tell Garrett to go on ahead."

As I was about to ask who Garrett was, Patrick nodded.

"Your new driver?" I asked.

Both men nodded.

Well, at least I had that answer.

The three of us rushed out of Sinful Threads, leaving Jana in charge with a promise to keep her informed. As the elevator neared the garage level, Sterling's phone rang.

His jaw clenched as he connected. "Stephanie, I told you that I wasn't to be interrupted."

Though we couldn't hear the other end and I wondered who Stephanie was, Patrick and I watched Sterling's expressions.

"She's there in *my* office?....Why?" His eyes closed as his nostrils flared. "I don't care. I can't be back to Michigan Avenue for at least ninety minutes...What does that mean?" He shook his head. "I have something else that takes priority."

When he disconnected the call, I said, "You don't need to tell me who Stephanie is. However, Winnie is staying at the Hilton. Is that far from your office?"

Patrick and Sterling exchanged looks.

Sterling's head shook from side to side. "No, it's not. I'll go with you to Winnie, and then Patrick can take you home or back to your office. I don't feel right about any of this."

I reached for his hand. "If that call was for business, you

have your own fires. The fire with Winnie is mine. I've asked you to respect my business. Sterling, I respect yours, too."

The elevator came to a stop. This garage wasn't like the one at the apartment building. This one was shared with others. Sterling's eyes were everywhere as were Patrick's, scanning the garage. I recalled the incident in Wichita when Patrick warned me against entering a parking garage, telling me the logistics were impossible.

A cold chill settled over me as Sterling gripped my hand tighter. "Hurry, we're getting into the car."

Our steps were quick as we rushed toward the black sedan. The locks beeped as Sterling opened my door and I entered, followed closely behind by Sterling as Patrick entered the front seat and we all let out a collective breath.

"That call wasn't about business," Sterling said. "Stephanie is my assistant at my downtown office. I told her I'd be unavailable for the rest of this morning. She knows better; however, someone is at the office, making a scene and demanding a meeting."

Though he hadn't spoken, Patrick's gaze was set in the rearview mirror, anxiously awaiting more.

"Who?" I asked, unsure if he'd answer.

"Judge Landers."

ARANEAE

y mouth opened yet no words came to my tongue.

First my aunt and now my mother.

"If you'd like, you can go to my office with me," Sterling said, "after we find Winnie."

My head shook as I blinked away unexpected tears. "No, I can't...not after that meeting with Mrs. McFadden. Can you please handle it? I think I should have taken you up on that getaway."

His large finger caressed my cheek. "Then that's what we'll do."

Patrick began driving toward the Hilton as Sterling reached again for my hand. "I fucking want to get you out of Chicago and naked on the deck of the yacht."

I sighed. "Only if you're dressed accordingly."

He looked toward the front seat. "I'll call Garrett and have him go to the office. Don't fucking let Araneae out of your sight. These two damn buildings are too close to drag this out any longer than necessary. Let's kill two birds. You two get Winnie. I'll find out what Judge Landers wants."

"I don't like any of this," Patrick said. "Reid's confirmed Winnie's phone is at the Hilton. We should also have Reid check security at both locations."

Sterling nodded.

I looked back to Sterling. "What are you going to do? What will you say to her?"

"Whatever needs to be done and said."

Suddenly, I didn't care that Patrick was in the front seat. All I cared about was the man who was now my lover, my family, and my confidant.

Leaning closer, I placed my hand on Sterling's chest. His heart beat under my palm, the steady rhythm reassuring me. "Please be careful. I-I..." I looked up to his eyes. "...fuck it. Sterling, I love you. I don't care who hears it. Don't take stupid chances by being a hero or a villain. I don't know what my mother or the McFaddens have in mind. My only concern is that everyone I love is safe. That includes you. Come home to me. I want to be on that boat."

One of his arms snaked around my back as his other hand lifted my chin until our gazes saw only one another. "Come home to me."

His lips crashed with mine.

My gaze followed Sterling as he got out of the car, his long legs walking with purpose as the Chicago wind blew his suit coat and he stepped regally toward the front of the building facing Michigan Avenue.

"Tell me that he'll be safe," I said to Patrick.

"Ma'am, he's had more difficult meetings. Let's concentrate on Winnie."

I looked down at my phone for the thousandth time. All of my calls to Winnie as well as my texts since we'd left the office had gone unanswered.

"I could try calling directly to her room."

"Reid saw her on the hotel's security go up to her room."

My head shook. "I don't understand what happened."

"Ma'am, I'm going in her room with you."

"I-I know that's what Sterling said, but if she's upset, your presence won't help. Could you please wait right outside? It's a hotel room."

For the first time, I saw the tells I noticed more in Sterling. The way Patrick's jaw clenched and the tendons in his neck tightened like cords being pulled taut.

"I'm worried," I said. "I don't understand why she apologized or what this is about."

"Ma'am, it's not too late to take you home."

The ma'am he'd reverted to calling me let me know that Patrick was slipping into full business mode. I didn't mind the loss of my name. It was as if he and Sterling both had their *tells*, as Patrick called them. "No. I want to see her."

"I'M ALMOST TO THE HOTEL. DO YOU WANT ME TO COME TO YOUR ROOM?"

· · ·

Before I sent the text, I looked up. "Do you have her room number?"

Patrick nodded.

Sending the text, I held the phone and prayed for a response.

"YES. PLEASE DON'T BRING THAT SCARY GUY OR MR. SPARROW. I NEED TO TALK TO YOU ALONE."

"Patrick..." I waited for his eyes again in the rearview mirror. "She finally texted me back. She's in her room and wants to speak to me alone."

"No, I'm sorry, Araneae. Sparrow will kill me if anything happens to you."

"What will happen? We're in a hotel room. Please wait outside and let me go in alone. Sterling said to listen to me. This is my good friend. She's upset." He didn't answer. That didn't mean I couldn't see the indecision on his face. "Please, Patrick. This is my friend. I've known her for..."

"Three years isn't a lifetime. It's not long at all."

I exhaled. "I suppose you're right. It seemed like from the beginning she fit in. I've known you and Sterling much less and yet you expect me to trust you."

"Ma'am, I don't expect anything. I watch. I listen. I make calculations and never assumptions. It's true you haven't known Sparrow or me longer. We, however, have known you. The last eight years have included watching, protecting, and observing."

Inhaling, I fought the tears. "I've lost a lot of people in my life. My friends are an elite group. Each one is dear to me for their own reasons. I would do anything not to lose one." I took another breath. "That includes you. I won't take any unnecessary chances."

We had now entered the hotel's parking garage. Once we were parked, Patrick motioned for me to wait as he connected a call.

I could only hear his end.

"What can you see?" He nodded. "Nothing after her. No room service? Nothing?"

He hung up and turned my way. "Reid confirmed that she entered her room over an hour ago. No one has come to the room since, not even housekeeping." He exhaled. "I'll wait right outside the door, but know that I'll be ready to kick it in."

My lips turned upward. "I like that you're scary."

"I'm scary?"

"Not to me."

Together we walked through the parking garage and entered the first elevator. It took us as high as the lobby. The hotel was alive with patrons as Patrick scanned each one and led me through the maze of people. A few minutes later we were on the elevator to Winnie's floor.

When we finally arrived at her door, he said, "I'm staying right here. Get her and bring her back. We'll go back to the office and forget this happened."

"You don't mean that."

"Please, Araneae, talk to her. If she intends to stay employed by Sinful Threads, she'll come back with you. If not, it's her choice."

"My company," I said with less zeal than before.

He didn't answer.

Taking a deep breath, I knocked on her door. When she opened it, her eyes were red and swollen, and her face and neck were covered in red blotches. "Winnie..." I wrapped her in my arms as we stepped inside. As the door closed, I asked, "Winnie, what is it?"

"Ms. McCrie?"

I gasped as I stood straight again, taking in the man who had appeared from the bathroom. I knew him immediately.

Knew was the wrong word.

I recognized him, his blond hair, and his boyish features. "Mark?" I questioned.

Hanging from his belt was a badge.

I took a step back, my shoulders colliding with the wall. "What is this?"

The man placed his finger over his lips. "I know you're being watched. I know there's a man outside who won't hesitate to enter. I need you to listen to me."

"I-I thought you were in trouble..." Winnie cried, her words surrounded by quick inhales of breath. "I-I thought..."

"What did you do?"

"Ms. McCrie," Mark said, speaking quietly as he came closer, "I'm certain you were told elsewhere. May I formally introduce myself? My name is neither Mark nor Andrew. I'm Wesley Hunter, a field agent with the FBI. For the last two and a half years, I have been infiltrating the world of Chicago's underground."

My lips came together as my head shook. "That-that has nothing to do with me."

"You didn't correct me on the use of your birth name."

"My name is Kennedy Hawkins." I fumbled with my purse. "I-I have my ID."

Mark, I mean, Wesley, lifted his hand. "If you want to play that game, it's your choice. You have a long history, Ms. Hawkins. Ms. Marsh. Or is it, Ms. McCrie? While infiltrating the world that *has nothing to do with you*, the FBI became aware of your connection—or should I say your father's? Because of that, there is concern for your safety. For most of your life you have been a sought-after individual. For that reason, once you were discovered, I tried to stop you from becoming involved. Wichita? Perhaps you recall? As you know, that didn't work."

My head was shaking. "This doesn't make any sense."

"Kenni," Winnie said, "I'm sorry. They came to me, told me you were in danger. Your behavior...I thought I was helping."

"Why?" I asked, this time louder. "Why not come to me?"

"I thought with the odd behavior," she said. "I thought...the FBI said...you were in danger...that you were being forced...and then today you said...I left the office to tell them they were wrong." Her head shook. "I'm sorry."

"Agent Hunter," I said, finding my voice yet purposely keeping it low so as not to alarm Patrick. "Am I under arrest? If not, I'm going to leave this room. I appreciate your concern; however, I guarantee that I'm safe."

He reached for a folder lying next to the TV and flipped it open, revealing Sterling Sparrow's picture. "Ma'am, this man is dangerous."

"He's in real estate."

"You're believed to have information that could be detrimental to him and his future. We have it on good authority that his plan is to get that information by any means possible. Are you aware of the information?"

What could I say?

"I don't have anything like that."

"The FBI is willing to offer you, Ms. Douglas, and the cofounder of your company, Louisa Toney, witness protection, in exchange for the information in question. Certainly, you want to save your friend's soon-to-be-born child?"

Oh my God. This was the same way Sterling convinced me in the first place—blackmail.

I shook my head. "I don't have any information."

"You have been marked by Sterling Sparrow."

He had no idea.

"We've tried for years to find something that would finally stick to Sparrow. We believe you have it."

I shook my head. "I'm leaving." I took a step toward the door.

"Upon further research," Agent Hunter said, "into Sinful Threads, it has come to the notice of the FBI that there are some unusual real estate deals regarding your properties that could be connected to Sparrow Enterprises."

"Yes, that company deals in real estate," I said, standing taller. "My company needs properties."

"The deals you received are significantly below market. That leads us to question the complexity of your agreements."

I shook my head. "Those agreements go back years. I only recently became acquainted with Mr. Sparrow."

"If you're not willing to share with the FBI the information that you have, possibly incriminating evidence against your new acquaintance, we are prepared to offer you an alternative. This is a onetime offer. Once it's made your decision must be imminent."

"I don't need an alternative offer. I don't have any information and I've done nothing wrong."

Wesley crossed his arms over his chest. "It's very easy. All you need to do is take my place, infiltrating and ultimately testifying against Mr. Sparrow."

"What?"

"The evidence regarding real estate combined with some questionable bookkeeping and inventory irregularities at your Chicago warehouse implicate Sinful Threads as a possible means for illegal activities. We have the records."

"No, that's impossible. Louisa and I go through every line. Besides, it couldn't be him. He's in real estate," I said again as if repeating it would nullify his other dealings. "And I just met him."

"Lying is what men like him do."

My phone buzzed and *STERLING* came onto the screen.

My mind was a battlefield as my lungs forgot to breathe, and my gaze went back and forth between Sterling's name and the FBI agent across the room.

Who should I believe? Who was telling me the truth, and who was telling me lies?

Sterling and Araneae's story concludes in the highly anticipated climax, PROMISES. You're not going to want to miss the final installment of this spellbinding story. Preorder Promises today.

WHAT TO DO NOW

LEND IT: Did you enjoy Lies? Do you have a friend who'd enjoy Lies? Lies may be lent one time. Sharing is caring!

RECOMMEND IT: Do you have multiple friends who'd enjoy my dark romance saga? Tell them about it! Call, text, post, tweet...your recommendation is the nicest gift you can give to an author!

REVIEW IT: Tell the world. Please go to the retailer where you purchased this book, as well as Goodreads, and write a review. Please share your thoughts about Lies on:

*Amazon, *LIES* Customer Reviews

*Barnes & Noble, *LIES,* Customer Reviews

*iBooks, *LIES* Customer Reviews

*Goodreads.com/Aleatha Romig

BOOKS BY NEW YORK TIMES BESTSELLING AUTHOR ALEATHA ROMIG

WEB OF SIN:

SECRETS

Coming Oct. 30, 2018

LIES

Coming Dec. 4, 2018

PROMISES

Coming Jan. 8, 2019

THE CONSEQUENCES SERIES:

CONSEQUENCES

(Book #1)

Released August 2011

TRUTH

(Book #2)

Released October 2012

CONVICTED

(Book #3)

Released October 2013

REVEALED

(Book #4)

Previously titled: Behind His Eyes Convicted: The Missing Years

Re-released June 2014

BEYOND THE CONSEQUENCES

(Book #5)

Released January 2015

RIPPLES

Released Oct 2017

CONSEQUENCES COMPANION READS:

BEHIND HIS EYES-CONSEQUENCES

Released January 2014

BEHIND HIS EYES-TRUTH

Released March 2014

THE INFIDELITY SERIES:

BETRAYAL

Book #1

Released October 2015

CUNNING

Book #2

Released January 2016

DECEPTION

Book #3

Released May 2016

ENTRAPMENT

Book #4

Released September 2016

FIDELITY

Book #5

Released January 2017

RESPECT

A stand-alone Infidelity novel

Released January 2018

THE LIGHT DUET:

Published through Thomas and Mercer Amazon exclusive

INTO THE LIGHT

Released 2016

AWAY FROM THE DARK

Released 2016

TALES FROM THE DARK SIDE SERIES:

INSIDIOUS

(All books in this series are stand-alone erotic thrillers)

Released October 2014

DUPLICITY

(Completely unrelated to book #1)

Release TBA

ALEATHA'S LIGHTER ONES:

PLUS ONE

Stand-alone fun, sexy romance

Released May 2017

A SECRET ONE

Fun, sexy novella

Released April 2018

ANOTHER ONE

Stand-alone fun, sexy romance

Releasing May 2018

ONE NIGHT

Stand-alone, sexy contemporary romance

September 2017

THE VAULT:

UNEXPECTED

Released August 27, 2018

UNCONVENTIONAL

Released individually

January 1, 2018

ABOUT THE AUTHOR

Aleatha Romig is a New York Times, Wall Street Journal, and USA Today bestselling author who lives in Indiana, USA. She has raised three children with her high school sweetheart and husband of over thirty years. Before she became a full-time author, she worked days as a dental hygienist and spent her nights writing. Now, when she's not imagining mind-blowing twists and turns, she likes to spend her time with her family and friends. Her other pastimes include reading and creating heroes/anti-heroes who haunt your dreams!

Aleatha impresses with her versatility in writing. She released her first novel, CONSEQUENCES, in August of 2011. CONSEQUENCES, a dark romance, became a bestselling series with five novels and two companions released from 2011 through 2015. The compelling and epic story of Anthony and Claire Rawlings has graced more than half a million e-readers. Her first stand-alone smart, sexy thriller INSIDIOUS was next. Then Aleatha released the five-novel INFIDELITY series, a romantic suspense saga, that took the reading world by storm, the final book landing on three of the top bestseller lists. She ventured into traditional publishing with Thomas and Mercer. Her books INTO THE LIGHT and AWAY FROM THE DARK were published through this mystery/thriller publisher in 2016. In the spring of 2017, Aleatha again ventured into a different genre with her first fun and sexy stand-alone romantic comedy with the USA Today bestseller PLUS ONE. She continued with ONE NIGHT and ANOTHER ONE. If you like fun, sexy, novellas that make your heart pound, try her UNCONVENTIONAL and UNEXPECTED. In 2018 Aleatha returned to her dark romance roots with WEB OF SIN.

Aleatha is a "Published Author's Network" member of the Romance Writers of America and PEN America. She is represented by Kevan Lyon of Marsal Lyon Literary Agency.

facebook.com/aleatharomig

twitter.com/aleatharomig

instagram.com/aleatharomig